<u>Special Thanks:</u>

To Alex—Cheers t̶o̶ gether! (And to not al̶r̶ ̶̶ ̶̶d̶o̶w̶n̶ ̶t̶r̶y̶i̶n̶g̶ to make popcorn again.) я тебя люблю!

To Stacia—Cheers to another year together, my fabulous half brain! You're stuck with me!

To my family, friends, and LaManna's Ladies, thank you for a wonderful 2018!

SHADES OF SUNSHINE

First edition. December 29, 2018.

Written by Gina LaManna.

To my husband!!

Synopsis

Lola Pink is all shades of concerned about the state of her wedding plans when her world is shaken as someone close to Dane Clark—her billionaire fiancé—goes missing. When the news of a kidnapping rocks the Clark Castle, Lola finds herself entwined in a mystery that could require a trip down memory lane.

However, a missing persons report is not the only thing on Lola's plate. There's a brownie rivalry between two of the town's oldest residents, a wedding cake that won't order itself, and a mother-in-law determined to ruin Lola's special day. But when the kidnapper's threats take a turn for the worse, suddenly, all bets are off. If Lola can't find a way to unveil the kidnapper's true identity, there won't *be* a wedding to ruin...

Chapter 1

"Annalise, don't cry again, please," I said. "I'm trying to kick off this emergency meeting, and I just can't do it with you sobbing."

"What does it *matter*?!" she wailed. "It's all my fault."

Babs shrugged and shot me an accusatory glance. "If you didn't say his *name* on the way up here, Annalise would never have started crying."

"She would have, too!" I argued. "The poor thing has a broken heart. She's been crying for a month. Annalise—" I beckoned her over—"come here, it's going to be okay."

Annalise plunked her head against my shoulder. I would've never expected that a body as small as hers with a tiny head to match could feel so heavy. I shifted into a more comfortable position as she laid her full weight on me and felt myself tipping dangerously close to the ledge. The three of us—the Sunshine Sisters—were sitting high above town on the water tower, our normal perch for meetings of the important variety, and it wasn't on my agenda to fall off this morning.

"Girls!" Mrs. Fredericks yelled from down below. "How much longer are you going to be? I have to run to the store for more ice cream to go with the special brownies. It'll only be a second. You've eaten clean through the gallon I had."

"We'll be a while, Mrs. Fredericks," Babs said, "but don't worry about the ice cream. I should lay off."

"You trying to get skinny for Lo's wedding?" Mrs. Fredericks hollered back. "What sort of diet are you on? I've been wanting to lose some weight too, now that they've set a date."

"But your legs look great," Babs said. "Look at those sunflowers all over your thighs."

Mrs. Fredericks was the sweet old lady who liked to think of herself as an honorary Sunshine Sister. Whenever she saw three sets of legs dangling from the water tower, she'd pop right over to her oven and throw in some cookies or other very appealing dessert that she'd use to eventually lure us back to the ground.

"Well, I need a walk anyway," Mrs. Fredericks said. "I'll get the ice cream, but don't y'all move before I get back. I can't finish off the brownies myself. By the way, Lola, when should I expect a wedding invitation? I have to know when to have my bikini body ready."

"Yeah, when should we expect invitations?" Babs turned her attention on me. "You've been engaged for almost two months. Get a move on, girlfriend."

"You just worry about that ice cream," I called to Mrs. Fredericks. "I'll drop one off soon."

"Nah, I want you to mail it," she yelled back with a half-hearted wave. "It'll make things exciting. All I get are bills."

"I walk past her house every day, and she wants me to mail it." I shook my head, turning to face Babs. However, I found no sympathy there, only demand. "Fine! I'll mail yours too. Sheesh! That's a dollar I'm out in unnecessary postage."

"You know that's not what I meant," Babs clarified. "Mrs. Dulcet called me the other day, and—"

"Why are you talking to Mrs. Dulcet so much?" I asked. "She's my fiancé's butler."

"Yes, but I'm one of your possible maids-of-honor, so I have a lot invested in this wedding. I mean, since Johnny and me sort of fizzled, I'm on the prowl." Babs shrugged. "What better place to look for a man than at my best friend's wedding to a billionaire? Maybe Dane has some available, hot friends."

"Dane?" I asked. "I love the man, but I don't think his friend list is as long as you think."

"You're right. He doesn't really have many friends, does he," Babs mused with a pout. "Do you think he'd ask Gerard to be in the wedding party? He's my Australian George Clooney, and I'm considering being interested. The age gap really doesn't bother me."

Babs—all blond hair, curves, and red lipstick with acerbic wit—could have just about any man she wanted. She was gorgeous and super smart, and she had a successful career as a lawyer to boot. Which didn't stop her from fantasizing about marrying a billionaire. The girl had a jeans collection to maintain, after all.

"I don't know," I said. "I haven't been all that involved in the wedding planning so far."

"What are you talking about? It's *your* wedding. Plus, it's going to be like—the biggest wedding Sunshine Shore has ever seen," Babs pointed out. "I'm expecting arches of flowers and a cake that I can bathe in. Do you know how big of a cake that is, Lola? I'm a generous-sized woman, and I want to be able to sit inside of your cake. You'd better get to planning."

"I'm trying to," I said. "But it's not as if I've been given much of an option."

"I'm still confused," Babs said. "Isn't it your day? Who else would plan it? Have you hired someone?"

"No, but Dane's mother seems to have hired herself."

Babs squinted at me. "Oh?"

"Apparently she's already ordered the invitations," I said. "I only heard that through Mrs. Dulcet. If it weren't for her, I'd have no clue. They should be in this week."

Babs frowned. "Okay, well, that sounds a bit rude. Maybe she's just trying to help?"

"She's vetoed most of the rest of my ideas." I shrugged listlessly. "I'm beginning to think it might be easier if I just forfeit all my planning duties to her."

Babs's nose wrinkled in concern. "Do you really want a wedding planned by Dane's mother? She's got... um, shall we say, a different style than you."

"It doesn't feel as if I have much of a choice at this point."

"Have you talked to Dane about it?"

"I don't want to bother him with little details. I know he doesn't really care, so long as I'm happy."

"Right." Babs stared at me. "And you're clearly not happy at your wedding planning being hijacked, so talk to him."

I shrugged. "I don't know. Maybe I'm overreacting. All that really matters is the fact that Dane and I get married, right?"

A small cry came from the petite figure next to me, interrupting my train of thought. Or rather, a pained sort of howl that sounded a bit like a tortured cat. "Annalise, what's wrong?"

"What's wrong?!" Her mascara was a mess. Her thin, limber gymnasts' body was contorted into some sort of pretzel that boggled the mind. Huge crocodile tears fell from her eyes. "Have you not been listening to me at all?"

I threw my arm around her shoulder. The circus performer was probably the naivest—and the strictest—of us all, and she'd just gone through her first heartbreak. Though Babs and I had been super sympathetic for the first two weeks, and then the third, and into the fourth, it was getting difficult to find new advice for Annalise. We'd covered a lot in the first forty-five emergency Sunshine Sisters meetings Annalise had called post breakup.

"It's going to be okay," I said soothingly. "Remember what we told you. If everything is not okay, it's not the end—er..."

"Everything will be right in the end," Babs corrected, and then translated. "If it's not right, it's not the end. Annalise, if you and Semi are meant to be together, then it'll happen. Maybe this is just a little bump in the road."

"But what if we're not meant for each other?" she said. "What then? How will I live?"

"I know it hurts," I said, rubbing her shoulder as my shirt slowly entered into wet T-shirt contest territory from her tears. "But you'll get through this. You're strong. After all, the breakup was mutual, wasn't it?"

"Yes, but not because I didn't *love* him," she corrected. "It was just too hard. We're both so busy, and our schedules were having a hard time matching up. We hadn't really seen each other for a month and a half! What sort of relationship is that?"

"I hate to sound crass, but the two of you didn't even date for six months," Babs said. "Don't you think it's a little premature to be mourning the guy for over a month? I mean, it's not like he physically went anywhere. If you miss him that bad, all it'd take is a quick trip to Clark Castle. I'm sure Semi still cares for you, too."

"But he hasn't called," Annalise said with a sniff. "Not once."

"Because you told him you needed space," I said. "He's being respectful."

"I don't want him to be respectful," she snarled. "I mean, I do, but I want him to respectfully chase after me."

"Oh, Annalise," Babs said, shifting her weight to rest her head in Annalise's lap. She bent her knees so she was laying and looking up at the sky. "I don't know what to tell you, honey. It'll get better. Time heals all."

I recognized Babs's movement for what it really was—a perfect sunbathing technique. I narrowed my eyes at her, but she couldn't see the dagger-glares headed her way because I had on these gorgeous yellow sunglasses I'd found at the thrift shop a week before.

They matched my yellow sundress, which was usually a great thing, except for the whole emergency meeting on top of the water tower—which required expert and Annalise-like movements to keep the fabric tucked under my legs. That was one show the Sunshine Shore did not need to see, even though my undies also had cute little sunflowers on them—also a sale item from the weekend's shopping trip. But more of a private little fact, and not something I wanted Mrs. Fredericks to know.

I felt myself blush as I remembered the look on Dane's face as I'd dressed this morning, his keen gaze taking in my cute little sunflower undies while he'd perused the newspapers in bed. He'd had a meeting to get to, which unfortunately had stunted our time together, but he'd given a whisper about finding some time to spend alone together in his afternoon schedule.

The thought made me jumpy to get back to the castle. I had work to do, and I missed Dane already. It was pathetic maybe, but I supposed that was the beauty of pure, sappy, unconditional love. I couldn't seem to be without him for very long at all.

"Annalise, I'm not sure what you want us to say," I said, running my hands through her hair. "Do you want me to talk to Semi for you? He's been a giant mope these last few weeks. Even Dane noticed, and he wouldn't notice an emotion if it slapped him in the face."

"Really?" She perked up, and the tears stopped at once. "You think he might miss me?"

"I know he misses you. You're both just too stubborn to make the first move," I said. "I hate seeing you this upset."

"Maybe you could just sort of poke around," Babs suggested. "Don't do all the work for Annalise, but just see if you can get a read on Semi's feelings."

"Yes," Annalise said quickly. "Do that."

"I don't like meddling in love lives," I said with a frown. "If I find out Semi's interested, I'll leave the rest to you."

"Or me," Babs said. "I love to meddle. I'm great at meddling."

"I'll handle it," Annalise said with a firm nod, a bit of light popping back into her eyes. "Oh, thank you, Lola. Will you call an emergency meeting as soon as you hear something?"

I raised two fingers. "I swear on it. Perfect timing because I have to get back to the castle, and anyway, here's Mrs. Fredericks coming back with the ice cream. Do you think she'll be offended if I ask her for a Tupperware to go? I really do have to meet Dane, but I'd hate to miss out on her brownies."

AS IT TURNED OUT, MRS. Fredericks was more than happy to put brownies and ice cream in a to-go container, which was only mildly problematic thanks to the heat. I hopped on my bike and headed for home. The Sunshine Shore burned bright with afternoon sun as I pedaled my legs just as fast as I could, trying to beat the melt.

Dane had continually promised he would outfit me with a car, but I kept refusing. I'd gotten along on my bike just fine for the last quarter century and more. Plus, he had enough motorized vehicles already. I could always bug Gerard, his garage manager, to use one in a pinch. Dane had made a point to insist that everything from here on out would be ours—his cars, his company, his house. I had my bike and a cool collection of sunglasses to contribute, which definitely made this marriage a fair trade.

I threw my newly refurbished bicycle into the handy dandy parking spot that Dane had asked Gerard to make for me outside the front door. I still wasn't certain if it was because having a bike in Castlewood's front lawn was an eyesore, or if he really wanted me to have a place for my things.

Either way, I wasn't complaining. Dane had made every effort to make the castle feel like mine since we'd gotten engaged. I'd sort of begun sleeping in his bed that very night and just never left. I supposed that meant I was officially all moved in.

"Hi, Mrs. Dulcet," I called as I burst through the front doors. "Melty ice cream emergency."

In a flurry of movement, I kicked off my shoes and jogged down the hall and into the kitchen. A few of the staff members were already there preparing afternoon tea, appetizers, and the start of dinner. I grinned to them as I threw Mrs. Fredericks's brownies into the freezer to harden up from the soupy mess they'd become.

Mrs. Dulcet somehow materialized while I'd stuck my head into the freezer to cool down, startling me as I shut the door and sending me lurching back in surprise.

"You scared me!" I pressed a hand over my heart. "I didn't think you'd heard me come in."

"The entire house heard you come in," Mrs. Dulcet said crisply. "It was like a herd of elephants arrived starved for dinner. That wouldn't be a container of Mrs. Fredericks's brownies in there, would it?"

"Um—" I hesitated, not sure if I should address the elephant bit or the brownie bit first. "Sorry if I was too loud, I'll—ah—not run in the castle."

"We love having you running around the castle," she said, confusing me with a frown despite her pleasant terms. "It's been too long since the castle has seen exuberant life."

"Okay?"

"It's the brownies that make me concerned."

I patted a hand against my stomach. "If you're worried my wedding dress won't fit—don't worry. I am considering ordering it a size larger just in case. You know, to make room for lots of stress eating."

"That's not my concern," Mrs. Dulcet said through gritted teeth. "Mrs. Fredericks and I have a history. We go way back."

"Way back to..." I shrugged. "Before her LuLaRoe leggings? I'm sorry, I'm not understanding the issue. She baked some brownies and sent them home with me. Usually I have time to stay and eat them, but—"

"Usually?!" Mrs. Dulcet sounded shrill. "She feeds you often?"

"Mrs. Dulcet." I put a hand on my hip. "Please tell me what's going on."

"Run away," one of the kitchen staff muttered as she walked past. "Rivalry."

I narrowed my eyes at the butler. "What rivalry? Between you and Mrs. Fredericks?"

"It's not a rivalry if my brownies blow hers out of the water," Mrs. Dulcet said with a superior huff. "It's just that the judge was compromised in the contest of '74."

"I don't understand. What contest?"

The woman who'd warned me to walk away came back, apparently too intrigued to leave the conversation alone. I'd heard her called Dahlia before. She was a friendly face in the kitchen who didn't mind all that much when I snuck pre-meal snacks from the cutting board.

"There was a brownie baking contest in 1974—I was just eight years old," Dahlia said with a smile. "Which dates me, but there you have it. I remember it vividly because everyone in town got to try a sample. Like a blind taste test. There were ten bakers who entered, but only two who had any real chance of winning."

"Let me guess," I said. "Mrs. Dulcet and Mrs. Fredericks."

Dahlia nodded. "Mrs. Fredericks won the contest, but Mrs. Dulcet contested the results."

"For a good reason," Mrs. Dulcet said sourly. "The judge was compromised!"

"How?" I asked. "How do you compromise a brownie judge?"

Dahlia leaned in. "You sleep with him."

"Oh—*oh*," I said in understanding. "Mrs. Fredericks slept with a judge, just so her brownies would win?"

"Well, the judge was her husband," Mrs. Dulcet said bitterly. "So, I suppose it makes sense, but that's hardly a fair and impartial judge."

"So why didn't you have a rematch?" I asked. "With a new judge?"

"The town was too distraught." Mrs. Dulcet sounded sniffy again and frustrated. "We couldn't handle another polarizing brownie competition. In addition, I do believe Mrs. Fredericks was too nervous to compete against me for a second time. But—"

I retreated at the glittering look in Mrs. Dulcet's eyes. "Oh, no," I warned. "I don't want any part in this feud."

"It's not a feud," Mrs. Dulcet said. "It's more like an unsolved mystery. You're good at mysteries, aren't you, Lola?"

"Not mysteries of the stomach," I said, tapping my head. "I focus on mysteries of the brain."

"Sure, honey." Mrs. Dulcet patted my arm. "Then that's settled. Don't you dare go eating that brownie yet. Wait until I make my own and then you can compare."

"It's hardly a fair comparison," I said. "Not if yours are fresh out of the oven and Mrs. Fredericks's are frozen."

"Well then, I'll just have you bike around some with my brownies," Mrs. Dulcet said pointedly, "and then you can pop them in the freezer as well. I'm not afraid of a fair competition, unlike my nemesis."

"I had no idea the feelings were so strong between you and Mrs. Fredericks," I said. "I don't want to come between the two of you, especially because you both play an important role in my dessert consumption."

"Don't be silly," Mrs. Dulcet said. "It's settled. I'll see you back here this evening. No—I take that back. Tomorrow. I'd like you to bike around in the sunshine so the conditions are exactly the same. No excuses this time when I wipe the floor with Mrs. Fredericks's brownies. Pardon my French."

As Mrs. Dulcet turned and flounced out of the kitchen, I turned to look at Dahlia. "I can't tell if she's serious."

The cook merely raised her eyebrows. "You have no idea."

"Oh, and Lola—" Mrs. Dulcet popped her head back in the kitchen. "Don't you go telling on me to Mrs. Fredericks or Dane. This is between me and you."

"But I have no stake in the matter!" I argued. "I'm just a pawn."

"Whose pawn are you?" The deep voice rolled through the kitchen, sending Dahlia and the rest of the staff into a flurry of excited movements. Clearly, they were not used to seeing the head of Clark Castle in the flesh.

Mrs. Dulcet stepped fully around the corner into the kitchen. Dane had entered from the other end through a pair of swinging doors near the dining area. While the two faced off, the chefs and other kitchen staff suddenly became very preoccupied with all sorts of chopping, washing, and peeling, their heads tilted down in concentration.

"Oh, it's nothing, sir," Mrs. Dulcet stammered. "It's, ah—"

"Wedding things," I filled in lightly, figuring it wasn't a lie if I was considering having Mrs. Dulcet just make the cake herself. "She wants me to taste different types of brownies in addition to cake to be sure I'm satisfied with the finished product."

I glanced at Dane, watching the man carefully to see if he'd buy it. As I looked at my future husband, I could see why the staff—including Mrs. Dulcet—might be intimidated. He had the build of a movie star with tall, broad shoulders and an authoritative stance that took over any room he entered.

His eyes were a piercing shade of blue that could wreck a woman's resolve and make her weak at the knees—save for a few moments when he softened, like when we lay in bed together in the late hours of the morning. Then, his eyes washed with sunshine and dripped with tenderness as his fingers traced soft lines down the bare skin of my back.

I shuddered, pushing aside the daydreams, thinking Dane's morning suggestions should be illegal. They caused severe distraction for the rest of my day. I frowned and crossed my arms, squinting at Dane so the sheen of his gorgeousness didn't affect me as much as if I stared directly at him.

Dane sensed a change in me and looked concerned. "Lola, may I have a word with you in private?"

I realized the rest of the kitchen had gone perfectly still and was waiting for my response. "Yes, actually—I'd like a word with you, too. Come along, Mr. Clark."

I grabbed his hand and dragged him from the kitchen, releasing Mrs. Dulcet and the rest of the kitchen staff from his piercing gaze. However, once we left the kitchen, Dane took the lead and strode toward the back of the estate.

He pulled me through a few of the dining areas, down the long hallway that led to a small common area off which little arteries petered away into private living quarters. There was a hall specifically for staff who lived on the premises, such as Mrs. Dulcet, as well as a guest hall—which contained my former bedroom and current closet.

Then there was the private wing that belonged to Mr. Clark...and now me: the future Mrs. Clark. The name almost caused me to choke as I thought it—though we'd been talking marriage for two months, it still seemed a novelty that we were soon going to be joining our lives together forever.

"Where are we going?" I asked again when he passed the bedroom. I wrinkled my nose as he pointed us toward the gym. "I thought I told you I wasn't really feeling the whole 'working out' thing."

"As much as the whole 'working out' thing should be mandatory with the amount of dessert you eat, that's not where we're going." Dane Clark stopped abruptly, his eyes sliding guiltily over to me. "I didn't mean—you're gorgeous, Lola, I just meant the amount of trans fat in your system—"

"Yeah, yeah, move it along, buddy," I said. "I know what you meant."

With a sigh of relief, he pulled me into the private area just outside of the gym. The long, narrow room had been outfitted with plush white carpets, a shower with four heads—a bit excessive, seeing as I hadn't figured out where to actually point each head—and luxury soaps and shampoos. Most people would call this a spa. Dane called it a locker room.

"I had time scheduled on your calendar," Dane said. "Don't you check your schedule anymore?"

"I do," I said. "I know exactly what I'm meeting you about."

Dane shut the door behind us and turned the deadbolt lock on it, an amused smirk on his face. The very action of it, along with the searing look he gave me as he turned around, sent the butterflies banging against my stomach. I knew that look. I liked that look—a lot.

"Is that right?" he asked softly.

I nodded. "It's about—"

Dane interrupted me by crossing the room and lifting me with gusto. He carried me over to the four-headed shower. It was like some sort of mythical creature for rich people. My legs wrapped around his waist as his lips hit mine.

"Look at you," Dane said, tugging at my bright yellow dress. My sunglasses had already fallen off to the soft carpeting of the locker room floor, and if the way his hands moved was any indication, he was about to get a second peek at my cute new undies. "You are all shades of sunshine today."

I laughed, nuzzling against him. "What's the special occasion? I wasn't aware of any meeting. I made that up."

"We didn't have a meeting scheduled," he murmured, his words hot against my ear. "But the thought of you has been driving me crazy all day. I have the most gorgeous fiancé in the world—and it's damn distracting."

"Oh, my," I muttered happily.

Then his lips hit my neck and sent shivers along my body as Dane declared our meeting officially commenced. And by the time the meeting was adjourned, I had a silly smile on my face and wobbling legs.

I also had a new appreciation for all four shower heads.

Chapter 2

"Cheers," I said, raising a glass of champagne and clinking it with Dane's. "To slacking off."

He gave a mock frown, but he, too, hadn't been able to wipe the goofy grin off his face since we disappeared into the shower half an hour before. After our shower meeting adjourned, Dane had suggested we take to the hot tub for a late afternoon soak.

"I thought you had working out on your schedule," I said, taking a sip of crisp bubbly. "Are you skipping that for today?"

He gave me some serious side-eye. "I got my workout in already."

I felt my cheeks turn red and mumbled some sort of apology that I didn't really mean. I took zero issue with Dane using me as a form of workout. "What do you want to do this evening?"

Dane cocked his head to the side and fell into deep thought. I knew from experience that it'd be a few minutes before he responded, so I sat back in the hot tub and took in the beautiful sunset colors while Dane disappeared into la-la land.

The hot tub was situated on the stunning back patio that Dane called the pool area. Really, it was like a piece of Roman history dug up and plopped right here on the Sunshine Shore. We sat in boiling hot water under a wooden gazebo. Every pole was covered in grape vines twisting and turning, tendrils of green reaching toward the fading sun. I reached out to snag one, munching happily on a sunshine-ripened bunch while Dane remained lost in thought.

The pool stretched before us, looking like it faded into an infinity of reds and pinks and yellows as sunlight dripped over the edge of it and the last heat of the day began to seep out of the Greco-Roman columns that stood mightily beside the lap pool.

Dane spent hour after hour swimming there, his body growing tan as he trained his muscles. I didn't partake in the training, though I was an absolute master sunbather by this point. Mrs. Dulcet usually found me stretched out on one of the loungers with a book or my work, sunglasses perched atop my head, coconut oil just inches from my fingertips. Sometimes it was still hard to believe this was real life.

I studied the man sitting next to me, admiring the sharp lines of his jaw and the tanned glow to his skin. He had a naturally harsh expression as his default, but after having known him intimately for some time now, I knew it was merely deep concentration. I was still drinking in the view of him, of the sunset, of the glittering pool when he startled me by speaking.

"Whatever you'd like," he said in a completely matter-of-fact tone, as if the conversation hadn't just stalled out for upwards of seven minutes. I'd munched through a bunch of grapes and topped off my champagne in the time he'd spent thinking. "I can be flexible with my schedule."

"You can?" I gasped. "This calls for a celebration."

He gave me a small, testing smile before easing into a full grin. I'd realized that's how Dane could tell whether I'd meant something as a joke: He would give a nonchalant smile that could be interpreted any number of ways, and then if I grinned back, he could tell I was kidding. The man might not have a ton of natural instincts when it came to socializing, but he was trying. He tried so hard it was adorable.

"Absolutely," he agreed amicably. "We'll probably need another shower after the hot tub, and then..."

I eyed him. "Mr. Clark, you're insatiable."

He raised an eyebrow. "It was just a suggestion. You wouldn't want to have chlorine all over your skin at the dinner table, now, would you?"

"Well, I suppose not," I said, humming with the prospect. "In fact, I'm about done here. How about one more glass of champagne each and then we hop out and get started?"

Dane eyed the bottle and saw there was approximately one pour left. "Have mine," he said. "I can see you eyeing it."

"I was hoping you would say that."

He laughed, the sound still a novelty after all these months. A true laugh from Dane Clark was a rare gem, and I sometimes felt like I was collecting them, one laugh at a time. I just wanted to bottle the joy and put it in my pocket for safekeeping.

"Um, sir—" The interruption came from behind the hot tub near the entrance to the locker room. Semi stood there, the tall, dark-skinned man who was responsible for the safety of Dane Clark and all that was his. "Excuse the interruption. I can come back."

"We were just relaxing," I called over to Semi. "You can come over."

Semi moved slowly, staring at his boss as if he'd never seen such a creature. Maybe this was the very first time Semi had heard Dane Clark truly laugh, and I understood why that could put him off-kilter. It wasn't a common occurrence.

"I apologize, sir—I didn't expect to find you here with your fiancé," Semi said formally, his eyes fixed intently on Dane. He shifted uncomfortably, as if the fact that we were both half-clad in bathing suits was an issue. "I can return later if—"

"We've no problem with talking here," Dane said, glancing over to me for approval. My nod came quickly—I'd grown up in a bathing suit running around the Sunshine Shore. A hot tub meeting was nothing. "What is it?"

"I believe we have a problem, and I'm not yet sure if it's of the personal or business variety," Semi said. "Would you prefer to speak in private, sir, once you're fully clothed?"

Dane's eyes flicked to me. "Whatever you need to say, you can say it in front of Lola. I'd rather not waste any more time if there's an issue. What is it, Semi?"

The man had gotten his nickname for very obvious reasons. He was about as big as a semi-truck; it wasn't exactly a creative name, but it was fitting.

Semi shifted his weight uncomfortably, and I could've sworn the cement creaked beneath his mass. I briefly thought of Annalise's small figure and reminded myself to speak to him about his feelings for the gymnast after whatever issue he had was cleared.

"It's about my brother." Semi's eyes flicked downward. "I think Trey's missing."

"Missing?" Dane's eyes snapped back to business mode, his deep, luxurious moments of consideration now whisked away in the wind.

"He didn't show up for work today," Semi said. "I asked around some—apparently he wasn't feeling great yesterday, so he left early, and nobody's seen Trey since then."

"He works in Warehouse 5?" Dane asked in Clark Castle short-hand. "Engineer?"

Semi nodded. "I went to his apartment already, took a peek. Nobody was there. His local hangouts have turned up nothing. I think something's wrong."

Dane processed all of this with more of that determined concentration. "What do you think happened?"

"Sir?"

"You know your brother better than I do," Dane said. "Do you have any theories? Was he worried about anything? Acting strangely?"

"I don't know. I hadn't seen him much lately; I've been busy." Semi gave a shake of his head, his eyes flicking toward me for the first time. "The trouble is, Trey wasn't the most upstanding citizen in his youth, and I'm afraid something in his past has caught up with him."

"You mentioned something about him once," I said, racking my brain for the story. "But I don't recall any specific details. Something about how you'd die for Mr. Clark because of what he'd done for your brother?"

Semi looked embarrassed and cleared his throat. "Sir, may I?"

Dane gave the 'go ahead' gesture.

"My brother and I were raised by a single mother," he said, speaking in a flat tone. "She wasn't the pinnacle of a good citizen either, but she tried. Unfortunately, she got sick and died when my brother was just thirteen. I was eighteen at the time and in no place to raise a kid brother who was going through some rough stuff. I wish I'd done a better job."

"You were just a kid too, Semi," I said. "And you'd lost a parent. I'm sure you did the best job you could."

Semi let my words bounce right off him as if he hadn't heard them. "We lived in a rough neighborhood because it was all I could afford. I was a bouncer at a local strip club just outside the Sunshine Shore—you can imagine the clientele wasn't pretty and neither was the pay, but I was an uneducated kid with a tough streak and size on my side. They didn't even bother with a background check before hiring me and paying me in cash."

"That all makes sense," I said. "You did what you had to."

"Sure, but my brother was left alone a lot during the nights. He fell in with the wrong crowd, started sneaking out—got into things he shouldn't have." Semi closed his eyes for a long moment. "I found out he was into drugs on his sixteenth birthday. I took the night off and brought the kid a cake thinking we could celebrate, and he'd already started a party of his own. He was a mess already, and somehow, I'd missed what was happening right underneath my nose."

"Semi, that's not your fault," I said. "You had to work. You supported him. You probably gave up a lot of your own dreams to take care of your brother."

"It wasn't enough," he said dryly. "After a few months of working with him—taking him to doctors, specialists—even a damn hypnotist—I couldn't get anything to work. He didn't want help."

"If he wasn't ready, there was nothing more you could do," I said quietly. "That's rule number one."

"I told him to clean up or leave," Semi said, letting out the first sigh, the first emotional note since he'd arrived at the hot tub. "He chose to leave. I looked around for him, but I couldn't find the kid for months. He'd racked up enough druggie friends to hide out on couches. Stopped going to school—everything. I tried, but..."

"I know," I said. "It's heartbreaking. I'm so sorry."

"Eventually, I got a job here," Semi said. "Apparently that caught the interest of my brother—the kid could smell money half a continent away. Showed up jonesing for cash one night—of course I didn't give him any."

"But," I said, glancing over to Dane. "That wasn't the end of the story."

"Not even close," Semi said. "The kid couldn't take no for an answer. He tried to break into Castlewood—wanted to steal from Mr. Clark here. I think he assumed that I'd choose my brother over my boss, but he was wrong."

"You caught him?"

"No," Semi said, embarrassed. "The kid knew my weaknesses and exploited them. He got through to Mr. Clark and demanded money. He had a gun, but even that didn't deter Mr. Clark, here."

"Deter him from what?"

"Offering Trey a job," Semi said with a vague smile. "I stumbled into Mr. Clark's office to warn him just as soon as I realized what had happened, and the two of them were negotiating salaries."

I blinked. "How did that happen?"

Dane gave the slightest, barely perceptible shake of his head. I'd never have noticed if I hadn't been staring directly at him, trying to see past the fissures in his unreadable face. He didn't give away anything.

"I don't know," Semi said. "That's the honest truth. Neither of them told me the words they exchanged that day, but so far as I can figure, Mr. Clark tapped into the kid in a way I hadn't ever been able to. The two of them connected—probably because they're both frigging geniuses—and came to an agreement."

"Trey agreed to go through an intense engineer training program under one of the mentors currently at the Clark Company," Dane said nonchalantly. "In exchange for cleaning up his lifestyle and habits, and of course ditching his old friends."

"And that went..." I hesitated, feeling like I was on eggshells. "Smoothly? Just like that?"

"He relapsed once," Dane said with a dangerous smile. "We talked, and it's never happened again."

There was a scary undertone to Dane's words, the sort that led me to wonder if it was possible to really truly know someone—inside and out. I knew that Dane was smart and kind, cunning and ruthless when needed, brilliant and daring in business and in life, but I was also sure there was more to him than all that.

There was so much I didn't know. Layers behind that blank expression, behind those bouts of deep, thoughtful silence. He was a man of many mysteries. A man I'd spend a lifetime unraveling.

In the pause that followed, Dane continued. "He's been with the Clark Company for quite some time now and is the head engineer in Warehouse 5. I am immensely pleased with his performance and would give him the highest ratings both on a professional and a personal level."

A flicker of something passed through Semi's eyes. It might have been pride, or concern, and I wondered if the fear of disappointment was there as well. Dane had clearly done so much for Trey already, and I could feel the worry radiating off Semi. If Trey let down Dane, Semi clearly felt it would reflect poorly on him. As if somehow Semi was responsible for all of Trey's actions as well as his own because they were brothers.

"We'll find him," I said. "I'm sure there's a perfectly logical explanation for all of this. Maybe he's not truly missing. There could be an emergency somewhere, or..."

"Or maybe he's been kidnapped," Dane said with ease. He didn't seem to register the weight of what he'd said and looked blankly around at the ensuing silence. "What? I find it more realistic to believe that someone took Trey than I do to believe Trey found himself in trouble again."

Semi heaved out a huge sigh. "I sure hope you're right, sir. Not that I want my brother to be kidnapped, but if he blew all those chances you gave him and is off on his own somewhere having a good time, I'll lock him up myself. I know how much you've given up for my kid brother."

"I haven't given up a thing," Dane said easily. "Trey is an excellent addition to the staff at the Clark Company. Good employees are priceless, and he is as loyal and hardworking as they come."

"You don't understand, Mr. Clark," Semi said, leaning closer to the hot tub, forgetting whatever discomfort he'd felt moments before in his proximity to us. "If you had sent him to prison, if you'd reacted in any normal way that day he broke into your office, he'd be dead."

"Don't be extreme, Semi," Dane said. "The police wouldn't have killed him."

"No," Semi said, "but he'd have ended up back on the streets, back with the wrong crowd, elbow deep in addiction. You pulled him out of that spiral, Mr. Clark. That's not me being extreme—that's a fact."

Dane shifted in the hot tub, sending the water rippling across the surface toward me. I set my champagne glass down along the edge, the celebratory beverage no longer appropriate. Seeing as Dane appeared paralyzed with discomfort at Semi's words, I took charge.

"We're going to hop out of the tub, rinse off, and change," I said with a quick flick of my eyes toward Dane to make sure he agreed. When he didn't give any sign of hearing me, I continued. "We'll meet you out front in twenty minutes—have a car ready. We'll find out what happened to your brother, Semi."

Chapter 3

U nfortunately, our plans to enjoy those four magical shower heads didn't pan out the second time around. We took plain old practical showers and rushed through the dressing process. I slipped into a fresh outfit—jeans and a bright blue tank top that subtly matched Dane's eyes.

The pair of us were quiet as we rushed through the castle. Dane stopped only to warn Mrs. Dulcet that he and I were headed out for a bit and that we'd be having dinner late.

"Tell her not to wait up," I whispered to Dane. "You know she always waits until you're back if you don't tell her to go to bed."

"Why don't you tell her?"

"Because she's your staff," I said. "I'm just—"

I stopped abruptly and looked to Dane, who gave me the most curious of expressions.

"You're just what?" he prompted expectantly. "My wife?"

"Well, I'm not your wife *quite* yet."

"Soon enough," he said with the slightest sign of a wink. "You might as well get used to the responsibilities of running Castlewood."

I cleared my throat and turned to the butler who had politely pretended to ignore our entire exchange. "Um, Mrs. Dulcet, if you feel like going to bed, you should. We might be out late, and so—ah...don't wait up for us."

Mrs. Dulcet gave a kind smile. "Thank you, Lola. Er—Miss Pink."

"Please, Lola," I said, waving my hands hurriedly. "Even after we're married. I can't bear to be called anything but my name."

She gave a nod of her head. "Of course, ma'am."

"Lola."

"Lola," she said with a smile. "Have a nice evening."

As Dane and I fled the castle and climbed down the stairs, he looked over at me with the beginnings of a smirk. "That was a very direct and decisive order you gave just then."

"Hey! That's not fair—I know you're mocking me." I put a hand on my hip as we slowed before reaching the waiting black SUV. "I'm not going to boss Mrs. Dulcet around—she's been a part of the castle longer than me."

"Relax." Dane hooked a finger in the top of my tank top and dragged me close to his side in an unusually suave gesture. "I love you—I'm joking. I'm trying to get you comfortable being here. It's your home, and my home. It's ours now."

I smiled and nuzzled against him, feeling warm all over. This engaged stuff was excellent. I just basked in the knowledge that we'd be together forever.

Semi cleared his throat from the driver's seat, startling Dane and me into stepping apart. Dane held open the door, and I slid in while he followed. I found it sweet when he slipped his hand into mine as Semi took off down the paved drive that led to the world beyond Castlewood.

"Take us to his apartment first," Dane said. "I assume you've called him several times already?"

"Yes, sir. I've gone to his apartment, too. My last phone call and message to Trey was at 6:42 this evening."

I glanced at the clock and saw it wasn't yet seven. "It'll be good to get a feel for how he was living," I suggested. "It could give us a clue about what he was doing before he disappeared."

It wasn't said, but my meaning was implied. We needed to determine first if someone had maliciously taken Trey without his permission—a.k.a. kidnapped him—or if he'd fallen into old ruts and had found his way elsewhere on his own.

We sat in silence as we drove across the Sunshine Shore, down Route 1, and into a tiny little subdivision on a cliff high above the water.

A new set of detached condos sat perched in a row just off the coastal road with magnificent views of both the town and the ocean. They'd recently been built and sold off to the highest bidder. Apparently, Trey was one of the highest bidders of them all because he'd managed to secure one of the best lots. Semi parked in front of a desirable corner plot with a clipped privacy hedge and a gorgeously landscaped lawn.

"This is not what I pictured when you said your brother lived in an apartment," I muttered as Dane popped the door open and we slid out one after another. "This is like a luxury retreat."

"Mr. Clark pays well," Semi grunted. "Trey bought the first condo available."

Mr. Clark didn't appear impressed one way or another about either the condo or the chatter about salaries, instead turning a calculating gaze toward the front. "Do you have a key?"

The three of us walked to the front door. I arrived first and gave Semi a sideways glance. "I don't think we need one."

Dane frowned as he peeked over my shoulder and saw the destroyed doorknob. "I see someone's been here."

"I was a little frustrated, sir," Semi said. "I thought...er, I assumed Trey had blown off work, and I'd come to give him a piece of my mind."

"Call Nicolas," Dane barked to Semi. "Have him send a contractor with a replacement doorknob immediately."

Semi gave a grateful nod. "Yes, sir. In the meantime, please let yourself inside and look around. Trey won't mind."

Dane and I kicked off our shoes before entering the beautiful new home. The sprawling rambler was much longer than it was tall, as were most buildings on the Shore, thanks to the too-frequent earthquakes that rocked the fault line beneath our town.

The condo had been manufactured with minimalist sharpness: Countertops gleamed in dark marble, while stark white walls gave contrast to the glittering blue water visible through the floor-to-ceiling windows along the coastal side of the house. As we made our way from the living room to the open kitchen, down past the first bedroom into the master suite, I watched the shifting views out the wall of windows.

"This is stunning," I said, taking in the view. "I bet this condo sold for a pretty penny."

"Would you like a better view at home?" Dane asked. "I'll see what I can arrange at the castle."

"I was just commenting," I said, shooting him a quizzical look. "You don't have to take everything I say to mean you need to change something. I'm just admiring."

"I want you to have everything you desire at the castle," he said. "I want you to feel comfortable at home. If there are changes you'd like to make, I'd be happy to work with you on them."

"Dane, I have everything I want." I wrapped my arms around him, savoring the rich softness of the deep gray sweater and the firm chest beneath it. "I have you. The rest is the icing. You're my cake."

"Cake," he said, musing. "Interesting."

"As much as I'd like to admire the view of *you* all day, I think we should get on with the investigation," I said. "Do you have any idea where Trey might be?"

"I don't think he's fallen into old ways," Dane said. "There would have been signs."

"Did you see him every day?"

"No, I rarely see any employee every day."

"Maybe we need to ask around Warehouse 5, then," I said. "Ask the people he worked with every day if there were changes in his behavior."

"Yes, we'll do that tomorrow," Dane said. "In the meantime, I think we should begin operating under the assumption that he's been taken against his will. I can't imagine why it would be a personal issue with

Trey, but I suppose it could be. I think we need to be cautious and not rule out the fact that it could be a work-related disappearance. Whether it is someone at the Clark Company, a competitor, or something else. We should keep the investigation as quiet as possible."

We began peeling through the layers of Trey's apartment. I picked through Trey's possessions with a light touch, carefully sifting through his belongings and then inevitably putting them back when they led nowhere.

By the time Semi finished up his phone calls as per Dane's instructions and joined the search, Dane and I had fallen into a concentrated effort to move quickly. The sun had finished its descent, leaving behind a twinkling blackness that blanketed the full-length view from every room in the house.

Semi flicked on a few lamps, modern little things that were slender and bendable, flooding the condo with a brilliant sort of light. I moved into the kitchen while Dane and Semi handled the bedroom. I sorted through the fridge, taking stock of the sparse, yet very organized, contents inside. A few bottles of condiments, a container of fresh salad greens, and one neat takeout box that looked to be Chinese food that hadn't yet gone bad. The man was impeccably clean.

"Normally, I'd be impressed at this level of cleanliness," I said. "But this is downright annoying. How are we supposed to learn about the man if he doesn't even have a photograph on the wall?"

"He works hard," Semi muttered. Then quickly corrected himself. "He had been working hard. Long hours at the Clark Company don't leave much time for a personal life. Not that I'm complaining, of course. Then again, I choose to live in the Clark Company residences, so I really don't get out much."

Dane heard our conversation from the next room over and came in. "Does that bother you?"

Semi looked startled. "No, sir. Not at all, sir. I was just commenting on my brother's lack of personal life. I enjoy my career."

Dane narrowed his eyes, but he didn't say much after that, turning instead to rifle through the edgy black desk protruding from the wall in the spare bedroom. I peeked my head in to make sure he was occupied, then hurried back to Semi.

"Speaking of a lack of personal life," I began. "I have been meaning to talk to you about something—"

"Oh, Miss Pink, it is totally worth it," Semi said. "Believe me, you are making the right choice."

"The right choice? About what?"

"You're second guessing your engagement to Dane? Worried it won't leave you much of a 'personal' life?" Semi guessed. "Listen, I'm telling you it will all work out. Working for Dane Clark is the best thing that's ever happened to me. I wouldn't trade it for anything."

"Not even Annalise?" I asked quietly.

"Oh." Semi straightened to his full massive height and stared down his nose at me. "You wanted to talk about me and Annalise, not you and Dane."

"Yes, and I know it's not my place, but she's one of my best friends, and I care a lot about Annalise. I care about you, too, Semi." I reached out a hand and touched him gently on the arm. "She's pretty torn up about your breakup."

Semi's face went blank. "She is?"

I nodded. "It's not my place to get involved, even though that's exactly what I'm doing. I just thought... well, I thought you should know. You don't have to say anything."

"I think we should keep looking for Trey," Semi said. "I'm still on the clock, and like I said, head of security for the Clark Company doesn't leave much time for a personal life."

"Of course."

"Lola, I—" Semi inhaled a deep breath. He glanced around the room, clearly scanning for Dane. When his boss was nowhere in sight, he relaxed somewhat. "It's not that."

"What is it then?" I pressed down on the button to release the garbage can lid, figuring it better for me to keep busy thumbing through things while Semi talked. "Semi!"

He crossed the room in two big steps to reach my side and glanced down next to me. "What'd you find?"

"Look at this," I said, reaching into the bin and pulling out a small Post-It note. All it had was a name and a phone number written on it. Billy Smalls, and then ten digits scribbled after it. "Do you think this is anything?"

I handed the note to Semi as I quickly rifled through the rest of the trash, but there was nothing else there to note. I spotted a few wrappers from cough drops, plastic that had been peeled from some sort of packaging, and that was all.

"I know this name." Semi stared at the paper, his eyes wide. "I know this guy."

"Who is he? What does he do?"

"Nobody good, and nothing good."

"Is he a friend from..." I hesitated. "Trey's past?"

"One could say that," Semi said dryly. "When I last knew him, he was stealing cars and selling marijuana. Real stand up guy."

"Can you think of any reason why Trey might be in touch with Billy?"

Semi gave a rough shake of his head. "Not unless Trey needed something he couldn't get legally."

"Semi, this is just a note in the garbage. It doesn't mean anything," I said, carefully patting him on the shoulder. It was like comforting a rock. "We're not sure he ever even called this number. We can't jump to conclusions."

"No, no jumping," Semi said.

At that moment, Dane Clark stepped out of the spare bedroom. Between his fingers, he held a baggie. One of his eyebrows raised. "I'm not a connoisseur of these things," he said carefully, "but I'm assuming what's in here is not a cooking herb."

A light went out in Semi's eyes, and his fist closed around the paper with Billy's name on it. "I'm sorry you had to find that, sir," he said. "I think we need to pay Mr. Smalls a visit."

"Yeah—about that, I'm going to need you to let go." I reached for Semi's hand and touched the outside gently, leaving my hand there until he unfurled his grip. I took one glance at the pulverized sheet of paper—now damp—and wrinkled my nose. "How about we grab Billy Smalls's address from Nicolas?"

"It's too late tonight," Semi said, "and I'm sorry, Mr. Clark, but this information isn't pointing to any sort of foul play except my brother's own bad decisions. I think we should head back to the castle. You can leave this mess to me—I'll take care of Trey."

The way Semi delivered that last line, I most certainly didn't want to be Trey when Semi caught up with him.

"We're not leaving you alone to deal with this," I said, "but I think you're right that it's too late tonight to visit Billy. First thing in the morning, we'll pay his friend a visit. Together."

Semi gave a quick, grateful look around the room, and then a nod. "I'd appreciate that."

Then he left the house and slammed the door behind him.

Dane and I shared an anxious look after him.

"It doesn't look good for Trey," I said to Dane. "If he fell in with his old crowd, it's going to be hard on Semi. He might even worry you'll take it out on him, and you have to reassure him that won't happen."

"Semi is not the same person as his brother. Why would Trey's actions reflect on Semi?"

"That's true, but Semi probably can't help but feel a responsibility for his brother. That's what family is all about." I sidled over and slipped under Dane's arm. "Just make sure Semi knows how much you appreciate him."

"Of course," Dane said, and his mind was already clicking away, digesting the information as always. Sooner or later, he'd have filed away enough signs of typical human behavior that he might be able to act like one himself. When I told him that, he laughed. Then he kissed my forehead. "Would you like that?"

"No," I said, resting my head against his chest as we left the condo. "I like you just the way you are."

Chapter 4

The drive home was uneventful.

Which was all sorts of wrong.

Dane stared out the window, lost in thought as he sunk into the darkness. Semi stared forward through the windshield, also lost in thought. Apparently, I was the only person who noticed the tail behind us—the small black car that dipped in and out of sight and tried to use other cars to cover up its tracks. It was a futile attempt, seeing as we were the only two vehicles on the road for most of the drive home.

I didn't notice the tail until we were over halfway back, and after I'd whipped my head around to look behind us, the car seemed to drop out of sight. Eventually, it disappeared.

I hesitated to say anything. There was a chance I was just being paranoid. I'd been involved in more freak investigations these past few months than ever before, and it might have messed with my mind. I supposed it was a perk of working closely with Dane Clark. The man, or rather his billions, had the tendency to draw out the cuckoos in droves.

Semi dropped us at the front door, and Mrs. Dulcet, no surprise, was there to greet us. I glanced over my shoulder as she ushered us inside, wondering where Semi would go for the night. What he'd be thinking. Would he be wondering about Trey? Missing Annalise? Traipsing across a dark, empty apartment alone?

"He'll be fine," Dane said in a rare moment of reading my mind. "Come on, Lola. You need some rest."

"You need rest," I said, but that wasn't entirely true.

Dane Clark slept for three to four hours a night, crawling out of bed at a ridiculous hour of the morning. But my favorite part of all was that he'd creep back into bed—changed back into pajamas and all—around seven thirty each morning.

He'd hold me until I woke some twenty minutes later as if he'd been there the whole time. I still hadn't figured out if he knew that I was aware of his little plan, or if he genuinely thought he was fooling me. Either way, I didn't want it to stop.

"I'm just worried about him," I admitted. "By the way, did you notice anything strange on the drive home?"

Dane blinked, as if surprised there'd been a drive home at all. "No, why?"

"I had the weirdest feeling we were being followed," I said, as Mrs. Dulcet ushered us into the dining room for a late dinner. "You didn't notice anything out of the ordinary?"

"No, but I wasn't looking, either," he said once we were seated at opposite ends of the long dining room table. "I just...what are we doing so far apart? I can barely hear you from here. Let's go into the living room to talk. We can eat later."

"Or, we can do this." I picked up my chair and marched it across the dining room and planted it right next to Dane. "How about that?"

He looked stunned at the rearrangement. "I never once thought to move the chairs."

"That's what you have me for."

"To move chairs?"

I leaned my head against his shoulder and tapped my noggin. "To think outside the box."

He wrapped an arm around me and kissed my head. "Did you see anything that might have prompted you to feel followed?"

"It's hard to say—it's late, and it was dark, and..."

"Lola?"

"I thought I saw a small black car. But when I looked back, it seemed to disappear."

"Semi is usually good about that," Dane said with a frown. "He rarely misses security issues. It's not as if we haven't been tailed by plenty of people before—media, reporters, and worse. He usually shakes them within minutes. I've never felt he missed a tail before."

"That's sort of my point," I said. "I think you need to be extra careful. Semi is a little distracted. It's natural—he has a lot on his mind."

Dane's lips pinched together. "But his brother's actions don't reflect on him as far as I'm concerned. I have worked with Semi for a decade. The hiring of his brother was completely separate."

"It's not only that, but he and Annalise also broke up, and I think they're still hurting."

"That was a month ago."

"I know," I said, patting Dane's leg. "But they really enjoyed being together. I know Annalise is still down in the dumps. I'm willing to bet Semi's not totally back to normal, even if he does a good job of hiding his emotions."

"How do I find out if he's too distracted to do his job?" Dane's eyes landed on me. "I thought you were just insisting that I ensure Semi knows I appreciate him."

"You should still do that," I coached, "but also keep your eyes peeled. You know, just be on high alert and be careful. I don't want anything to happen to you."

Dane's eyes roved over me. "What about you?"

"I'm not involved in this thing like you are," I said. "I'm just your peripheral help. I poke through the garbage."

"Emotions are so difficult."

"I know." I sighed. "Tell me about it. I'm a woman—we have some rough hormones to top off the party."

"Don't you think he should be over his breakup by now?"

"I don't make a point to think about how someone should feel," I said. "It's how they actually feel that matters. I mean, if something happened to me, would you be over it in a month?"

"No, but that's different."

"Maybe a little," I said. "But it's still—"

"No," Dane said, utterly serious. "I don't believe it's the same at all."

I turned to face him. "And why's that?"

"Because I don't think there's anyone in the world who can love someone else as much as I love you." His eyes darkened, he leaned in, and his kiss stole my breath.

My heart burst with the sweetness of him, and even if he couldn't possibly know any such thing for a fact, I could tell that in his heart, he believed it to be true. And isn't that what mattered?

"I think we should skip dinner," I said, grasping his hand and pulling him to his feet. "Maybe we can have someone from the kitchen send it to our room...later."

The dark in Dane's eyes danced. "I'm catching onto your insinuations quicker, don't you think?" He stood, his arm wrapped possessively around my waist as his lips came down to nip at the back of my neck.

"Mmm..." I let him nuzzle me, pressing into him. "Well, you know what they say—practice makes perfect."

Dane's fingers slid across the top of my jeans and hooked through the belt loops as he nearly dragged me out of the dining room, down the hall, toward the bedroom. Which is why Mrs. Dulcet found the table empty when she appeared with trays of food, and it's why she gave a little smile and hummed to herself as she sat the trays under warming lids and gave her staff instructions to leave it outside the boss's bedroom sometime later.

DANE CREPT BACK INTO bed later than usual the next morning.

I was already awake when he slipped into the room just before eight. In fact, I'd snuck out of bed myself and brushed my teeth, added a little makeup, and wiped the sandman from my eyes because two could play at this game. Then, I had feigned sleep as he slipped under the sheets and pulled me tight to his chest.

He'd gone through the effort of changing back into his pajama bottoms but had deliciously foregone a shirt, which did wonderful things for snuggling. I sighed, easing back into him, stretching as I pretended to wake.

"Good morning, sunshine," I said, turning to face him with a bright smile. "How did you sleep?"

"Excellent!" He made do with a horrible fake yawn. "And you?"

"Great! The sun is shining, my fiancé is next to me, and..." I frowned. "What's wrong?"

"Nothing's wrong," Dane said, but he, too, was frowning. "Did you brush your teeth?"

"Um..."

"Were you already awake?"

"Why are you ruining our game?" I asked. "I like the way we do things."

"The way we do things?" Dane leaned up on one elbow. "What are you talking about?"

"You know, the whole, you pretending you've been asleep all morning when really you've already changed into your suit, spoken to Japan, read fifteen papers, and put in a half-day's work before you change back into pajamas and climb into bed with me thing."

"That's not true," Dane said. "I didn't do that."

"Oh, really?"

"I talked to China, not Japan."

I burst out laughing. "Oh, well, excuse me," I said, reaching forward to rake my hands over his chest in playful tickles. "Then I'm allowed to brush my teeth and pretend to sleep so that you're not scared away by morning breath."

"I'm not scared away—"

"Just...shh," I said, smothering his lips with a kiss. "It's too early to dissect things. Let's just enjoy."

"You should know," Dane said with a groan, "that I've made Mrs. Dulcet pencil in relaxation hour from seven thirty to eight thirty every day on my schedule."

"That sounds stressful," I said with a wink. "I guess we have half an hour left. Best get to work relaxing..."

Our attempts to relax one another were rudely interrupted a few minutes later by a hesitant tap on the door. "I apologize," Mrs. Dulcet called through after waiting the appropriate amount of time. "But Dane, I must talk to Lola."

"Is it urgent?"

Mrs. Dulcet cleared her throat. "In a way, yes."

I sat up in bed, clutching the sheet around me. Relaxation hour had kicked off with a magic act that involved disappearing clothes and magical fingers. "Oh, um, give me a second and I'll be right out! Sorry about this," I whispered to Dane, pulling his head close to my chest and planting a firm kiss on the top of it. "To be continued."

His groan was one of serious disapproval, but he diligently rose and began dressing in a clean suit. When he caught me staring, he stopped. "What are you looking at?"

"Do you go through two suits a day now?" I asked. "An early morning suit and a..."

"A pre-Lola and post-Lola suit," he said with a smile. "Mrs. Dulcet isn't thrilled."

"Yeah, I imagine not."

"I don't wear the same clothes twice in a month."

I blinked at him. "Seriously?"

"I have forty-suits," he said. "They're all nearly identical. I just rotate through them in order."

"Yeah, but that only gets you through..." I hesitated, struggling to do math before coffee. "Twenty days of the month if you're doing double duty."

"I ordered twenty more. Which will be fine except for months that have thirty-one days," he mused, the corners of his mouth pinching together. "I suppose I should have two more ordered."

"You're ridiculous." I slid into my attire for the day—a set of slouchy jeans with some rough holes around the knees (Babs had assured me they were totally in style), and another tank top. On went the pink flip flops and the pink shades perched on my head. I surveyed myself. "I don't think I look like the wife of Dane Clark."

Dane smiled. "I think you look perfect."

As usual, he looked smashing in his suit, and I wanted to push him out onto a runway somewhere to show him off to the world. But instead, I pulled him closer to me and fell into him for a hug because that way, I didn't have to share.

"Good luck with Mrs. Dulcet," Dane whispered against my head. "I have a meeting with Germany in twenty minutes. After, I'll gather Semi and we'll pay a visit to Billy Smalls. Nicolas pulled through with the address late last night, but we were—ah—otherwise occupied."

I was giggling as I yanked the door open with Dane just a breath behind me. I stopped dead at the sight of Mrs. Dulcet's face. She wore a severe frown, and in her hands was a silver tray.

"Get your bike," she said blandly. "It's time."

"Time for what?" Dane asked, then waved a hand. "Never mind. I have to prepare for Germany. I'll be in my office."

"You interrupted Dane's relaxation hour for this?!" I gestured to the Tupperware full of brownies that Mrs. Dulcet held out to me. "Some stupid contest between you and Mrs. Fredericks?"

"It's not stupid," she said blithely, "and don't think I'm not aware of what relaxation hour is, missy. How often can the two of you *relax*? You relaxed all of last night during dinner, after I'd spent my night preparing to serve you."

"We ate the meal," I said sheepishly. "And that's not fair you're guilt tripping me into going along with this contest! I am allowed to relax with my almost-husband as much as I like."

"Sure, then eat some brownies and replenish your relaxation energy supplies," Mrs. Dulcet threw a conspiratorial arm around my shoulder and led me toward the front of the castle. "I need you to be biking around at the same hour as yesterday so that the circumstances are exactly the same. We need to achieve the same level of meltiness *that* woman's brownies had when they went in the freezer."

I rolled my eyes. "You're ridiculous, Mrs. Dulcet. I love you, but this is insane."

"I love you, too. Now help out the old woman who you blew off last night for your fiancé," she said, smiling as she shoved the tray into my hands and pointed me toward the front door. "While you're at it, the invitations came in last night, but I didn't have time to show you. Why don't you drop a few off while you bike around? I think twenty minutes should do it, don't you?"

I hesitated to agree, wanting instead to focus on the issue of Semi and his missing brother, but I couldn't do a whole lot without Dane and Semi. Since they were occupied, I might as well get my wedding obligations out of the way in the meantime.

"Fine," I said, snatching the brownies from her hand. "Where are the invitations?"

Mrs. Dulcet produced them from a counter somewhere behind the front door and with loving care, held them to her chest. "Aren't they just gorgeous?"

"I wouldn't know," I said dryly. "I wasn't consulted on them before they were ordered."

"Oh, Lola—are you upset?" Mrs. Dulcet's brow furrowed. "Amanda was just trying to help—she wants the best for the two of you."

"Sure," I said, spinning around to head down the front steps without looking at them. "I'll look at them later. I'm not really in a festive mood at the moment."

"Here, just take one of the extras in case you change your mind." Mrs. Dulcet popped an envelope on top of my tray. "In case you're curious. If you don't like them, Lola, we'll get something else. I promise."

"Alright, thanks." I shifted the envelope higher on the brownie container.

The envelope itself was made of fine material, thick and shiny, and I expected that the invitation inside was equally as elegant. Too bad I didn't know what it said, or what it looked like, or where it'd come from. I wasn't even sure how many invitations Dane's mother had ordered. She probably had her own guest list sorted already as well.

"By the way," Mrs. Dulcet said, wringing her hands together as she watched my expression carefully, "I have samples of flower arrangements being sent to the castle today. Maybe you'd like to join me in reviewing them with Amanda this afternoon?"

"How kind of Amanda to have invited me."

"It's not..." Mrs. Dulcet hesitated. "I can reschedule if it doesn't work for you."

"Why don't we do that," I said. I cocked my head to the side, contemplating. "I'd prefer to go to the florist myself. I'm busy today, but—"

"Tomorrow then," Mrs. Dulcet said, excitedly patting her hands against the apron across her lap. "Tomorrow. It's a date—I'll clear your schedule for the afternoon, and I'll let Amanda know."

I felt the smile falter on my face. "Wonderful."

Before Mrs. Dulcet could ask why I seemed less than thrilled about the idea of Amanda joining us for a visit to the flower shop, I hopped the rest of the way down the steps and wedged the brownie Tupperware into my basket. I carefully arranged the invitation so it balanced securely on top, and then nudged up the kickstand and took off without looking back.

The air felt good flowing through my hair, the sun beating on my shoulders as I raced down the road to the Sunshine Shore. I loved living at the castle more than anything. Mostly because Dane was there. But there was something about being close enough to walk to the waterfront that I missed, despite all the luxuries of Castlewood. I'd grown up with the beach at my front door, and sometimes I just needed to see the water. To plop down in the sand and think.

Babs found me with my toes in the sand, flip flops scattered next to me, the sample invite squished between my fingers an hour later.

"Brownie soup," she said unceremoniously. "Yum."

"Oh, *crap*!" I glanced at the Tupperware. "Mrs. Dulcet will kill me. Quick let me have your sweater so I can give it some shade."

Babs happily handed over a bright orange sweater that perfectly matched her bright orange stilettos. Then she kicked off her heels, smoothed her business-black dress over her backside, and eased onto the sand next to me. "What's up, buttercup?"

"Semi's brother is missing," I said. "Don't tell Annalise."

Babs leaned closer, her eyebrow raised. "Is he cute?"

"Babs," I said. "You're missing the point. He's gone. Hard to be cute if he's disappeared, don't you think?"

She gave a shrug. "Is it serious, like, something happened to him?"

"I don't know," I said. "But he does have a past. I was wondering if you might poke around in it for me. See if he served jail time, see if he had any close friends. Dane and team are looking into things, but Semi is...well, he's distracted."

"A broken heart and a missing brother," Babs said. "That's a lot."

I nodded. "I'm almost certain he's not over Annalise. I almost got him to talk to me about it yesterday, but then we got caught up searching for his brother and the moment passed."

"They'll figure it out," Babs said confidently. "They're both just stubborn. Maybe if we can figure out a way to get them together somehow and force them to talk, they'll kiss and make up."

"Knowing them, they'd just make out and not talk," I said with a wry smile. "I don't know if that would help or hinder their case."

"True," Babs said. "What about—oh, Lola! Your wedding! We can get them to go as dates. Even as just friends, and then they'll fall in love all over again. It'll be great. Speaking of, I'm going to need a copy of the invite list."

"Why do you need a copy of that? Even I don't have one."

"Didn't you make it?"

"Not really," I said with a quizzical smile. "I mean, I have a list of my invitees: you and Annalise, and about four other people that are somewhat of a stretch. I am sure Amanda Clark has her own list. However, I haven't seen it."

"She's really starting to bother you, isn't she?" Babs frowned. "I think you need to talk to Dane about his mother's involvement. I mean, it's great if she wants to *help*, but not so much that it's making you unhappy."

"It's fine." I brushed Babs off. "I have bigger things to worry about, and you still haven't told me why you need the invite list."

"Because I need to stalk potential candidates for me to make out with while Annalise and Semi are busy falling in love again, and you're busy getting married and having babies," she said. "It doesn't have to be Mr. Perfect, but I'd take a Mr. Right Now. You know, handsome and single. It's not like my standards are over the moon."

"Well, aside from the fact that's creepy, I'll ask Mrs. Dulcet. Maybe she knows what's happening with the list because I certainly don't." I handed the invitation to her and watched carefully as Babs fingered it, pulled the paper out from inside. "This came today."

Babs's eyes scanned it approvingly while I did the same over her shoulder. "It's beautiful. You hate it."

"I don't hate it," I said. "They will be very nice, and I'm sure they were the *most* expensive option. I just...they don't feel like mine. This is the first time I'm seeing one."

"You've got to talk to Dane about this," Babs urged again. "It's your wedding. Well, Dane's too, but you're the bride. Amanda already had her wedding. It's not your fault it was, like, a century ago."

I laughed and leaned my head against my friend's shoulder. "How'd you find me here?"

"Mrs. Dulcet called to ask me where her brownies had gotten to," Babs said. "I figured you were probably in need of some thinking time."

"You know me so well," I said, smiling. "I should have you plan the wedding."

"I've been begging to do it," Babs said. "But, I probably wouldn't be as nice about Amanda Interference as you."

"It is odd," I admitted. "She never quite shows her face around the castle, but things have been happening lately that have her stamp all over them. The invitations and guest list, least of all."

"What else?" Babs asked. "You haven't told me any of this."

"Because I might just be a paranoid wackadoodle."

"You are not a paranoid wackadoodle."

I crossed my legs, soaking in the energy of the sun as it hit our skin, and faced Babs. "The other day, I suggested these adorable, individual sized Bundt cakes for the wedding reception instead of a traditional cake. Mrs. Dulcet and I found the perfect place for them, and initially, they said they'd be happy to do it for us."

"What flavor?"

"A bunch of flavors," I said. "Everyone could have their pick: red velvet, confetti, pecan praline, carrot cake, strawberries and cream—"

"Say no more." Babs held up her hand. "I'm sold. What went wrong?"

"They called back a few days later and said they were no longer serving Bundtlets for weddings. I called a few other bakeries, and they all told me the same thing."

Babs squinted. "You think Amanda did that?"

"I don't know. It's about the first thing with the wedding I took initiative on," I said. "You know I love my cake."

"I do know that."

"Then out of the blue, we were sent this gorgeous, traditional style miniature cake to sample, along with the promise that the bakery could make it full size." I shrugged. "It was very good, but it was plain white and all fancy decorated, and...not me, you know?"

"I'm sorry, Lo," Babs said. "That sucks."

"So, I've been thinking that it might be better to give up," I said. "I mean, these invitations are stunning. I'm sure our wedding will be beautiful. The cake Amanda selected was exquisite. But, I just don't really feel connected to any of it. Honestly, I'd rather marry Dane at the courthouse, so long as it's our decision and not hers."

"Maybe you should," Babs said. "That'd show her, and you'd get what you want—you'd be married to Dane."

I sighed. "It doesn't work like that. I'll be part of Dane's family forever. I don't want to upset his mother from day one."

"Too late for that," Babs said. "She thought you were the maid."

"Yeah, well, I thought she was coming around to me," I said. "But it turns out, it's just a show. She's trying to control me like a little puppet."

"You don't have strings, Lola," Babs said. "She can try, but it's futile. Why are you letting her have all this power over your wedding? Is that why you haven't gone dress shopping yet since we went browsing?"

I gave a sullen nod. "I liked that dress we saw down at Monique's Bridal, but when I called back the week after, they were completely out of stock."

"That's impossible," Babs said. "They'd just ordered in five new ones."

"My point exactly." I swirled my pointer finger around and jabbed it forward like magic. "She's got powers, Babs. Amanda has her hands in everything. She must have called the store after we left and instructed them not to sell us anything without her stamp of approval first."

"That's ridiculous. Lola, you *must* talk to Dane."

"It's not worth it. I promise I'll stop complaining now. I just needed to vent after this morning. The invitations, the flower shopping..." I brushed the sand off my legs and stood. "It's not like I have a ton of guests coming to the ceremony, anyway."

"What's that supposed to mean?" Babs struggled to stand. Her dress was far too tight for her to be jumping up and down, and her legs got stuck.

I extended a hand and helped pull her to her feet. "Does it really matter what I want if all the guests are Dane's? I have you and Annalise, sure, but that's about all that really matters to me. I don't have family coming—I have no father to walk me down the aisle and no mother to fuss over my dress. I don't have relatives asking me where to stay when they come to town, and even..." I hesitated for the most painful memory yet. "Even Dotty can't make it."

Babs opened her arms, her face crumpling. "Honey, come here."

I fell into Babs's arms, feeling the tears prick at my cheeks. I hated to cry over something as silly as a wedding—it was meant to be a celebration of love, not a stressful game with my future mother-in-law. "I don't care about the wedding, really. I just care about marrying Dane."

"Dotty will be there," Babs said, and I felt her own shudder of sadness as she squeezed me close. "And this is your day—with Dane. You should have it how you like it."

I gave her one last good embrace, and then I stepped back and wiped my eyes. "This has helped a lot," I said to Babs. "Thanks for finding me here and listening."

"So, you're going to confront Amanda?"

I smiled and shook my head. "Nope."

"What?! What about everything we talked about?"

"I'm going to see if Dane wants to get married at the courthouse."

"But Lola, no!" A look of horror crossed Babs's face. "Why? You shouldn't have to give up your wedding just to avoid Dane's mother!"

"I'm not," I said with a tense smile. I gathered up the invitation and brownies. "It's fine, Babs, really—I've already come to terms with it."

Babs was still staring after me with her mouth parted in surprise when I climbed on my bike. I glanced down at the brownies, but as Babs had suggested, they were nothing more than a sugary soup of frosting and brownie crumbles.

My ride back to the castle was a quick one, and I ignored the pinching in my gut as I flounced back into the castle and handed over the brownies without a word. Mrs. Dulcet wisely didn't say anything as she popped them in the freezer, scurrying after me down the hall.

"What did you think of the invitations?" she asked. "Did you show Babs? Did she like them?"

"Babs thought they were nice," I said, turning to face Mrs. Dulcet. "But that's a silly question. Amanda doesn't choose anything that's not *the best.*"

Mrs. Dulcet's face went as white as sheet cake.

I frowned. "And the sample cake sent here, that was her doing, I imagine? The wedding dress out of stock?"

"Miss Pink, she's only trying to help," Mrs. Dulcet said. "It's in her nature to interfere, and—"

"Thanks," I said shortly. "I'll try your brownies tomorrow."

Before she could argue, Dane and Semi appeared, their heads together as they murmured about something confidential, as evidenced by the fact that they stopped abruptly the moment they spotted company.

"Mrs. Dulcet," Dane said with a bob of his head in her direction. "Lola, come with us. Please. We have a visit to make, and I have your updated itinerary."

"Okay," I said with a frown. "Updated itinerary?"

Dane handed me a sheet of paper while simultaneously dismissing Mrs. Dulcet with a hand gesture. It took only a second to realize that the sheet of paper wasn't an updated itinerary.

I gasped. "A ransom note?"

"One million delivered at midnight," Dane said with a thin smile. "The money's not the problem, but the Clark Company will not be blackmailed."

I flicked my sunglasses down and gave him a wan smile. "Agent Pink is ready for action."

Chapter 5

B illy Smalls's apartment was everything that Trey's apartment wasn't. Run down in a corner of the Sunshine Shore that I hadn't even known existed, the place looked like it was barely standing on its ragged old cement foundation.

"Semi, what's your brother's last name?" I asked. "Is it the same as yours?"

"No," Semi said, climbing from the SUV with a frown. "I don't have a last name. I'm just Semi."

"And Trey's last name is..."

"Hampton." His eyes flicked toward me. "Trey Hampton."

"Semi Hampton." I tried the name on for size, then scrunched up my nose. "Yeah, you're right. Doesn't work."

Semi barely managed a smile before leading us to the door where he pounded on the cracked wood with enough force to shake the house's foundation.

The ransom note had been dropped at Castlewood's front door by a private courier. Mrs. Dulcet had opened the door and claimed the package, and by the time the letter had been delivered to Dane and opened to reveal its ugly nature, the delivery boy had been long gone.

Mrs. Dulcet was working with Nicolas and the security team to grab footage of the kid and chase him down, but we all knew it'd be a dead end. Surely he'd been paid off to deliver a package—three steps removed from the real kidnapper. If someone was out to kidnap one of Dane Clark's employees, they'd be smart. And probably crazy. Because no sane person messed with the Clark Company.

There was no answer at Billy's door. Semi pounded again and muttered a few choice curse words under his breath, then continued to batter the door until Dane rested a hand on his shoulder.

"I don't think we're getting in through the door," Dane said. "He's not home."

Semi eyed his boss. "Yes, sir."

I left the front steps and wandered around the back of the house—if it could be called that. The thing was two floors high made from some odd combination of cement, old wood, and peeling blue paint. I suspected the paint just barely held together the rest of it, and scotch tape might've done a better job. One hint of an earthquake and the thing would come tumbling down, no question about it.

My purpose in accompanying the men behind the house had mostly been as a support person. I wasn't as strong as Semi or as smart as Dane, but I'd watched enough detective shows with Babs to know a few tricks of the trade, and I had a good idea of a way to get inside.

I wasn't normally a huge rule-breaker, but the ransom note had sufficiently freaked me out. The kidnapper had requested Dane leave a million dollars at midnight tonight for Trey's safe return... or else.

We had no leads as of now, which made the whole thing even worse. The closest thing we had to a trail on this kidnapper was a dead-end courier and a Post-It note with the name of Trey's old friend on it. If we didn't move soon, Dane would be out a million bucks and we still might not have Trey back.

This kidnapper was smart and ruthless, and I suspected he hadn't gone after Dane Clark for a measly million. That was petty cash in the world of the Clark Company. I hadn't told Dane yet, but I suspected there was more to the story. I only wanted to find Trey Hampton before the other shoe dropped.

It was with this conviction that I surveyed the pile of rubble that qualified as a backyard. Carefully selecting a rock the size of my fist, I took aim at the small window beside the back door and lobbed the stone through. There was the crash of smashing glass, and it was a testament to how dangerous the area was that none of the neighbors even poked their heads out of the windows.

Dane and Semi, however, came wheeling around the corner at the speed of light. Quite impressive, considering Semi's size. He had the grace of a slightly fat antelope. It was kind of neat to watch.

"Lola!" Dane's eyes were wide. "What happened? We heard glass?"

"I have no idea! I heard something and then this window shattered," I said, gesturing toward the doorway. "I think that means we should go inside and try to help."

Dane's eyes narrowed at me. "I don't believe you, and you know how I feel about lying."

"I didn't lie," I said. "None of what I said was a lie."

Dane thought back over what I said. "You heard something..."

"A bird chirping."

"And then the window shattered," he continued, sizing up the hole in it, "from a rock you threw at it."

"Wanna get inside or not?" I asked. "Have Nicolas send a guy out here to repair the window after we're done. It wouldn't be the first time we've *accidentally* let ourselves into a place."

I carefully picked my way across the lawn as Semi elbowed out the rest of the glass from the frame then reached around to unlock the door.

"Thanks, Lola," Semi murmured, before Dane joined us.

I gave him a thin smile as Dane appeared at my side looking quite disgruntled with our methodology.

"We're in," Semi said, nudging the door open and stepping through. "Let me clear the house before either of you step inside."

I blinked as Semi rested a hand over the butt of a metal weapon on the inside of his suit coat. My eyes bulged. "You carry a gun?!"

Both Dane and Semi gave me a quizzical look.

"You just broke into a house," Dane said dryly, "and now your moral compass decides to point north?"

"I just..." I trailed off. I should've figured Semi carried a gun, seeing as he was protector of the billionaire Dane Clark, but it was still jarring to me to consider that my future husband had an armed body guard at all times. "Forget it. Go ahead and do your thing."

Semi quickly prowled the ground level. His heavy footsteps climbed the stairs and a second later he gave the all clear.

"Stay alert," Semi said, returning downstairs. "The last time I saw this kid, he was armed, high, and stealing a car. I have no clue what he's into these days, but based on his living quarters, I'm guessing he didn't see the light."

"What are we looking for specifically?" I mused aloud. "Do we really think that some low-life druggie came up with a plan to blackmail the Clark Company?"

"We need to focus on the link between Billy and Trey," Dane said. "We can't assume they're into anything at all. We have to find out why Billy's name was in Trey's garbage. Were they working together on something? It might not be drug related at all, and we have to be careful not to limit our focus."

Semi gave a nod. "Yes, sir."

We each went a different way to begin our search. I took the kitchen because I'd had good luck last time in Trey's garbage. Dane took the living room, which unfortunately smelled like dead rats. Semi got the joy of ascending the stairs to clear the second level.

A quick search of the kitchen turned up nothing but rotted lettuce in the fridge and over a hundred different Taco Bell hot sauce packets in a bowl on the counter—a few of them opened, leaving a sticky residue on my fingers as I thumbed through them. I frowned, washed my hands, and then returned to examine the exterior of the refrigerator/freezer, which was very...colorful.

Tacked to the freezer door was a collection of interesting artwork featuring well-endowed ladies in suggestive positions. I studied the images for a few moments, looking for scribbled phone numbers or hasty reminders, but quickly realized there was nothing there I wanted to see. I moved to the cupboards instead, which were quite bare.

Dane also seemed to be striking out in the living room. I was just on my way to join him when I heard several clanks and a *thunk*, followed by some more choice words that had wormed their way into Semi's vocabulary over the last few hours. He was normally calm, collected, and quietly strong, but when his gigantic legs came pounding down the stairs, his face was livid.

"Keep that thing holstered!" I said, throwing my hands in front of my face. "I hate guns."

Semi leveled his gaze at me. "This one isn't mine. Look at the thing—it's ugly. Serial number is scratched off, so it wasn't obtained legally. Also, Mr. Clark, I think it's safe to say my assumptions were correct."

Semi respectfully laid the gun on the table, clicking through a few quick motions that I suspected meant he'd relieved the thing of bullets. Next to it, he dropped a huge wad of cash that was slightly damp around the edges, and several baggies of powders that could only be one thing. It was obvious by his stash that Billy liked variety. Semi held a bag of a white-colored powder, one with a crystal-like substance, and a few more that I didn't recognize.

"Quite the connoisseur," I muttered. "Do you think he's dealing? Why else would he need a gun?"

"Plenty of reasons, though I wouldn't be surprised to find out he was selling this garbage."

"What are the other reasons he might have a gun?" I asked. "Carjacking?"

"Yeah, could be," Semi said. "People don't like when you steal their cars. People don't like when you steal their other shit. People don't like when you lie to them. People don't like when you don't pay them their money." Semi shrugged. "There are a lot of reasons someone like Billy might find themselves in need of a gun—and drugs are just one of them. He could've been in debt, jacked someone's wheels—hell, he could've looked the wrong way at someone's girlfriend."

"Sounds like Trey had some lovely friends back in the day," I said. "I suppose that confirms our theory that Billy hasn't changed much since that time, but Trey has. I'm not convinced he was calling Billy to get back into this mess. It just doesn't make sense. Someone could've easily given Trey the number and he threw it away and wanted nothing to do with it."

"People don't make sense when they're stupid," Semi said.

The statement sounded dumb at first, but the more I thought about it, the more it made sense. "Fair point. But I'm not convinced Trey was acting stupid. He was smart, he had a great job...what would've caused him to reconnect with Billy?"

"I don't know," Dane said, hesitant. "But I suggest we ask him."

Without warning, Dane flew toward the front door. He was faster than Semi, even though the bodyguard leapt to attention at almost the same time as my fiancé. Dane had the front door to the house pulled open and a kid on the ground in the next moment.

Though kid was a loose term. When the guy on the ground looked up, he was older than I'd initially thought—probably somewhere around my age, give or take a few years. But I was still replaying the last seconds in my mind, trying to figure out when Dane had become a karate master in his "spare" time.

"I know Jiu-Jitsu," he said, glancing at my expression. "That, and swimming keeps my cardio up."

"Of course," I said. "Well, I know rhythmic, ah, napping, so there."

"Rhythmic napping?" Dane asked, driving his knee harder into the kid's back until he groaned. "What the hell is that?"

"Forget it," I said quickly. "We should focus on this guy. Are you Billy?"

"You can't be attacking me in my own place!" Billy snarled from the floor. Billy was a skinny white kid with a huge row of pimples on his forehead and a splotchy little goatee. "Get off my property. You're not the freaking cops."

"How do you know?" Dane eased up just slightly. "Why do you have a gun here, along with a drug buffet?"

I was trying to pay attention to Billy's answers, but it was much more romantic for me to replay Dane's super-stealth moves. I didn't always think of him as Mr. Tough Guy, but there was something very sexy about Dane's understated confidence when things got physical.

I told myself now was not the time to feel thrilled all over again at the fact that this guy was marrying me, but I couldn't help it. He was my own personal superhero. With a billion bucks to his name. Who needed Tony Stark, anyway?

While I forced my daydreams into a neat little box I could open and review at my leisure, Dane and Semi wrangled Billy into a seated position on the couch. His hands were cuffed behind his back courtesy of Semi. Neither party looked happy.

"We want to make sure this goes smoothly," Dane said, his voice firm and calculating without a hint of give in it. "Please answer our questions, and we won't bother you any further."

"Who are you people?" Billy spit, studying the three of us. "I'm calling the cops on you, and they're going to arrest you for trespassing."

"Yeah right," Semi said with a snort. "The cops are the last people you want in this dive. I don't think they'll appreciate your drug collection as much as we did."

"What are you talking about? I don't do that garbage anymore," he said, and then he did a huge double take at Semi. "Oh, my God—you're *that* guy. You're Trey's old man."

"I'm his brother," Semi corrected. "And if you knew what was best for you, you'd have left Trey alone."

Billy blinked. "Right. Like he'd even talk to me anymore. He blew this popsicle stand years ago. I haven't heard from him in ages."

"Then why did he have a Post-It note with your name and number on it?" Dane asked. "In his house? He got in touch with you, didn't he?"

"Trey? No. I'm telling you, I haven't talked to the dude in years." Billy looked too calm to be lying, though his eyes were livid as he glanced at the sight of three strangers in his living room. "If he had my name written down, someone else gave it to him. He hadn't used it yet."

"You're lying," Semi said. "He'd tossed the number which means he used it."

"Dude, listen to yourself," Billy said. "Trey left this scene. He got himself a fancy new job with a fancy-ass new condo. It's not like he invited the rest of us over for parties at his new digs, you know? We weren't good enough for him. Even if he had my name for whatever reason, I'm telling you—he wouldn't have used it. He wanted nothing to do with us."

A sheen of satisfaction slid over Semi's face, but he didn't let Billy's statement derail him. "What's with the gun, the cash, and the drugs? You dealing? Let me tell you something, Billy. If you're honest with us, we might just let you off the hook."

"I'm telling you, that's not my stuff," Billy said. "Do I look like I'm high to you? I am not into drugs anymore. I don't need a gun."

"Still stealing cars?"

"Ha-ha," he said. "No. I work at a gas station. I know it's no fancy-ass job like your brother got," he said with a simper, "but it's real work. So, get the hell out of my house."

"Dude," Semi said. "This stuff is in your house. How can you deny it's yours? You're telling me someone crept in here and loaded up your toilet with all their extra cash?"

"Dude," Billy said, sarcastic. "No. I'm telling you I have a shitty roommate. I've been trying to kick him out, but it's not like the gas station is paying for all my bills. He's been here awhile. I let him stay so long as he doesn't get me in trouble."

"Your roommate?" I asked in the deafening silence. "What's his name?"

Billy shifted uncomfortably. "I'm not ratting anyone out."

"We'll find him either way," I said. "And it's in your best interest to help us."

Billy considered, then shrugged. "I guess I don't care. His name's Darius. I don't know the guy's last name. He pays cash, and the utilities are in my name. He works...er, you can probably find him on the shore. He likes to steal stuff from the tourists."

"What an upstanding guy," I said. "I thought you didn't want to get in trouble, yet you're living with a known thief?"

"I told him it's stupid what he's doing, but he doesn't listen," Billy said. "All I want is five hundred bucks a month and he can sleep in the bed. I don't care what he does when he's not in my house."

"Fine. Where's Trey?" Semi said. "We know you know something."

"Know something about what?" Billy's eyes found their focus on Semi, and he narrowed his gaze. "Uh, oh, Trey-boy's in trouble, ain't he? What'd he do this time? He fall back in with the wrong crowd? Shame he didn't call me."

"Shut up," Semi said. "Where is he?"

Billy's eyes gleamed as he took in Semi's worried look. "He's in bad trouble. Come on, share some gossip with an old friend. Maybe I'll even know where to look."

"He's been kidnapped," I blurted. The room stalled as Dane and Semi turned to look at me. "It's not like we have a choice—we have to do everything we can to find him. Time's running out."

Billy's face paled. "I don't do that sort of thing. I told you—honest job here. I don't know anyone who's into kidnapping these days."

"What about that roommate of yours?" I asked. "It sounds like his moral code might be gray. Think he borrowed Semi's brother for a quick payout?"

"He's too dumb," Billy said. "A kidnapper's gotta be smart. But hang on—doesn't the kidnapper want someone with money? No offense, but I don't think Semi here's rolling in it."

"Familiar with the name Dane Clark?" I asked, nodding my head toward my blue-eyed hero.

Billy's eyes went from interested to greedily selfish. "Dude, I swear I don't know why he had my name on that slip of paper, but there's one guy who might know more than me. He knows everything. If Trey *was* looking for me—for whatever reason—he could've gone to Fat Jim."

"Fat Jim?" I said. "Really?"

"He's fat," Billy said, as if that explained everything. "He knows what goes on in the, ah...shadowy side of the Sunshine Shore, if you will. You can find him at the casino most days and at the strip club most nights."

"Wonderful," I said. "And you think Trey might've contacted him to get to you?"

Billy shrugged. "It's the only thing that makes sense. I certainly didn't reach out to him, and he didn't contact me. I can only assume he was going to do it before someone swiped him first. Why? I have no idea."

"Thanks for your time," Dane said, standing. "If you happen to hear anything else, give me a call."

"I don't have your number," Billy said. "How should I call you?"

"Ask around." Dane's voice was dangerous. "You'll figure it out."

Semi moved across the room to Billy's side. "I'm going to let you go, but one wrong move, and I won't be so nice next time."

"Dude, you broke into *my* house."

"Yeah, and that's exactly how the cops will see it when they find a load of drugs in *your* house," Semi said. "Let's call it even, shall we?"

"It's not even yet," Billy said, his eyes calculating. He pointed a finger toward Dane. "I want some compensation for my information."

"Fine," Dane said easily. "If Fat Jim pans out to be a good resource, you'll be paid. No answers, no money."

We filed out of the house, me first, Dane second, Semi third—the latter keeping his eye on Billy the whole way to the car.

"Well, he's a whole bag of problems," I said, as we climbed into the SUV and pulled away. "Anyone think Billy's lying?"

"He's not Honest Abe, that's for sure," Semi said. "We've got two names. Darius and Fat Jim."

I grinned at Dane as Semi pulled away from the curb. "This morning you have meetings with executives in China and Germany. This afternoon, you've got a meeting with Fat Jim. How far the mighty have fallen."

Dane pulled me closer to him, took a whiff of my hair, and backed away. "You smell like hot sauce."

"Yeah," I said. "Well, let's just hope Fat Jim likes the scent of Taco Bell."

Chapter 6

"Do I smell Taco Bell?"

"Aw, really?" I turned to the man who'd asked and frowned. "Is it that bad?"

The man who'd spoken sat in front of the casino where Fat Jim supposedly spent his daytime hours. He was dressed in ragged old clothes and had a nub of a cigarette dangling between his lips. "Got any you could share?"

"Just the aroma," I said dryly. "We'll see if we can find you something inside, okay? Do you know a Fat Jim?"

The guy cackled. "Fat Jim doesn't like to share his food."

"So, he's in there?" I persisted, stepping closer. "What does he look like?"

The guy looked up at me like I was stupid. "Fat."

"Yeah, thanks," I said to him, and then turned to Dane and Semi. "I think we've got the right place."

Semi had driven the infamous Clark SUV and parked it outside of the Sunshine Shore's only casino. Because there was only one casino for miles, it saw quite a mix of clientele. The lights blinked and blazed, drawing visitors and locals alike through the magical doors of this miniature Vegas.

There were the high roller sections that drew the tourists, and the slot machines where weathered old women held cigarettes in one hand and oxygen tanks in the other. There were blackjack tables and roulette, and the flashy games that drew new eighteen-year-olds toward their first taste of gambling. Lastly, there were the seedy rooms in the back, and that was where we found Fat Jim.

As we strolled under the arches and blinks and whirs of various machines, my nervous system seemed to short out with all the stimulation happening around here. I'd stepped foot in the casino once before for one of Babs's birthday parties, and we'd stayed in the politely pink section that was tame and subdued for those of us who were terrified of the dark and dangerous world of casinos.

Dotty always told me that her psychic visions didn't include reckless activities such as gambling, so we'd never dabbled—despite her talents. I'd tried to convince her to play the lottery once upon a time, but she'd refused.

Fat Jim, however, didn't have a problem with taking money from other people. He was situated at a high stakes blackjack table and appeared to be sitting on piles of cash—quite literally, seeing as he sat in a custom-sized chair with hundred-dollar bills printed along the outside in a tacky pattern. Then again, everything about Fat Jim was gloriously tacky.

The man looked like he was the king of the casino. He had chunky gold chains over a chunky bare chest. Thick black hair that looked sturdier than a Brillo pad spread over a Hawaiian shirt open down to his navel. There was a lot of Brillo pad on Fat Jim.

I winced, glanced away, but my gaze was sucked back to him like a magnet. There was just so much more to see. His earring studded lobe sagged from the weight of the gold. The shorts he wore were so short they sort of just disappeared into him. He appeared naked from the waist down unless I looked really closely, and I didn't exactly want to spend my time looking really closely at Fat Jim.

The man in the money chair glanced over the tops of his cards toward Dane, Semi, and myself as we approached. We probably looked like an odd trio—not the lunchtime regulars at the Sunshine Slots—and he took notice of us with a big, cheery old grin. Something about his unabashed brashness almost made me like him. He knew exactly who he was. A girl had to respect that sort of confidence in a man, even if his name was Fat Jim.

"What's up, my friends?" On his money throne, Fat Jim gave us the hang loose sign. "Call me Fat Jim. You looking to play or just admire?"

"We're looking to talk," Semi said, taking the lead. "How about a word?"

The man's almost friendly smile took a dive straight into frownsville, and he gave a quick shake of his head. "I'm busy."

"We'll wait," Semi said. "We'll wait as long as you need."

"You don't understand," Fat Jim said. "I'm always too busy for you."

"Hey, nobody needs to get upset," I said, waving a hand. "We just want to chat. Surely you can spare us a few minutes?"

Fat Jim gave me the once over, then fished around in a fanny pack that was hanging over the arm of the chair next to him. It probably didn't fit around his waist. "You're pretty enough, but I'm gonna guess you're taken."

I felt Dane tense next to me as he rested a hand on my elbow.

"She's taken," Dane said, his voice soft, deadly. "How about a chat, Mr. Jim?"

Dane's tone caught Fat Jim's attention. Apparently, the latter could recognize power and wealth because he surveyed my fiancé with a critical eye. It took a long time before he gave a nod of agreement.

"I'll keep my hands off her, then," Fat Jim said, as if that was supposed to solve everything.

Nobody appeared to consider my say in the matter, which was mildly annoying. I pulled my soapbox right over and climbed up, prepared to give Fat Jim a piece of my mind when Dane shook his head.

It didn't stop me. "We're here to talk to you, and it's serious. We think you might have information on a kidnapping case, and if you don't help us, an innocent kid might die."

"Sorry." Fat Jim raised his hands. "I can't help you. I don't do kidnappings, everyone knows that. I've been here for most of the day, and I came straight from the strip club where I spent all of last night. There's my alibi."

"You didn't go home in between?"

He shrugged. "Why? I'm headed home after this—figured I'd get a few rounds in, make a quick buck before I do that. I'll sleep this afternoon before I head back to the club tonight."

The rest of the group appeared entirely uninterested in their cards at this point. There were three other players at the blackjack table: A grandfatherly old figure in a clean suit, a man in jeans and a button up shirt who could barely see straight, and a woman in a tank top that should really be a corset, and nothing much in the way of a skirt. The dealer, a completely unforgettable middle-aged man, had the look on his face of someone in a deeply hypnotized state.

"I'll play you," Dane said easily. "Half an hour of blackjack. Whoever comes out on top wins."

"I'm already winning," Fat Jim said. "Why should I play you?"

Dane Clark reached into the pocket of his glorious suit—number twenty-four of forty, if I had to guess—and pulled out a business card. It was shiny, solid, and said only the name Dane Clark on the front. I'd never seen him use one before.

He pressed it on the table and slid it toward Fat Jim.

"Holy crapola," Fat Jim said, picking it up. "Is that a titanium business card? Wait a second, you're..."

"Dane Clark," Dane said. "Take your pick of winnings. I'll bet you anything you like."

"Anything?"

"Sure," Dane said easily. "Not that it matters, since you won't be collecting the prize."

To anyone else, Dane's words sounded like a threat. To me, they sounded like fact. I wasn't sure Dane even knew how to trash talk, but he was pretty damn confident in regular talk, and it gave me some real flutters inside. The King of Castlewood versus the king of the casino in his fat old money chair—it hardly seemed fair.

"Dane, you don't have to do this," I said. "Come on, we'll just leave him alone. He probably doesn't know anything anyway."

"I know something about everything," Fat Jim said. He surveyed Dane. "If you're so confident, you won't mind betting your girl on it."

"She's off the table," Dane said sternly.

"Um, yeah, I was never on the table," I interrupted. "I'd just like to throw my two cents in there. You can't bet over a person, anyway. That's illegal."

"Honey..." Fat Jim shook his head, as if disappointed at my naivete. "Fine, whatever. Double my winnings from the evening in cash and we'll call it a deal. You win, I'll tell you what I know."

Dane extended a hand. I cringed as Fat Jim extended a chubby set of fingers, and the two shook on their arrangement. The king of the casino gave a smug look and made a gesture around the table that had the other players scattering without comment. The dealer snapped out of his trance and swiped the cards on the table out of game play.

"Dane, a word?" I put my hand in his and tugged him off to the side without waiting for permission. Once we were in a quiet corner—as quiet as a casino could be—I gave him a strange look. "What do you think you're doing? You don't gamble."

"No, I don't."

"So, what are you doing? If you lose, not only will we not get information, but you'll have to pay out money to Fat Jim along with whatever money is needed for Trey's ransom."

"We need the information." Dane's jaw set into a firm line. "I am normally not a fan of breaking into others' houses, nor am I a proponent of gambling away hard-earned money for pleasure. It's senseless and risky and dangerous."

"Exactly."

Dane's eyes narrowed. "We can't go to the police or they'll kill Trey—you saw the note as well as I did. I will not have the death of Semi's brother on our hands."

"It's not on our hands! And he's not going to die," I said quickly. "We'll figure it out, Dane, you don't have to lose to Fat Jim. It'll just waste time."

"Oh, I don't plan on losing." His eyes twinkled. "Lola, I just told you I don't gamble. I make educated guesses and calculated risks. This is hardly the riskiest business move I've made today."

I blinked. "It's barely lunch."

"Exactly. Now, may I finish what I started?"

I sighed. "I'm not going to talk you out of this, am I?"

"No."

"Then at least let me give you a kiss for good luck."

"I already told you, Lola—I don't need luck." Dane gave me a brilliant smile. "But I will take a kiss."

I groaned, but Dane cut me off mid-grumble. He put his hands on either side of my face and pressed me hard to him, his lips soft, the tension high, the heat level just north of scorching.

"Damn this kidnapping." I sulked as he pulled away. "I smell like hot sauce, and I can't stop dreaming of that four-headed shower. It's like a mythical creature."

Dane brushed his fingers against my chin. "The wait always makes things better. Unfortunately, we do have a deadline to hit, so I'm in a bit of a time crunch. I apologize for the shortness of the kiss."

My grumbling was silenced as we returned to the table. Gossip and tension seemed to travel across the casino like a virus, sucking people in, pulling folks away from their pre-scheduled activities to watch the face-off between the two royalties.

My heart began to pound for Dane as the dealer introduced himself as Dan. It was understood that whoever won more over the course of the next thirty minutes would be declared the unofficial winner of a bet that wasn't *really* happening according to casino rules. Either Dane would be out a lot of money, or we'd acquire some much-needed information.

As much as I trusted Dane, I had serious doubts about his ability to gamble successfully. He was as clear-cut as people came: Good and evil, light and dark, business or pleasure. Except the latter. I suppose we'd done some mixing in the business and pleasure arenas lately. Regardless, he wasn't a gambler by nature. I hated to think he might be out money, or worse. Word traveled around the Sunshine Shore. It would be big news if Dane Clark lost serious cash to Fat Jim.

"Semi, have you ever seen Dane gamble before?" I asked his trusty old friend and bodyguard. "In all the years you've known him, has he stepped foot into a casino?"

"Rarely, and if so, only for business meetings or the like," Semi said, his hands crossed over the front of his body, his eyes fixed on the game before us. "You worried, Miss Pink?"

I shrugged, noticing that Semi had left his gun locked in the safe in the trunk of the car. Weapons weren't allowed in the casino—probably for the best, seeing how much money was won and lost between these walls on any given night. Hopefully Semi's size would be enough to ward off any unsavory advances.

"My advice?" Semi spared me a quick glance. "Don't be worried."

"How can I not be concerned?" I hissed. "That's my fiancé over there."

"He's got enough money to buy this casino."

"I'm not worried about the money; I'm worried about him. If he loses, I don't know what that'll do to him. Does Dane Clark ever lose anything he puts his mind to?"

"No, ma'am," Semi said. "And that's exactly why you shouldn't fret."

"But this is different. Gambling is all luck of the draw and unpredictable."

"For some," Semi admitted. "For most, sure. But Dane Clark isn't most people."

I squinted, shifting uncomfortably from one foot to the next as I watched the first round of cards go out. Dane had an eight and a ten, and he instructed the dealer to hit.

I closed my eyes just after the dealer flipped a face card and Dane busted. When I reopened my eyes, Fat Jim was rubbing his chunky hands together and grinning. "Down a grand already? That was fast."

"They're playing a grand a hand?" I felt my face go pale. "Oh my. That's—that could add up quickly for the next thirty minutes."

Semi's hand came up to mine and he squeezed my shoulder. "Do you trust your future husband?"

"Yes, one hundred percent."

"Then just watch."

"But I don't know if I trust the casino," I argued, "and that's what worries me."

"Mr. Clark factors in every variable," Semi said. "Now with all due respect, Miss Pink, shut your mouth and watch."

I did as Semi had suggested, fretting more each time Dane's pile of chips disappeared. There must have been at least thirty grand on the table—I'd missed them cashing in for chips when I'd been talking to Semi, so I couldn't say for certain, but there was something horribly upsetting about seeing all of that money laid out for fun and games. That could've fed me easily for the next decade.

Dane's playing befuddled me. Though I understood only the basic rules of blackjack, I knew one shouldn't hit over sixteen, and one should definitely hit when the first two cards totaled under ten. But Dane didn't seem to be playing by any discernable rules so far as I could tell. He seemed to hit willy nilly and stay when it made no sense. And still, his pile of chips continued to shrink.

"Sir," the dealer said, taking sympathy on Dane when he gestured to hold on nine. "May I recommend you hit?"

"Considered," Dane said shortly. "Hold, please."

Meanwhile, Fat Jim was accruing a nice little pile of chips under his massive arms. He had this way of pulling it toward him like a dragon hoarding its loot, his beady little eyes glancing around at the gathering crowd. It seemed the faster Dane lost, the more rapidly the crowd grew.

People wanted to watch the King of Castlewood flame out like a burning star. It irked me to see them drooling over him like hyenas, just waiting for the half hour clock to run out and see how he reacted to a loss. I was just about to start telling off the crowd for their leering, mocking laughter at Dane's choices to hit and stay, when a very peculiar thing happened.

Dane began to win.

Suddenly, his peculiar choices began to make a lot of sense. His bets got larger and larger, and after four winning hands in a row, Dane shoved a huge pile of chips toward the table and arranged them in a complicated little pattern. I wasn't sure exactly what was happening, so I turned to Semi.

"Should I look?" I asked, covering my eyes with my hands. "How much money is on the table? Tell me when it's okay to look. Oh, I can't look. Just make me go sit in the car—I'm going to get an ulcer from this."

Semi gave a nervous laugh. "He just bet fifty grand, Miss Pink."

I groaned. "How much time on the clock?"

"Approximately thirty seconds, ma'am."

I forced my eyes open and saw Fat Jim sweating bullets. I could tell this was the hand that would win or lose everything. Even Dan, the dealer, had little patches of sweat on his underarms. I clearly wasn't the only one deathly afraid of seeing that much money vanish with a single hand gesture.

The dealer flipped over four face cards for both Dane and Fat Jim. It was a good hand, I understood, based upon the reactions of the crowd.

"If they both win this one, Dane will lose," Semi explained. "He doesn't have enough bet to bridge the gap between them. Dealer likely has nineteen under there, so they'd both be good. Dane would need to hit twenty-one to pull ahead."

The dealer looked first to Fat Jim, who gestured to stay on twenty. The logical choice. Dan cast a wary glance to Dane, looking like he didn't even want to ask.

"Hit me," Dane said, as casually as if he were ordering a diet coke from a passing waiter.

Dan cleared his throat. "Sir—"

"Hit me," Dane said evenly. "Please."

Dan winced as he drew the card that would end everything. He needed an ace. Anything but, and he'd lose in a big, huge way. The crowd was squabbling with jeers and laughter as they waited to see the huge bust.

And then the card flipped, and it was an ace.

Stunned silence followed. Nobody moved. Even Dan the dealer froze, and he had unturned cards on the table that needed flipping. The crowd of onlookers shut their mouths, and even Fat Jim's huge lips drew into a pudgy line.

"Flip," Dane said to Dan.

Dan quickly flipped his cards and revealed a nineteen, as Semi had predicted.

"Great," Dane said without fanfare. Then he looked to Fat Jim. "Let's talk."

"Sir, your winnings!" Dan said as Dane pushed back his chair. "Your chips!"

Dane reached for a chip that Semi had informed me was worth a thousand bucks and flipped it to the dealer. "Thanks," he said simply. "I'll have my bodyguard collect the chips—I have business to attend to, and the clock is ticking. Let's go, Jim."

Fat Jim couldn't push himself back from the table. He merely sat there in stunned shock. Finally, he stumbled onto some words and threw a pointed finger in Dane's direction. "How did you...how could you?! That's illegal."

"What is?" Dane spread his hands wide. "Everyone watched me lose for twenty-six minutes straight. I just hit a winning streak there at the end, and I know when to stop. Let's go."

"You counted the cards. You did all that on purpose," Fat Jim spluttered. "You knew the whole time what was happening and did this for laughs. You were making a mockery of me!"

"It's gambling," Dane said with a shrug. He wrapped an arm around my waist and pulled me close, giving my forehead a kiss. "And I happen to have an excellent good luck charm."

"You little cheat."

Dane raised an eyebrow. "Where would you like to talk, Jim?"

"It's Fat Jim," he growled. "Use my name. And we'll go in the back—Dan, send in some wings. I'm hungry. You lot—follow me. You've got ten minutes. Let's move."

FAT JIM WADDLED INTO a back room of the casino off the main floor. It wasn't anything particularly special, though it had the look of an old speakeasy that'd been revamped in the eighties with a minimal budget. The room was a little too dark, the furniture a little too big, the dressings a little too gaudy.

Fat Jim took a seat around a circular mahogany table, and Dane, Semi, and I filtered in across from him. Semi held a small parcel that I suspected contained a wad of cash from his boss's winnings.

A plate of wings arrived seconds later, along with a round of soda for each of us. The wings looked brilliant red and burned my nose with the smell of 'flaming hot'. Fat Jim didn't offer to share.

"What do you need to know?" Fat Jim asked. "Hurry up. I don't have time for this."

Dane's eyes flashed with a hint of frustration. More than anything else, he was a man of his word. He'd won the deal fair and square, and it was easy to see Fat Jim's lack of the same moral code bothered him fiercely.

"Trey Hampton," Dane said. "What do you know about him?"

"Long rap sheet," Fat Jim said. "But all that was a while ago. I take it this one's his brother? I always knew there was an older brother who wasn't in the picture much."

Semi's hands clenched tightly. "Yes, I'm the brother."

"Well, if you want to know about Trey Hampton, I don't have much for you unless you want a history lesson," Fat Jim said, digging into the wings and dipping one into a vat of blue cheese dressing. "He was into it all back in the day—light drug use, a few theft charges, possibly one for impersonating a police officer, but I think that was a misunderstanding. He hung out with some car thieves, but I don't think he was directly involved in that. There you have it."

"You're lying." Dane surprised me by leaning forward across the table. "What've you heard about Trey recently?"

"I told you, nothing," Fat Jim said. "He hasn't been in my realm. Last I heard, he got a real job and cleaned up. That's about when I cut ties with folks, like it or not. That's why you came to me, isn't it? So, none of that should be a surprise."

One of many things that impressed me about Dane was his seeming lack of fear. He had a confidence in facts, in all that was good and right in the world, and nothing deterred him from going after the truth. If I'd been sitting across from Fat Jim alone, I'd be sweating—and not only because of the spicy wings. He had the look about him that said crossing him wouldn't end well—and that was the understatement of the century. Dane didn't seem to notice.

"You're lying," Dane said again, adamant. "What do you know about Trey Hampton?"

"I told you, mate, I don't know—"

Dane stood, accompanied by a violent screech of his chair as it flew backward. His eyes held a livid anger in them that sent Fat Jim spiraling into a whole new level of perspiration. Fat Jim reached for the napkin and began dabbing his forehead under Dane's deadly stare.

"Trey Hampton isn't back into drugs," Fat Jim said. "That's what you came to ask, isn't it?"

Dane rested his clenched fists on the table, leaned forward, and met Fat Jim's eyes with a pitiful expression. "You've wasted my time, Jim, and I don't appreciate that. I held up my end of the bargain, and I'm disappointed you aren't showing me the same respect. We're leaving. Lola, Semi—now."

Dane stormed toward the door of the back room and reached it before I'd managed to pull my jaw off the floor. I'd never seen him in such a rage before.

With a start, I realized that Dane was worried about Trey—seriously worried for the kid's life. Despite the bravado in which he'd promised Semi we'd find his brother, it appeared there was a very real chance things were heading south, and fast.

"I hope you're happy," I said, standing over Fat Jim who hadn't bothered to stop eating. "You've pissed off Dane Clark and aided kidnappers in keeping Trey away from us. If that kid doesn't make it out alive, that's on you, Jim."

"It's Fat Jim!" he roared after us.

I filed out of the room first, followed by Semi, and Dane slammed the door shut behind all of us. He reached for his temples and massaged his forehead in obvious frustration.

"Shit," he cursed.

Dane wasn't big on cursing, which drew my attention. "What is it?"

"Prick," Dane muttered under his breath. "Waste of time. Come on, let's talk to Darius."

"You can go back in there," I said. "Why did you give up so soon? He might have talked if you put a little pressure on him."

"He'll talk," Dane said. "He'll come to us, but he has to do it on his own time. His ego's too big. I miscalculated."

"That's not your fault—you beat him fair and square," I said. "It's lousy he's not following up on his end of the bargain, but there's nothing you can do."

"Come on," Dane said again. "Darius first, then back to the castle. Fat Jim will be there within three hours."

"How can you be sure?" I asked him. "How can you predict what he'll do?"

"Did you see that game of blackjack?" Semi muttered as we strode through the casino and toward the front doors. "I think you need to start having a little faith, Miss Pink."

"Hey, hot sauce," the man outside the door called as we plowed into the warmth of sunshine and inhaled fresh air for the first time in an hour. "Did you find Fat Jim?"

"Yeah, and he didn't share his wings," I said. "Thanks for the tip."

Dane gestured to Semi, who reached into the parcel of cash and doled out a stack of hundreds as thick as my thumb.

"Merry Christmas," Dane said, and handed it over to the man. "Don't spend it all in one place."

The guy reached forward, his eyes widening. "You sure, man? What'd I do for you?"

Dane didn't answer. He was already opening the car door, holding it wide for me to enter first. Semi climbed into the front, and as I slid in, I gave our newfound friend a little wave. Then my future husband eased into the car next to me, and I nestled my head on his shoulder.

"You're hot," I told him. "You know that?"

"Warm?" Dane asked. "Me?"

"Nah," I said. "I mean you're sexy."

"What'd I do to make you say that?"

I pulled him close to me and kissed him on the cheek. "You're a good guy. Sometimes, that's all it takes."

Semi pretended not to listen as he pressed his foot to the gas pedal and sent us shooting in the direction of the Sunshine Shore to face our next target. No rest for the wicked.

Chapter 7

We found Darius slumming on the beach as Billy had suggested. Darius was short and compact, muscled and intimidating, despite his five-foot stature. Next to Semi, he looked like an ant. A very buff ant.

"You Darius?" Semi asked gruffly. "We need to talk."

"Sure, man, what's cracking?" Darius turned a million-watt smile onto Semi. "What can I help you with, brother?"

I had to give the guy credit. He didn't look the least bit intimidated by the nearly two-foot gap in height between himself and the bodyguard. Darius just kept right on grinning up at Semi as if he'd seen Santa Claus.

The constant grinning seemed to confuse Semi, and the bodyguard struggled to speak properly. I gently elbowed him out of the way, earning another bruise to my arm in the process, and faced Darius.

"We're looking for some information. Do you think you can help us?" I asked. "We're not trying to get you in trouble."

"Good, good," he said still grinning widely. "I'm not looking to get in trouble, either. I'm just over here minding my own business. But if I can help a pretty thing like you out, it'd be my pleasure."

From behind me came the clearing of a throat. Dane didn't sound happy.

"Aw, man! This is your girl?" Darius gave Dane the thumbs up. "Nice job, man. Don't worry. She's not my type. I'm just admiring the female figure, you know what I'm sayin'?"

When nobody commented, I cleared my own throat. "We hear you live with Billy."

"That's right, he's my landlady," Darius said, then guffawed in laughter. "Get it? He's a dude. I just call him my landlady because he's all nagging and shit about me paying the rent on time. He can be a real drag."

"Not all ladies are nags," I said, "but I suppose that's not the point. We happened to find a gun, some drugs, and a load of cash in the toilet. Are those yours?"

"Yep."

I blinked, shook my head. "You just admitted to having a gun, a plethora of drugs, and a wad of cash in your toilet."

"Well, it's technically my landlady Billy's toilet, but yeah. I keep my special objects there. Did y'all put it back?"

"Um, sure," I said. "We left it there. About the plethora of drugs—"

"Lady, I've got cocaine, weed, ecstasy, and a few other knickknacks, but I haven't heard of this 'plethora' you speak of. That a new drug?"

"Uh, no," I said. "It just means you have a lot."

Darius nodded, grinning. "Yeah, I do. It's kind of a collection of mine, but don't worry. I use them responsibly."

"There's no such thing as using them responsibly," I said. "They're completely illegal. You shouldn't have them at all—we should be reporting you to the police."

"I know, but y'all said you didn't want to get me in trouble, right?" Darius gave the thumbs up gesture again. "I trust you, so I'm here to help. What can old man Darius do for you?"

I couldn't handle him anymore. I turned to face Dane, massaging my forehead as I debated whether this was all an act, or if Darius was just a giddy, stupid soul who trusted strangers implicitly. My gut told me the latter was probably true.

By the time I turned back to face Darius and gathered my thoughts and my patience, he was looking more curiously at us.

"Who are y'all anyway?" he asked. "You're from around here, right? Most tourists don't know of Darius, and that's why I can scam them."

I shook my head, convinced that this blissful stupidity wasn't an act and was, in fact the real deal. "You scam tourists?"

"Yeah. Beg, scam, whatever I can do to get some cash," Darius said with a nod. "After all, I've gotta get the landlady paid. Every single month, believe it or not. She's a real pain in my ass. But don't you worry—as soon as my bills are paid, I stop the scams."

"Why not just get a real job?" I asked, unable to help myself. "It would probably save you a lot of time and effort."

Darius flexed his fingers. "This one really gets my creative juices flowing. Plus, with the police always just a step behind, it keeps the thrill level high. And if I get caught, it's not like a huge loss. They put me in jail and feed me three meals a day, and I don't gotta pay rent. Plus, I'm a friendly guy. The inmates like me and leave me alone. Hell, I even get my own little toilet."

"Okay, that's bizarre," I muttered, "but moving on, we're here because of something bad that's happened. We are hopeful you might have some information for us."

"Anything for the pretty lady," Darius said, then gave Dane a playful smirk. "I'm just kidding, man. I'd do it for you, too. You're a handsome fella yourself—but not my type."

"Trey Hampton," I said, "do you know the name?"

"Oh, yeah. He's an old timer around here, but he don't come around much anymore," Darius said, scrunching up his face in thought. "In fact, I ain't seen him in quite some time. He used to run around with Billy. They might be in contact."

"They're not, that's why we're here. We're talking to anyone who might have an idea of what he's been up to lately. We believe..." I hesitated, glancing to Semi and Dane, both giving me a nod of encouragement. "He might be in trouble. Someone's after him, or has taken him, and we need to find out who."

"There ain't that many people around into *that* level of bad stuff," Darius said with a frown. "This is the Sunshine Shore. We keep things pretty light and friendly around these parts, and we leave the murderers and serial killers and kidnappers to flock to other towns."

"You said there aren't *many* people into bad stuff," I said. "Does that mean you know someone who is?"

Darius tapped on his lip. "You know, some people flow in and out of here, and it's hard to say sometimes. There's a new, ah, ring of folks selling drugs around these parts, but I haven't gone to them yet. I like to stay with the tried and true locals."

"Any idea where we might find these people? Do you think they're capable of a kidnapping?"

"Capable? Sure," Darius said, "but I don't know much more than that. Have you talked to Fat Jim? Just about everyone on the shadow side of the Sunshine Shore has to go through him."

"What do you mean go through him?" I asked. "Like, he knows about it?"

"Like, pay him money," he said. "Fat Jim has a little protective service on the sly for people into that sort of thing."

"Are you into that sort of thing, Darius?"

"Me? Nah, if I get in trouble, I face the consequences. I'm not stupid," he said with a shrug of his shoulders. "I know when I break the law—that's my own choice. If I get caught, I pay the price."

"Then what does Fat Jim do for his subscriber base?" I asked. "You know, the people paying him taxes."

"Fat Jim's got a few powerful dudes in his fat pockets," Darius said. "He's been known to help people out of a scrape a time or two. Not worth it to me, but to some of those bigger charges, yeah—they're paying Fat Jim to make problems go away."

"Powerful dudes," I said. "Do you mean cops?"

"Cops, lawyers, judges, and probably more that I can't even pronounce," Darius said. "I mean, it takes a whole army to fool the justice system."

"If that's true, Fat Jim might know who's moved into town," I said with a shake of my head. I faced Dane. "You're right—he was lying, big time."

"Fat Jim knows something about everything," Darius said. "If he wasn't being helpful, it was on purpose. Did you piss him off?"

Dane winced. "Possibly."

"Well, that'll do it. He doesn't take kindly to being embarrassed," Darius said. "And you look like a slick man. I doubt you punched him, so you must have outsmarted him."

"Look, Darius, thanks a lot for your help," I said turning back to him. "I'm begging you, if you hear anything else, please give us a call. A kid's life is at stake, and if we don't get more information before midnight on who took him, things won't look good."

"I read ya," Darius said. "I'll give you a call if you hand over some digits, pretty lady."

"I'll let my fiancé take care of that," I said pointedly, stepping back and letting Dane fork over another titanium business card. "Call us, okay?"

"What the hell is this thing?" Darius flipped it over. "Can I use this as a charge card?"

Dane cleared his throat. "Business card. Call the number on the back and you'll be routed through to my personal line. If you misuse it...well, don't."

"Gotcha, boss-man," Darius said with a salute. "I hope I see you all again soon. It was nice chatting with you. By the way, what sort of car do you drive?"

I frowned. "Black SUV, why?"

"Great!" He chuckled good-naturedly. "Would hate to steal one of my new friends' cars."

"Try," Semi said. "And you're dead."

"On that note," Darius said, leaning back on a heel. "It's time to take my leave. Adios, *muchachos*."

Darius continued his stroll down the beach, flicking a pair of cheap sunglasses onto his head as he did so, surveying the crowd of tourists and locals alike as they basked in the sun on blankets.

"He's a piece of work," I said, as we walked back to the SUV to find it mercifully still had all its wheels attached. "What a nut."

"I dunno," Dane said. "I sort of liked him."

"Really?"

Dane shrugged. "He didn't lie, and he smiled at me. What more can I ask for from a stranger?"

"Huh," I said, and that was the end of it.

"Back to the castle," Dane instructed Semi once we were all in the car. "It's time to start an investigation on the home front, but I would prefer to keep this quiet—even from Nicolas and Mrs. Dulcet for the time being. If it's an inside job, the fewer people to know about it, the better."

"Agreed," I said. "Where do we start?"

Dane offered a grim smile. "At the start. And for Trey, the start was Warehouse 5."

Chapter 8

"Lola, may I steal you for a second?" Mrs. Dulcet had clearly prepared for the pounce. No sooner had Semi, Dane, and I stepped foot through the front door, and she was herding me into a corner like a lion separating an antelope from the herd. I dodged her and slipped in place next to Dane.

"I'm sort of busy," I said. "Can it wait?"

"I'm sorry about earlier." Mrs. Dulcet didn't give up easily. As Dane and I began walking behind Semi, she fell into stride next to me, keeping up at the quick clip. She had shorter legs than everyone in the trio so she was practically running to keep up, and her skirt swirled around her ankles like a parachute. "Please, just a few minutes. Mr. Clark—"

"A minute," I told her, taking pity on her little legs. "Dane, where should I meet you?"

"Semi and I will be in my office," he said. "Come up as soon as you finish."

"What is it, Mrs. Dulcet?" I put a hand on my hip. "We really do have important business to take care of today."

"The Clark family always has important business to take care of!" Mrs. Dulcet said with a scowl. "I thought you were different, Miss Pink. There is more to life than working."

"You don't understand," I said. "It's bigger than that. It's very important, I promise."

"Well, fine." Mrs. Dulcet arranged her face into a quiet form of protest. "I have amended your schedule for tomorrow to include a flower appointment at Sunshine Gardens at two in the afternoon. I checked your itinerary for the day and that time appeared open."

"Great," I said, and turned to head up the stairs. "Thank you."

"Lola," Mrs. Dulcet said. "Don't you walk away from me! I'm not done with you."

I turned to face the butler, surprised by the raised tone in her voice.

"Are you excited by your wedding at all?" Mrs. Dulcet blurted. "You seem very indifferent about it."

I thought of the wedding invitations that didn't really feel like mine, and the dress I hadn't been able to order. I thought of the cake Amanda Clark had practically ordered for me, and the flowers I was sure she would choose tomorrow.

I didn't want to lie to Mrs. Dulcet, so I shrugged. "Mostly, I'm excited about marrying Dane."

"You only get married once," Mrs. Dulcet said. "I just wish you were having a better time planning your day."

"Planning my day?" I gave a thin smile. "It doesn't feel like I'm planning much of anything."

"This is about Mrs. Clark, isn't it?"

"Partly," I said. "She hasn't shown her face around here once since our engagement, and I know she's pulling strings and talking to you behind my back to organize this wedding. If she wanted to help, why didn't she just say so?"

"She didn't want to interfere."

I snorted. "Which is why she called the cake place and encouraged them to be out of Bundtlets and helped the wedding dress shop to remember they were suddenly out of stock of my favorite design. I've no doubt this flower showing tomorrow is just a formality for me. Mrs. Clark will choose what she wants."

"Lola..."

"Look, I've come to terms with it," I said. "Let her plan the wedding. Who cares? I'll show up in whatever dress she chooses, holding whatever flowers she wants, standing in whatever shoes she prefers. The important thing is that I end up married to Dane."

"But Lola—"

"It doesn't matter," I reiterated. "I've come to terms with it. Like I told Babs this morning—it's not like I even have a say in the guest list. I can count my guests on one hand. The entire rest of the venue will be filled with Amanda's friends. The ceremony is for her, apparently. But the marriage is all mine. I've chosen my battles, and this is not one I'm fighting."

I hesitated for a mere second, feeling the urge to apologize without knowing why. I puzzled on that for a second until I saw understanding register in Mrs. Dulcet's eyes. With that, the battle was done.

"I'm sorry," I said anyway, and I turned, leaving her to watch me as I ascended the staircase to Dane's office.

I found Dane and Semi pacing in the tower that served as Dane's office. It was a turret at one of the highest points in the castle with a huge mahogany desk perched in the center of the room and a large circular window lodged behind it with a view over Castlewood grounds. Dane was looking through the window, surveying the campus in his backyard that looked eerily similar to the inside of a snow globe.

I crossed the room to stand next to him, quietly counting the huge warehouses that lined the outer rim of the quad. Each Warehouse was an individual silo that housed interesting and unique projects worked on around the clock. I felt a little like an evil overlord standing so high up, looking down at people the size of my thumbnail as they crossed over the grassy green fields or rode the train from one warehouse to the next.

I spotted Warehouse 5 easily and flicked my glance up at Dane. "Is the project inside confidential?"

"All of our projects are confidential," he said. "I didn't think Warehouse 5 was particularly high risk—Warehouse 9, maybe, and Warehouse 10 most certainly, but 5..."

I shuddered, not daring to ask what went on inside 9 or 10. No matter how long Dane Clark and I lived together, there were some things I preferred he kept secret. "Can you tell me?"

"Can I? Of course," Dane said. "You can know whatever you'd like about the Clark Company, Lola. Just ask."

"I'll wait outside, sir," Semi said. "As we've discussed, it's best I know as little about the company as possible—unless utterly necessary."

"It's utterly necessary," Dane said shortly. "I'll not have you waiting outside on this one, Semi, but I am not the person who should be explaining a project to you. Follow me."

Semi and I followed Dane back down the stairs and outside to a small platform where the train ran, round and round, day and night. It was for looks as much as convenience, and for the seldom rainy days that plagued the Sunshine Shore. Dane had always loved trains.

I went to drop my phone into the miniature lockers on the side of the station, but Dane stopped me with a simple shake of his head.

He took my hand and pulled me onto the platform. "You're mine, Lola."

"I don't need special treatment," I muttered. "I can lock my phone up like everyone else."

"You're to be my wife," Dane said, giving me a quizzical look. "It's expected you get special treatment from me, and it'd be a shame if you didn't."

Semi looked away as I felt my face blush. "Well, okay then. If you say so, but I won't make any calls."

Dane gave a short laugh, not the boisterous one I loved, but that was to be expected. There wasn't much that was funny about a looming midnight deadline and the possible death of Semi's brother. The laughter would have to wait until we had something to smile about.

Dane must have flashed the appropriate swipe card because the train arrived in front of Warehouse 5 without any additional signal. The three of us disembarked and made our way across the short platform to the huge, steel-reinforced doors of a building that looked part bomb shelter, part high-tech laboratory. In essence, that was exactly right.

Dane led us through the front doors and straight upstairs to the Eagle Office. Each warehouse had one—a large office situated well above the lab where the project manager and a few select staff held important meetings and confidential conversations. Dane swiped his all-access pass again and let us into the office without further ado. Then he sat down behind the desk and waited.

Semi and I stood uncomfortably along the wall until Dane gave us a curious look. "What are you doing?"

"Um, waiting," I said, "but we're not sure why."

"Ah, there he is," Dane said easily, gesturing toward the floor where a man in jeans and a button-down shirt separated himself from a machine and began an awkward jog toward the stairs. "The project manager for Warehouse 5—Dean Gobbler."

Dean Gobbler looked like his name sounded. He appeared to be the quintessential nerd trying to be cool and somewhat succeeding, thanks in large part to the fat salary he earned that could buy him nice clothes and fancy glasses.

Dean burst into the Eagle Office and wiped his forehead of perspiration from his short jaunt up the stairs. "Mr. Clark, welcome. What brings you to Warehouse 5 today?"

"A few questions," Dane said smoothly. "Please take a seat. Are you alright? You're sweating incredibly profusely."

"I'm nervous," he said with a high-pitched giggle. "It isn't every day the boss makes his appearance."

"You obviously know Semi, and this is Lola, my fiancé," Dane said, gesturing toward us respectively. "You shouldn't hold anything back from them or me today. Understood? Everything that's spoken here is completely confidential."

"Sir, it's understood the Eagle Office is always confidential," Dean said quickly. "I'd never dream of repeating this conversation anywhere."

"Good," Dane said. "Please explain quickly—high level overview—of the current project in Warehouse 5."

Dean's eyes flashed. "Here in Warehouse 5, we're working on a revolutionary piece of technology. It could change the face of politics, government operations, and covert operations on its first deployment. Eventually, it'll change the way in which the world communicates."

"Huh?" It wasn't the most eloquent of answers, but I was a little blindsided. "Did you say covert operations? Like spies?"

"The way it works now, whenever government personnel are deployed or otherwise in the field, they are somewhat limited by their training," Dean went on to explain. "Language barriers. We're aiming to not only break them, but to blow all of them fresh out of the water."

"How do you plan on doing that?"

"With an implantable device." Dean gave a giddy smile. "We've been working on the technology for two years. As you can imagine, it's very...ah, sensitive to get something past all the requirements that will allow us to put a device into the human body. At this time, we're finalizing the software that goes inside. The next phase will be focused on the packaging, sizing, and general requirements that will allow this to become a legal and safe procedure."

"What does it do?"

"It's essentially a translator," Dean said. "Or it will be. It won't help you to speak another language, but while wearing the device, you'll be able to clearly understand three hundred and seven languages with a ninety-eight percent accuracy. We're working for closer to one hundred percent accuracy, and I fully expect us to be there by the time this chip launches."

"When do you expect it to launch?"

Dean glanced quickly at Dane, as if checking to see whether he'd overstepped his bounds, and then turned back to me at Dane's stony expression. "Honestly, we'd love to hit the one-year countdown. It's looking like two years at this point, mostly due to legal approvals, copyrights, and other red tape issues that are generally out of our control."

"I see," I said, though half of what he'd told me felt completely out of reach for my measly old brain. "When you say you're finalizing the software for the device..."

"I mean it's nearly ready," he said with a hint of pride. "You can test it out if you'd like."

"I'm not ready for an implant today," I said. "But thank you for thinking of me, anyway."

"No, no!" He laughed, as if I were a silly child struggling with my multiplication tables. "That's not what I meant. We have an over the ear packaging system for trials. Obviously, we needed to be able to test the device without implanting it into someone every hour of the day. Would you like to see it? Assuming, of course, it's cleared by Mr. Clark?"

"That would be lovely," I said. "Assuming Dane's okay with it."

Dean laughed again and glanced toward his boss. The sound of his laughter grated against me, and I found myself taking a sort of instant dislike to him. Just because I didn't have a brain the size of Uranus didn't make me totally stupid. But listening to him talk, one would think I didn't understand English.

"Of course," Dane said. "Please send us one of the lead engineers who works with Trey Hampton."

"Sir." Dean cleared his throat. "Trey Hampton has been out of work for two days now."

"Yes, taking sick time cleared by me," Dane said dismissively. "I apologize if the memo got lost somewhere in the system, but when he returns, he should not be reprimanded nor should he be punished in any way for his absence."

"Understood," Dean said with a nod. "Hope everything's okay for the guy—he's one of the good ones."

The four of us stood around in awkward silence. It was so clearly a fishing attempt for information that even my non-genius brain could understand it. I couldn't help myself smirking at the look of discomfort on Dean's face as he quickly excused himself and began a return jog down the stairs of the Eagle Office to the main floor.

From our vantage point above the lab, I watched as Dean shuffled toward a tall, leggy woman with luxurious blond hair and a gorgeous figure. Dean began talking rapidly, and it was followed by a few nods and a smile from the woman. She wore a seriously gorgeous shade of red lipstick, and I reminded myself to ask her where she'd gotten it as the pair on the floor glanced upward at the Eagle Office. Dean made a gesture for us to come down, so Dane, Semi, and I headed out.

"Hi, I'm Stacey," the blonde said, sticking out her hand for a shake. "Obviously, you're Mr. Clark, this is Semi, and you must be..." She trailed off glancing at me. "You must be the boss's fiancé?"

"Bingo," I said, taking an instant liking to her despite her unfair beauty and brains combination. Obviously, she was ridiculously intelligent, or she wouldn't be in Dane Clark's laboratory at all. "Nice to meet you, Stacey."

"I hear you'd like a small demonstration of our latest design," she said with a pleased smile. "I'd love to show you—if you'll just follow me into Demo A."

Dane, Semi, Stacey, and I filed quickly into a small-ish room with hefty soundproofing visible along the sheer-white walls. The ceiling was lofted high above with huge, greenhouse-style windows that let in lots of light and reflected an almost blinding whiteness.

"We never test products outside of a Demo room," Stacey explained as she closed and locked the door behind us. "They're all soundproof, blast proof, and high security. There are no cameras or audio devices inside the Demo rooms."

"Soundproof and blast proof?" I gave a shudder. "I thought this was a translator."

"Yes, of course." She gave a tinkling laugh. "But in all of our prototype devices we have an auto-detonate feature built in that can be activated by voice command or remotely. So, if something is stolen, it's easily taken care of."

"Gee," I said dryly. "I'm not sure I'd want an automatic detonating device implanted into my head."

She laughed again. "We remove all capabilities of that nature before implantation. It'd never pass regulations otherwise of course."

"Yeah, of course," I said. "Well, anyway, carry on, I suppose."

"I hear Dean has already explained what our project here does?" Stacey looked to me for confirmation. When I nodded, she continued. "Great. Who wants to give the product a try?"

The room fell silent.

"Fine," I said a second later. "I'll do it. But don't blow me up, please."

Stacey laughed, but I noticed she didn't give me any reassurance. "Here, put this on."

"It won't auto-detonate?" I asked, taking a small tube from Stacey and fitting it into my ear, sort of like a miniscule earbud. "You're sure?"

She laughed again, giving a cute wrinkle of her nose and a shake of her head. "You really are funny."

"I'm also serious," I said. "It won't—"

"Okay, look at my lips," Stacey said, bending down from her perch on long, slender legs to look me in the eyes. "You don't speak Norwegian, do you?"

I shook my head and kept my eyes fixed on her lips.

"Great. Here we go. Watch my lips but listen through the translator."

My eyes zeroed in on that super gorgeous lipstick color. I was in the middle of reminding myself that I'd need to ask where she'd bought it when a strange rush of bouncy syllables came at me. I wasn't an expert lip reader by any means, but I couldn't pick up a thing she'd said from watching her mouth, and my open ear told me she'd spoken in a language that barely even registered in my brain except as some sort of bizarre-sounding song.

However, while my brain was struggling to process everything happening at once, a cool, calm metallic voice spoke in my ear: "How are you doing today?"

"Fine," I said, and then started. "Wait, what just happened?"

"Don't!" She spoke again in a foreign language as she raised a hand and patted the bud in my ear to stay in place. "I'm speaking to you in Norwegian, but you are understanding me. Yes?"

"Yeah, I can hear you just fine," I said, responding to the pleasant metallic voice in my ear. "This is bizarre!"

"See?" Stacey pulled back to her full height and grinned at the group. "It's almost real time, and it's very effective. Eventually, the goal for this project is to provide everyone in the world the opportunity to travel freely between countries with little hassle due to language barriers. Of course, that's still years away."

"Dean said you were aiming to launch a different wave first?" I said, barely realizing that Stacey had switched back to English to include Dane and Semi. "Government officials and spies?"

Her eyes flashed quickly at Dane, then back to me. This time, her laugh was stilted and uncomfortable. "Well, that's a little dramatic sounding, but that's just Dean. We do expect the first wave to help foreign dignitaries and possible law-enforcement types."

"Like spies," I said, insistent. "It'd be great for them; they would be able to listen in on a zillion more conversations without learning every nuance of three hundred and seven languages. That would be huge."

"I suppose," she said, rushing the conversation along. "Who else wants to try? Say something to Lola in another language."

"Have any of the devices been deployed yet?" I asked. "Are any of them out there in the wild, working away in some spy's ear?"

"I am not at liberty to say," Stacey said shortly. "I'm merely an engineer on the product, and I have nothing to do with when or if it goes to market."

"Interesting," I said. "I bet this technology is in high demand."

"I imagine," Stacey said. "Then again, everything at Clark Company is generally in high demand. Mr. Clark is the best at what he does—and the world knows it."

"Yes, maybe so, but this—"

A short burst that sounded like German hit my open ear, and less than a millisecond later, the charming female voice radiated from the bud in my ear.

"Lola," Dane said through the female robot. "What's wrong? You're acting strangely."

I gave a shrug because the one flaw with this little earbud was that it couldn't make me talk back in German. It would be a very one-sided conversation with this thing unless the other person had a similar device.

"You work with Trey Hampton, don't you?" I asked Stacey. "What's he like?"

Stacey's eyes flicked toward Dane for confirmation before she spoke.

"Please, answer the question," Dane said. "He's one of the reasons we're here today. I trust we have your utmost confidence on the subject? Your project manager—nor anyone else—is privy to the conversation we're having in Demo A."

"Yes, of course." Stacey easily clasped her hands before her body and smiled. "Trey is excellent at his work, of course, but that's standard. I realize it's not humble of me to say, but Dane Clark only hires the best."

"Tell us a little more about Trey and his work ethic," I prompted.

"As you know, we're both lead engineers on the project," Stacey said. "We report directly to Dean. I handle more of the software, the translation side of things, while Trey works on the packaging."

"Who added the auto detonate?" I asked. "Was that Trey?"

She nodded. "Physical hardware, etc., is all within his realm of expertise. He's also an efficient coder and can handle software, but he prefers the physical aspect of development."

"Any changes in behavior lately?" I asked. "For better or worse?"

She hesitated, her eyes flicking around the room.

"Nothing you say will reflect on Trey's status, salary, or position within the company," Dane said. "We're dealing with a time-sensitive matter and are looking for anything you can give us that might help."

"Something's happened," she said, her sharp eyes widening with alarm. "Something's wrong, isn't it? That's why Trey hasn't shown up to work these last few days. I knew it wasn't just an illness."

"How did you know?" I asked. "Did he give any other signs?"

"No, that's the thing," she said. "He was working harder than ever on the project. Late nights. Except for Wednesdays, of course, but that's been going on for a few months now."

"Wednesdays?" I asked, shooting Dane and Semi a curious look. "What about Wednesdays?"

"Oh, um, he had a standing obligation on Wednesday evenings. He always took off around seven, which for Trey was leaving early. He worked seven a.m. to midnight most days."

"Except Wednesdays," I said again. "Do you have any idea where he would go? Or what this obligation entailed?"

"No, I'm sorry. Trey and I didn't discuss our personal lives much. I prefer to remain private, as does he. It makes for a very efficient engineering team since our entire professional relationship is focused solely on the project and its progress."

"Thank you. This might be really important," I said, calculating in my head. Today was Friday. That meant yesterday was Thursday, and the night before—his last day at work—would have been a Wednesday. I could see Dane and Semi calculating along with me. "He would have left early this week too, yes?"

She frowned. "Yes, I'm sure he did. Let me think...the days all start to run together."

I nodded impatiently.

"Yes, we had a meeting about the project Wednesday in the early afternoon—it ended at three p.m. He mentioned not feeling well during it, and I believe he left sometime after our meeting, but I'm afraid I can't give you an exact time. I noticed his station was cleaned up before I had dinner at seven."

"Were you here all evening?"

"Yes, I stayed here until midnight," she said. "As I've mentioned, Mr. Clark strives to hire the best, and the best tend to enjoy their work—myself included. The long hours are a choice."

"Trey has been leaving early on Wednesdays for months?" I asked. "Yet he hasn't said once whether it's for a personal or business reason?"

"Of course it was personal," Stacey said. "Which was why I didn't press him on it. He could have been spending time with a significant other, taking a cooking class, or playing in a chess club—among a million other things. I'm sorry, I just don't have the answer for you."

"It's really important!" I said, pleading. "If you can think of—"

Another flurry of a language I didn't understand hit my open ear in Dane's voice. Meanwhile, the metallic female trickled the meaning through the earbud. "She said she doesn't know, Lola. I believe her, and I think you do, too."

"But we need to figure this out," I said in English, and Stacey glanced to me curiously. I turned to her. "I'm sorry if I'm coming off as harsh, but like Dane said, this is a very time sensitive matter. If there's anything you can think of—anything at all—please don't hold back."

Stacey clasped her hands before her body once again and gave a demure shake of her head. "I'm sorry, but there's nothing else I can tell you. I have no idea where Trey went on Wednesdays, and when he stopped showing up for work yesterday, I heard it was because he was ill. If there's more to the story, I'm afraid you're asking the wrong woman."

It was with a seriously heavy weight on our shoulders that we tramped out of the room—all four of us—and left Stacey and Dean behind at the front doors. Semi, Dane, and I hopped onto the train that zipped back to the castle and let us off. Mrs. Dulcet was there waiting.

"Sit down," she said, pointing behind her in the general vicinity of the dining room, "and eat. You've been running around all day, and I insist you feed this poor girl, Dane."

Dane gave one look at me, and as if on cue, my stomach growled.

"Sorry," I said, wincing as I hugged my arms over my stomach. "I can't control those sounds. We can keep going—I'll grab a granola bar."

Mrs. Dulcet looked at me as if I'd suggested giving myself a lobotomy. "A granola bar? I've cooked you a full meal. A healthy meal. Dane Clark—feed your bride. She won't be alive to marry you if you starve the poor thing to death."

"Fine," Dane said, scratching his head at Mrs. Dulcet's attack. "We need to figure out our game plan, anyway. I suppose we can eat and talk at the same time."

"Very good," Mrs. Dulcet said. "Take a seat, and I'll tell those detectives they can just wait for a few moments."

"Detectives?" I asked, frozen solid. "Why are there detectives here?"

Mrs. Dulcet paled. "I'm not sure, dear. They said they would wait while I went to find you. Then you all popped up here."

"Tell them we're not back yet," Dane said, "but that you called us and we're on our way. We need five minutes, Mrs. Dulcet. Stall them if you can."

She nodded. "One look at my cinnamon buns, sir, and they'll be occupied for the next ten minutes. Fifteen if I bring them coffee. I'll let them know you're on your way."

Chapter 9

While Mrs. Dulcet entertained the detectives with her cinnamon buns, Dane Clark led the way through a winding passage of halls until we reached the kitchen via a back route. At one point, I could hear the detectives complimenting Mrs. Dulcet's baking, followed by her high-pitched offer of coffee. Our time was running low.

"What are we doing?" I asked Dane as he blew through the kitchen before the surprised gazes of his staff. "Where are we going?"

On the way, I yanked one of the cinnamon rolls fresh from the pan, nearly burning my fingers in the process. I plucked a napkin as Dane breezed through to the opposite end of the room and stopped dead before the set of swinging doors.

"This is poor timing," Dane said, facing Semi and me, his voice low. "According to my calculations, Jim should be here at any moment."

"Jim?" I sorted through my thoughts. "Who's Jim?"

"Fat Jim," Semi said.

"Oh, right. You thought he was coming over here," I said. "What makes you so certain?"

"Trust me." Even as Dane spoke, however, his eyebrows furrowed with concern and he flicked a glance at his watch. "In fact, he should have been here already."

"What if he's not coming?"

"He's coming," Dane said firmly. "I know his type well. His ego can't handle being left out of the loop. I'm especially certain after what we learned from Darius. If he has his sticky little fingers in everything, he won't want to miss out on a chance to find out what we know."

"The guy has major FOMO," I said. At Semi and Dane's blank stares, I shrugged. "Fear-Of-Missing-Out. It's what all the cool kids are saying these days. It just means he's got to be involved in everything possible."

"Yes, FOMO," Dane repeated, his voice clipped. He moved closer to one of the high windows along the kitchen, scaring a thin little man away from his stove to cower in fright over a fresh basil plant. "He should be here. Where the hell is he? Semi?"

"Sir?"

"Why isn't he here?" Dane grew more and more agitated by the second. "I had a plan. He's not following the agenda, and it's frustrating. What could be the hold up?"

"Maybe there's no hold up. Maybe he just decided to let this one go. You're an intimidating bloke," I said, trying for a joke as I watched the cowering little man staring up at Dane in awe. "Maybe he decided to stay away."

"No." Dane's answer was firm, resolute. "I'm not wrong about these things."

"Okay, then. As you wish, sir." I gave a pointed tinge to my words, but Dane was too distraught to notice.

"Would you like me to return to the casino?" Semi asked quietly. "I can provide surveillance and let you know his movements. It's possible Fat Jim has decided to seek extra protection or advice before coming here, and that's what delayed him."

"No, I can't have you leave now." Dane turned away from the window, a frown on his face. "I need you on the lookout. If Jim shows up while the detectives are here, it will not go over well, and we can't take the time to explain it. We can't tell the police Trey is missing this close to the drop—it'll only cause problems. We all read the ransom note. It's obvious we need to handle the money drop ourselves or risk losing Trey."

"Yes, sir, I see your point," said Semi. "I will run interference at the front gates on the off chance that Fat Jim arrives. Should I detain him in the garage until after your meeting with the detectives?"

"That would be fine." Dane and Semi had some sort of unspoken code that must have signaled the conversation was over because at once, Semi launched his hulking form toward the swinging doors and let himself through while Dane faced me. "Ready?"

"For what? I'm a few steps behind," I said. "You think Fat Jim's going to arrive and ruin everything with the cops?"

"He's got a bad reputation, and we don't want the detectives asking questions. It's too dangerous for Trey's safety. I'd prefer it if the three of us handle the situation on our own—at least until we learn more about who took Trey."

"I understand, but this is the first I've heard of you actually planning to make the drop," I said with a wave of my hand. "Are you sure that's a good idea? Once they get the money, what's to stop them from killing Trey anyway?"

"Nothing," Dane said evenly. "But a million dollars is disposable. Trey's life is not; if we're out the money, we're out the money. Worst case scenario—they won't kill him, they'll simply ask for more. A million is not a lot, Lola. I suspect it's not their end game."

"Uh, yeah. A million is a lot!" I said. "We have to think this through, Dane. I'm not convinced making the drop is the best choice. Are you sure we shouldn't tell the detectives what's going on?"

"That's the only sure path to Trey's death." Dane's expression was grim. "Whoever has taken Trey is smart enough to capture a Clark Company employee. They will be taking precautions to ensure the drop is safe. If they catch a whiff of police, they're gone, and so is Trey."

"Maybe," I said, "or maybe not. What if it's not some evil genius who took Trey, but merely someone he knows?"

"What?"

"Stacey just said that Trey went somewhere on Wednesday nights. That means he had a standing meeting with someone, or something. Whether he just liked to watch a certain television show in peace, or met a girlfriend for drinks, there was a definite pattern. I think if we figure out where he was going, we might find some clues as to what he was into outside of work."

"He wasn't into anything outside of work," Dane said. "As Stacey said, Clark Company employees tend to live and breathe their jobs. There's just not much time left for auxiliary activities."

"Maybe so, but something was important enough for Trey to skip out on a few hours of work every Wednesday night," I insisted. "What if he was meeting a friend? Better yet, a girlfriend? What if that's the route the kidnapper took to get to Trey? For all we know, Trey could've gone to his Wednesday night obligation and never returned. All we know is that he didn't show up to work on Thursday."

Dane considered this and culminated his thinking with a nod. "Fair enough, but still, whoever took him is smart enough to have not left a trail. Even I must admit we're grasping at straws."

"True," I said, feeling a sinking in the pit of my stomach. "Which means maybe Trey's kidnapper knew him. Maybe he or she is an evil genius."

Dane pursed his lips.

"There are only so many brilliant people on the Sunshine Shore," I said, taking baby steps with my next suggestion. "I think we need to look closer at the employees of the Clark Company, Dane. Trey knew them, and most of them are incredibly intelligent. They'd know how to not leave a trail. And they'd likely not be involved with people like Fat Jim and Darius, so there wouldn't be any trace there, either."

Dane heaved a sigh that sounded like agreement. "Internal investigations are not easy."

"I know, and I'm sorry," I said. "I wouldn't suggest it, but time is running out, and I'm desperate to find something that will work."

"Me too," Dane said, leaning against the counter and gazing out the window. "Me too. Now where the hell is Jim?"

"Mr. Clark—" Mrs. Dulcet burst through the kitchen doors. "The detectives have finished their cinnamon buns, and I'm afraid the coffee is wiring them up. It was a mistake to give them caffeine, I think. I can't cover for you much longer."

"Thank you, Mrs. Dulcet." Dane tipped his head toward her in acknowledgement. "We're ready for them. Please bring us a round of coffees and a cinnamon roll." Dane's eyes flicked toward my sticky fingers and the dirty napkin in my hand. "A second one."

I gave a sheepish grin, stopping at the nearest sink to wash my hands. I dumped the napkin, then followed Dane out of the kitchen and down the hallway in a more direct route to his web of sitting areas and sun rooms.

Two male voices filtered out from behind a closed door. Dane raised a hand to let himself in, stopping abruptly at the last moment. Instead of pushing the door open, he faced me with a quizzical expression. "Lola."

"What?"

His raised hand reached toward me, and he gently removed the ear bud. An eyebrow raised. "Speaking of thieves..."

My face colored. "I'm so sorry! I didn't realize—we rushed out of there so quickly, and then with all the detective talk about Fat Jim...I'm so sorry. Stacey's probably peeing her pants with worry."

"Um, what?"

"It's an expression," I said quickly. "Just tell Mrs. Dulcet to let Stacey know that her demo thingy is safe."

Mrs. Dulcet appeared with a tray of coffee in hand and gave a nod. "Tell Stacey demo thingy is safe. Understood."

"Really?" I asked. "You know what I mean?"

Mrs. Dulcet gave me a patronizing smile. "I've worked here for longer than you've been alive, sweetheart. Now, why are we waiting at the door? You'll be much more comfortable inside the room."

Mrs. Dulcet brushed past us as Dane gave me a quirked smile and a halfway shake of his head. "You never cease to surprise me."

"Give me," I muttered, taking the earbud from Dane's outstretched hand. I quickly tossed it into one of the secret pouches in my purse and zipped it up for safekeeping. At Dane's questioning glance, I shrugged. "You don't want to have to explain that to the detectives, do you? I'll give it back, I swear."

Dane gave a bark of laughter and put his arm around my shoulder. It was in this position—laughing, curled against one another, that we appeared before the detectives. Unfortunately, their faces didn't reflect our joy in being together, and slowly the room deteriorated into a grim standoff.

"Well, I'll be going," Mrs. Dulcet said when she finished pouring four dainty cups of coffee. "Warm cinnamon rolls, coffee, and I'll be back shortly with fruit."

"Gentlemen," Dane said with a frown. "It's been a while."

"Not long enough," Detective Plane, the taller, more athletic of the two men said. "Normally, we prefer not to pay visits to the same people over and over again."

Dane ignored the barbed comment and pulled me over to sit in two elegant, high-backed chairs that looked like antique treasures. Mrs. Dulcet had cleverly arranged the two detectives so that they were squished together on a dainty little love seat well below our eye level. Smart woman, I marveled. It was nice to have the homefield advantage for once and watch the detectives squirm with discomfort.

Detective Ross, the chubbier of the two, had a ruddy face and permanently pouted lips. He stared greedily at the cinnamon rolls on the table, but he refrained from taking one under the stare of his partner.

I didn't feel the same pressure. I reached for the coffee first, then a cinnamon roll, and I alternated the flavors as Dane Clark reintroduced us to the detectives and asked the nature of their business at Castlewood.

Detective Plane cleared his throat. "There's been a murder."

I froze, my fingers turning white around the handle of the coffee cup, and I felt Dane's hand on my leg tense.

"A murder?" Dane asked, organizing his voice in a calm, nonchalant manner. "I'm sorry to hear that, but what does this have to do with us?"

"Do you recognize the name Jim Gordon?" Detective Ross asked.

"Fat Jim?" I inhaled a gasp. "Fat Jim is *dead*?!"

"I can see you're familiar with the man," Detective Plane said dryly. "When's the last time you saw him?"

I glanced guiltily at Dane. I probably should've tried to hide my reaction better than a huge gasp, but I was an open book when it came to reactions. That was sort of my thing. Maybe I'd have to practice at holding back now that I'd be marrying into the Clark family and that sort of skill would be required more often.

"I wouldn't say familiar," I said. "I just learned his name—er, Dane?"

Dane squeezed my leg progressively harder until my mouth stopped spewing words on its own. "We're familiar with Jim," he said when I finally fell silent. "Why? We most certainly didn't kill him."

"You know, it's strange us being here on two separate murder investigations within a year," Detective Ross said. "And we don't like coincidences."

"Then we have one thing in common." Dane gave a thin smile at the detective. "You still haven't told me what brings you here today. I think I'll get my lawyers on the phone, so if you'll hold—"

"Wait!" Detective Plane stood and held out a hand while shooting a glare at his partner. "We just have a few questions to ask. You're not—we have nothing on you. If you can give us an alibi for this afternoon, we'll be on our way. We're just looking for your help."

"Obviously we have no idea what time Jim was murdered," Dane said evenly, "since only the murderer and the cops would know such a fact. I only know it must have been after..." He frowned, glanced again at his watch. "Twelve thirty."

The detectives looked at one another. Eventually, Ross shifted in his seat. "Yeah, about two hours later."

"He only knows that because we left Fat Jim around that time," I said, my nerves sending more spouts of words from my mouth. "When we left, Fat Jim was still alive. I swear it; he was eating hot wings!"

Detective Plane stared darkly at me for a long moment, as if waiting for me to break. I took heart in knowing that what I'd said was the truth, but it made me nervous nonetheless. I could see how detectives roped false confessions out of surprised interviewees. This questioning business wasn't for the faint of heart.

Finally, the detective's face cleared. "That matches up with what we learned at the casino," Plane said finally. "Where did you go after you took your leave of the casino?"

"We went down to the beach," Dane said. "To talk to—"

"For a stroll," I said smoothly, reaching for Dane's hand and giving the officers a cheesy grin. "You know, romantic walks on the beach and such."

Dane gave a nod. "Exactly."

Plane glared at me. I could see in his face that he knew I'd interrupted whatever Dane had been about to say for a more convenient story. The difficult part was that we *were* hiding something; it just wasn't what the cops thought. It was hard to appear innocent when we had a kidnapping weighing us down.

"Right, a nice stroll along the beach," Plane said. "Did anyone see you there?"

"Yes," Dane said. "There was—"

"There were a lot of people," I interrupted, waving a hand nonchalantly. "I mean, if you asked around, I'm sure some tourist or another saw us. And of course Semi, Dane's bodyguard, drove us there and kept an eye on us, so he'll be able to corroborate our story."

"You didn't talk to anyone else specifically?" Plane asked, looking solely at Dane. "Not a soul?"

"It doesn't matter much," Dane said, "since we couldn't have been there more than twenty minutes—thirty at the most. Which means we were back at Castlewood by one—one thirty at the very latest. Any number of people can verify our whereabouts since we returned home. In fact, you can even check my swipe pass. We were in Warehouse 5 at the time of the murder."

"It'll be on camera," I said, remembering Stacey's words. "I mean, the security footage. Plus, all of Warehouse 5 saw us, and we can give you their names to check out our story."

"We'll be doing that," Plane said, taking out a notebook. "Names?"

After Dane listed off a good ten or fifteen people we'd passed at some point during our afternoon on company grounds, the detective looked up, resigned. I could see he believed us. Then Dane called for Mrs. Dulcet and spoke quietly to her. When they finished, she waved toward Detective Ross.

"I'll take you to the security office now," she said. "You can check the footage yourself."

"What was your business with Fat Jim earlier this afternoon?" Detective Plane said, watching as his partner left the room. "You both are intelligent people. I'm assuming you know he's an unsavory sort of fellow."

"What do you mean?" I feigned ignorance. "We only met him today. It was hard to get a read on him."

"Right," the detective murmured. "I know you're hiding something from me, Miss Pink. I assume Mr. Clark is in on it as well, though he's got a much better poker face than you do."

"We didn't murder anyone," I said. "You've heard our alibi; check it out."

"Detective Plane, I believe we've already helped you out plenty today," Dane said. "If you have any more questions, I'll have you talk to my lawyers. It's none of your business what I was doing at the casino."

"It is when the murdered victim is found dead in his car with his GPS pointed toward you." Detective Plane didn't bother to rise from his seat. He knew his announcement would shock us; I could only assume he'd been saving it for this very moment. "What was Fat Jim coming to discuss with you, Mr. Clark?"

"How should I know?" Dane asked, his voice relaying a calmness that I most certainly didn't feel. "It's not my place to know why someone is coming to pay me a surprise visit. You may check my calendar, detective. You'll find a detailed itinerary down to the minute. There is no meeting with a Jim Gordon on there."

"It's true," I said, adopting a nervous whisper. "It's sort of weird how accurate his schedule is. He even schedules his leisure reading. His agendas are legendary around here—just ask anyone."

Detective Plane continued to ignore me. "Mr. Clark, let me paint you a picture."

"I have quite enough art," Dane said, and I worked hard to suppress a smile. "I'm running low on patience, detective."

"A billionaire and his bride-to-be," Detective Plane began quickly, "who rarely leave Castlewood grounds decide that all of a sudden, they'd like to visit the Sunshine Slots on a perfectly normal day for no reason at all."

"There was a reason," I said. "Entertainment. Why else would we go to the casino?"

Still ignoring me, Plane spoke to Dane. "You and your entourage show up, beeline straight to Fat Jim himself, and you strike up a challenge."

"Mmm," Dane murmured noncommittally. "Is that how it happened?"

I wanted to applaud Dane's sarcasm abilities, but I refrained. I'd hold my applause until the end of the show.

Plane's face melted into annoyance. "There are multiple eyewitnesses to confirm the story."

"Did I deny it?" Dane raised a hand in question. "It's an enthralling story. Do tell what comes next."

Plane shifted uncomfortably in his seat. "That's where things get a little—ah, murky."

"How unfortunate."

"I can't seem to find what it is the two of you bet on," Plane said, "but I figure it must be something big. The King of Castlewood doesn't leave his throne for petty cash. Fifty grand is a sneeze to you, Mr. Clark."

"Mmm." Dane was on-point with his murmurs. Each time he answered with one, Detective Plane grew more and more irate.

"Then two hours later, Fat Jim gets in his truck to come here, and someone wants to stop that from happening. Who could that be?" Plane pressed. "Why? What were you discussing that was so important it got Fat Jim killed?"

Dane's face paled.

I recognized it for what it was: a sudden bout of guilt.

"Hey, that's not fair," I said. "Dane didn't cause Fat Jim to get killed—none of us did. If Fat Jim ended up dead, it's his own doing. You said it yourself: He was an unsavory type. Sometimes unsavory types find their way into unsavory situations."

"And sometimes, others help it along," Plane said, finally swiveling his gaze to me. "Is that what happened? Fat Jim was going to reach a grisly end anyway, so you just sped things along?"

"You know that's not what I meant," I retorted. "We don't have any say over what Fat Jim's involved in—it's common knowledge he has a hand in the shadow side of the Sunshine Shore."

"I thought you just met him today. You seem pretty familiar with his work," Plane said. "Why are you so interested in him?"

"This conversation is over." Dane stood, his voice prickly thin. "Have a nice afternoon, Detective Plane. You can see yourself out. Mrs. Dulcet!"

The butler hurried through the doors. She'd clearly been on stand-by awaiting orders. Dane Clark and Mrs. Dulcet had been running this schtick for years and had their movements choreographed to a fine art.

"Please see that Detective Plane and his associate vacate the premises at once," Dane said. "Lola and I will be in my office."

"Yes, sir. Detective Ross is currently with Semi in the security room. I'll have him removed." Mrs. Dulcet bowed her head toward Dane with exaggerated obedience, and then turned to Detective Plane with a bright smile. "Did you enjoy the cinnamon rolls, sir?"

"Er—yeah, thanks," he said, still glancing after us. "Mr. Clark, this isn't the last time we'll be back. You might not have killed Mr. Gordon, but he had something to tell you—and that *did* get him killed. Whatever you brought on him this morning, ended him this afternoon."

Dane was out of the room, a door slamming behind him before Plane finished his sentence. I stayed behind with Mrs. Dulcet, one last question burning on my tongue.

"Detective," I ventured slowly. "How did he die?"

Plane shot me a look of venom. "Painfully."

Mrs. Dulcet cleared her throat in the ensuing silence. It snapped Plane and I back to reality. While I turned on a heel to follow Dane, the detective stomped out the opposite pair of doors ahead of Mrs. Dulcet.

I found Dane pacing out back on the patio. He hadn't gone to his office as he'd said, and I suspected it felt too confined. Dane paced up and down the length of the pool, his gaze fixed on the ground. He must've done a mile in five minutes at the rate he was moving.

"Hey," I said softly, easing beside him and giving a half-jog, half-skip to keep pace. "I loved your joke about the art back there. I just didn't laugh because, you know, it would have sounded very immature."

Dane flicked his gaze to me. "You're sweet, Lola. You don't have to make me feel better."

"It really was great," I said, slipping my hand into his. "Your jokes have come a long way."

"I started at ground zero. It's not as if the bar was set particularly high."

I gave another peal of laughter that eventually faded into silence, and then a somber echo as the late afternoon sunlight began to slip beyond the horizon. "What are you thinking?" I ventured. "If it's about what that detective said...you have to let it go. If Fat Jim was involved with the kidnapping, he knew what he was getting into. Plane had a point in calling him an unsavory type."

"Yes, but what if he wasn't involved?" Dane looked pained. "What if my questioning him led to his death—and he was innocent?"

"He was coming here to tell you something," I insisted. "That means he likely wasn't innocent. In fact, I'd reckon a guess that he was feeling guilty and was on his way here to confess something to you. Maybe he figured it wasn't too late, or maybe it was selfish and he was just hoping you'd give him a fat payout in exchange for information."

"I would have done exactly that."

"I know, and he knew that, too," I said. "Your plan worked—he really was going to be here when you said, but someone beat him to it."

"Someone wanted him silenced." Dane's eyes turned icy blue. "Someone involved with Trey's kidnapping."

"That's my thinking, too."

Dane blinked. "What the hell was Jim trying to tell me?"

I shook my head. "I'm not sure, but if we find out, I think we might find Trey."

"We don't have time." Dane's face fell, and he shook his head. "We have to prepare for the drop."

"But Dane, if we can just—"

"We can't risk it," he said, crossing his arms as he studied the horizon. "We've got to get the money and a plan. If we do everything right, we can end this tonight."

Chapter 10

The next few hours passed in a flurry of preparations. Semi joined us under the grapevine gazebo. While I munched on the vine-ripened fruit—a girl needed energy for a ransom exchange—Dane quickly caught Semi up to speed on our visit with the detectives and the evolving plan.

"Sir," Semi said as soon as Dane finished. "Trey is my brother, and I'd do just about anything for him. But a million dollars—I can't ask that of you. Especially not after all you've done already."

"You've never asked me for a thing, Semi." Dane's gaze swiveled to face his bodyguard. "It's not about keeping score. This is about getting Trey Hampton—a good engineer and a good man—back from the bastard who took him. The Clark Company won't be threatened."

"But if you pay the ransom, aren't you giving in to the kidnapper?" I asked. "No negotiating with terrorists—the government is always talking about it."

"This is just the start, Lo," Dane said. "The money exchange is the beginning—*we* will determine when it has ended. Now, we need a plan for tonight, and I think I have one."

Dane's plan was relatively simple: The three of us would gather up a million dollars from the Clark Company slush fund. We'd take the SUV away from the castle to a neutral location to wait for the kidnapper's call. The third rule was to stick together, and the fourth element was to wait.

I fretted over the simplicity of the plan, but the truth was that any way we looked at it, the options weren't good. Alert the police, and Trey would most certainly die. Stay at the castle, and everyone here would be at risk.

If the three of us stuck together and delivered the money at the designated time and place, that should in theory provide us with the safe return of Semi's brother. Any further planning would quickly become irrelevant because the only thing certain about this whole evening was that the three of us were going in blind while the kidnapper had a plan.

Gathering the money, piling into the car, and finding a secure location to wait didn't take as long as I'd thought. The money had been double counted and stuffed into a large duffle weighing, as Dane calculated in his head, a mere 22.05 pounds.

I lifted the duffle into the car and bit my lip. "Huh. I always thought I'd feel a lot more impressive carrying around a million bucks than I do right now."

Dane raised an eyebrow. "You have a lot more than a million dollars to your name now. You can carry around as much as you'd like, though I wouldn't recommend it. That's why I have a credit card."

"It's not in my name," I scoffed. "I wouldn't want you to put your money in my name. I wouldn't even know where to begin spending it. I mean, I could do some damage online shopping, and I do like keeping fresh flowers around the house, which adds up. My favorite ice cream is five bucks a pint, so that's a real splurge, and..." I shut up. "Right. Kidnapping—let's go."

Dane had the ghost of a smile on his face as we slid into the backseat and Semi took the front. After a short drive, Semi pulled into a parking spot not far from Trey's condo, giving us a view over the city, as well as a central location to just about everything on the Sunshine Shore. We fully expected to receive a phone call telling us to meet elsewhere and that's when the improvising would kick in.

Dane snuck a glance at the clock. I followed suit. 10:58 p.m. One hour and two minutes to go, if not less. I tried to ignore the panic building in my chest at the thought of not knowing where we'd all be within the hour.

"I got an interesting phone call today," Dane said, breaking the silence at 11:09. Both Semi and I swiveled our gazes to face Dane. We waited for him to continue with bated breath.

"Um, okay," I said. "Is it relevant to the kidnapping?"

"No," he said thoughtfully. "But I can feel your breath on the verge of hyperventilating, and I was wondering whether it might help you to talk."

"Oh, okay, sure. Who called?"

"Babs," Dane said. "She was in quite a tizzy. Something had gotten her worked up, and she used some strong language to convey her meaning."

"Is she okay? I just saw her! Why would she call you and not me?" I asked, vaguely aware of Semi opening the driver's side door and sliding out, then closing it behind him and standing respectfully outside the car. "What happened to Babs?"

"I don't know if anything happened to Babs, but she made me swear that I wouldn't let you get married at a courthouse." Dane turned to me, his gaze passively open. "Is there a chance you know anything about that?"

"Oh." I flinched. "Possibly. But it was just a little freak out, I guess. Nothing big. I don't need to get married at the courthouse."

"Are you anxious about the wedding?" Dane cleared his throat.

"I'm not—well, I know I haven't been much help in planning, so I apologize. If you'd like me to take more off your hands or perhaps hire a professional to take over, I would be more than happy to do so."

"No, Dane, it was just an overreaction." I sighed. "Our invitations came today, and they were—well, I didn't expect them."

"Why not? I thought you were working with Mrs. Dulcet to pick out everything."

"Well, Mrs. Dulcet is lovely. There are just a few things that aren't—ah—working out as I wished," I said. "It's my fault for not being flexible."

"Why would you prefer to be married at the courthouse?"

"It's not that I'd *prefer* that solution! I didn't mean that at all. When I was talking to Babs, I was just expressing my frustration. The most important thing in all of this is that I get to marry you. If, at the end of all of this, we're happily wedded, our ceremony will have been a success whatever it looks like."

"What do you want it to look like?"

"I—er, I don't care."

Dane slipped his hand over mine and squeezed. His cheeks held the slightest tinge of color, which had me wondering what was going through his mind.

"Dane? Are you okay?" I asked. "I'm not sure I've ever seen you blush."

"I had some wedding magazines delivered after Babs's phone call this afternoon and glanced at them while you were busy," he said in a rushed voice. "Every magazine has pictures of brides grinning and laughing and smiling, and articles about choosing flowers and colors and twirly things over chairs. Are you not interested in any of that?"

I gave him a smile. "You read a bridal magazine?"

"That's not the point," he snapped. "Why don't you want a wedding, Lola?"

I froze. "Is that what you think?!"

"What am I supposed to think?!" When he looked at me, the expression in his eyes was dulled and worn. "Am I not enough for you? I'd rather know now if you'd prefer not to be married to me."

I gave a light laugh which sent him spiraling into frustration. Throwing my arms around his neck, I leaned against him. "That's the exact opposite. I want to be married to you, but this wedding planning business is a mess. I thought I wanted to plan everything, but then your mother—"

"Hold on a second." Dane sat up straighter which jerked me back to my own seat. "Is this because of my mother? I knew she would do something. She pretended to be happy for us, and then she turns around and does this. By the way, what is "this" exactly? I'll need to know when I contact her and suggest I'll revoke her invitation if it continues."

"Stop. Chill," I instructed Dane. "It's not a big deal. I'm probably blowing it out of proportion. I'm sure this is your mother's way of trying to help."

"It's not helping if you're unhappy."

"I think she's trying to guide me to the perfect wedding for the Clark family," I said, and then I quickly explained about suddenly unavailable caterers and cakes and dresses, and the arrival of invitations I'd never ordered. "It would probably be best if I just went along with her choices. The most important thing is that you never doubt I want to be married to you."

"I love you, Lola, and I don't doubt you love me." His fingertips reached out, tilted my chin upward. He dusted a kiss across my lips. "But I will have a word with my mother."

"Please don't do that," I said. "You've already had to defend me to her more than once. I'm going to look like a wimp and a complainer, and I get the feeling that your mother doesn't respect wimps."

Dane's eyes crinkled with a smile. "A wimp? Lola, you are the least wimpy person I've ever met. You bike everywhere you go. You solve million-dollar mysteries and face off with murderers. You are the strongest person I know in every way."

"Well, that's mighty sweet of you," I said, sidling up against him. "But let's not make a big deal about it. I would prefer to just get the wedding over with so we can start our happily ever after already."

"Did I hear that you have a flower appointment tomorrow?" Dane raised his eyebrow at my confused glance. "Your itinerary is linked to mine. You shouldn't be surprised that I know where you are every second of the day. Or at least, where you should be."

"Careful who you tell that to, Mr. Clark. That sounds quite creepy."

He smiled. "I'm going with you. We'll choose flowers together, and I'll invite my mother along."

I groaned. "That sounds miserable. Just give me a bouquet of dandelions."

"If you don't want me to talk to her," Dane said. "You can do it yourself. I'll be there for moral support."

"Ugh, there's no way around this, is there?"

Dane's gaze softened. "Not if you want to take care of it yourself. I'm sorry, Lola. I know my mother is difficult, and I promise to take care of things if you prefer."

"No—no," I said with a huge sigh. "You're right. I need to do this. I'll have a word with her tomorrow. But you should know that I'm dreading a date at the flower shop with your mother more than I am dreading the idea of facing off with a murderous kidnapper."

Dane's eyes flicked to the clock. Under twenty minutes to go. He brushed a kiss against my forehead and scooted closer. "I feel the same way, sweetheart."

"Where'd you pick up the endearment?" I asked. "Usually you just go with Lola. Those bridal magazines making you soft?"

Dane turned an embarrassed gaze out the window. "I used them for kindling, I'll have you know. I thumbed through a few pages and realized it's no wonder brides go insane. There's more work that goes into planning a wedding than in running a billion-dollar company. If I had to choose which I'd prefer to do—"

At that moment, a phone rang. Semi threw open the front door. He was in the seat with the car running by the time I realized it was my phone.

"Well, that's weird," I said, glancing at the unknown number dotted across the screen. "If this is our kidnapper, we have to assume he's watching us. How else would he know he could use my phone?"

"I think that's a safe assumption," Dane said. "Would you like me to answer?"

"He called me for a reason," I said. "Let's find out what it is."

Chapter 11

"He wants you to do *what*?" Dane squinted, studying me as I hung up the cell. "No, that's not happening."

"We don't have a choice," I argued. "The instructions were clear. If we don't move and drop the money by midnight, Trey's dead."

I had put the phone on speaker during my call with the kidnapper. The man—or woman, I supposed—had used a voice changer and what I assumed was a burner cell to make the call. There'd be no clues even if we had all the hottest tracking gadgets on the market—which we didn't.

"We heard Trey's voice," I said. "That was him, right, Semi?"

The large man closed his eyes and nodded.

"So, we know Trey's still alive, and we have simple instructions. It shouldn't be hard," I said. "I'll just...do what he said."

"Lola Pink," Dane said harshly. "The man asked you to get on a bicycle and pedal down a dark path at midnight to leave the money on a rock. Alone. I'm not letting that happen."

"He won't hurt me," I said. "I'm engaged to you, Dane. You have a million bucks riding on this. Semi has a brother out there. A lot of people want this guy. If he hurts me, he'll never get away with it. His incentive is to take the money and run—that would be the smart thing for him to do, and he's not stupid."

"But—"

"I'll take Semi's gun," I said. "If that will make you feel better."

"Do you know how to use a gun?" Semi asked. "Ever fired one?"

"Nope and nope," I said. "But I'm assuming you sorta point and pull the trigger if the movies are to be believed. Look, we have to move. Drive, Semi. You heard the drop spot."

Semi began to drive because there was nothing else he could do. The kidnapper had instructed us to pull the SUV down to the parking lot where old Mr. Reynolds's grocery store used to be. There, on the rack out front, a bicycle would be waiting for me.

From there, I was supposed to bike—alone—down the trail behind the new condos to a small clearing behind the lake. I knew the place well—during the day, it was a bright park complete with a children's playground, a miniature rock-climbing wall, and a small little dock where kids fed ducks and ran away from an extremely aggressive infestation of geese.

I was to leave the duffle bag, which would be slung over my arm while riding, on the park bench nearest the dock. I knew the one—it was the coveted lunch bench that was taken by ten thirty every morning and not vacated until after sunset. At midnight, however, the park would be vacant.

The evil beauty of the kidnapper's plan was that no cars could reach the drop spot easily. Neither could a person on foot, and by giving me a bike, it ensured I'd be moving a lot faster than either Dane or Semi could follow. It ensured that I would be utterly and completely alone.

"You're not going in there," Dane said. "I won't allow it."

"I'd never ask you to do that, Lola," Semi said. "Let me go. We'll take that risk. He'll get his money either way and that should be enough."

"I'm choosing to go in there," I said. "He asked for me for a reason. Probably because I'm the weakest link, and he knows I'm not going to put up a fight. He wants the money, and he wants to be sure there's nothing funny going on during the drop."

"That's a stupid thought on his part," Dane said. "Because the last man who picked a fight with you took a dive off a cliff. You're not the weakest link, Lola."

I smiled. "Let him think so."

"*I* don't think so," Dane said. "I couldn't handle it if anything happened to you."

"You'll be waiting in the parking lot. Give me five minutes and if I'm not back, rush in with guns blazing," I said. "He won't be able to get far. If anything, this is an advantage for us. He can't have a car in there either. He'll have to be on foot or bike or something similar."

"Give us a minute, will you?" Dane asked, giving my hand a squeeze. "I need to talk to Semi."

"Sure, fine," I said, "whatever."

I tried not to give away the fact that my feelings were slightly hurt. The three of us were supposed to be in this together. It was frustrating that Dane and Semi felt as if they couldn't trust me to do the job—and worse, that they didn't feel I needed a say in the matter.

Dane and Semi had stalked a good twenty feet from the car and still, their voices carried. I couldn't make out the exact words of their conversation, but I knew they were discussing what to do about me and how to handle the drop. Without me.

Slowly, I went from annoyed to upset. As I watched them, my gaze caught on the duffle shoved on the floor in the backseat. Inside was the money.

A glance through the windshield told me the bike the kidnapper had promised was waiting for me. One last look over my shoulder told me that Dane and Semi were going in circles with their argument and wouldn't be back in the next few minutes.

The clock clicked to 11:56. Four minutes until drop time. The two men would still be arguing when the clock struck midnight at this rate, and I wasn't letting Trey die on my watch.

Snatching the bag—all 22.05 pounds of it—I hoisted it onto my shoulder and cracked the door open. I slid out on the opposite side of the vehicle to where Dane and Semi stood arguing, and I crouched out of sight.

I left my purse and all other items behind as I eased the door mostly shut, stopping just before the click. I needed to buy another minute or two without them noticing my absence. Once I was on the bike, I would be as good as gone.

Nobody could keep up with me on a bicycle. I'd been riding the trails of the Sunshine Shore since my fifth birthday, and not only did I know the routes backward and forward, but I had thighs like Tony the Tiger. At least, that's the way it felt when I was sailing down a big hill and flying at top speed. That is not how I felt when I was going up a huge hill and had to walk my bike to the summit.

"I know we can't ask her to go in there," Semi was saying, "but she volunteered. The kidnapper asked for her. I don't like this any more than you do, but—"

Go, Semi! I thought. At least he was talking sense.

Until Dane cut him off. "No. Absolutely not. I'm not letting her out of my sight. I am not risking her life. I'm sorry, Semi—I'll go in there myself before I let Lola go in there alone."

The sentiment was sweet, and my frustration at being left out of the argument wavered somewhat. It was replaced by sheer nerves and sweat as I reached the bike rack.

I was going to have to make a sound, I realized. There was no way the bike was coming off that rack silently, and when I made a noise, I had to be ready to fly. I held my breath, listening for a loud point in Semi and Dane's conversation, only to realize that the world had gone silent.

"Uh, oh," I said, turning around to find Dane and Semi staring at me from across the lot, frozen. "I guess I wasn't as quiet as I thought."

"Lola!" Dane and Semi unfroze at the same moment, both men launching toward me with their distinct styles. Dane like a leopard, all sleek and dark, and Semi like a charging bull.

"I'm sorry!" I yelled as I swung a leg over the bike. "We have only two minutes to get to Trey or he's dead. I'll be right out—give me five minutes alone and then you can come in."

They were still rushing me, not appearing to listen to a thing I was saying—as had been the trend tonight—so I gave a frustrated huff of breath and launched into pedaling. I was a little lopsided at first thanks to the 22.05 pounds of money, but I righted myself quickly thanks to years of practice balancing everything from eggs and milk to Babs on my handlebars.

"Stop, Lola!" Dane called after me. "Don't go in there."

"It's the only way to save Trey!" I yelled back. "I love you, Dane!"

I heard Semi mutter something about going after me, but Dane must have responded in the negative. There was no way the two could keep up with me, and even if they could, that would be a breach of the kidnapper's rules. While they'd been willing to break the rules with an alternate plan, it was too risky with such a last-minute ploy. Especially since the kidnapper had proven, with the murder of Fat Jim, his willingness to kill somewhat innocent bystanders.

And with that, the trees engulfed me and the money, and the darkness swallowed us whole.

THE PATH BETWEEN THE parking lot from Reynolds's old place and the park wasn't long—maybe half a mile of winding, bumpy dirt paths. My legs pedaled like the world was ending. Then again, Trey's world might be ended if I didn't move fast enough.

Branches *thwacked* at my face, hedges scraped at my legs when I took corners too tightly, and random sticks in the middle of the road made for a somewhat painful ride, though I barely noticed any of it. Only after I skidded to an abrupt stop in a cloud of dust did the sting of my cuts and bruises begin to ache.

The bench the kidnapper had specified was next to the path and overlooking the lake. On a normal day, it was a gorgeous little nook, somewhat private, tucked away for young lovers and old hand-holders. Tonight it was for cold, hard cash.

I dumped the bag on the bench. "There," I called into the night. "You have your money—let Trey go."

As instructed, I hadn't brought my phone, my purse, or any other belongings. I had no clue if the kidnapper had a way of checking me for them at a distance, but I couldn't afford to take any risks. He'd proven that he watched me carefully and was smart and ruthless. He'd also upped his status from kidnapper to full-blown murderer.

"Where's Trey?" I called back. "It's all in there, I swear. It's been double checked. We just want Trey's safe return. Please. We followed your orders."

A phone rang then, crystal clear in the cooling night air. An annoying sort of ring that came standard on a cheapie mobile—another burner phone, no doubt.

I bent over, running my hands through the decorative grasses around the bench until I caught sight of a faint glow. Nabbing the device, I picked it up and threw it against my ear, answering while trying to catch my breath.

"Where are you?" I demanded. "Where's Trey?"

"You say you played by the rules," the kidnapper's voice—autotuned to mask gender and other defining characteristics—"but that's a lie."

"What are you talking about? We brought the money, and it's all there. I came alone. I have no phone, no purse, no wires. Nothing."

"I know, but this afternoon, rules were broken, and now you'll pay."

"What rules?" I felt panic and frustration rising in my chest. "If I don't see Trey, I'm taking the money and leaving."

"You spoke with the cops." The kidnapper actually *tsked* at me like a disappointed grandmother. "That's a big no-no, Lola Pink. And as you saw this afternoon, I don't like tattlers."

"You killed Fat Jim."

"Lola..." The voice hesitated.

I had to keep him talking, had to listen for Trey's voice and ensure his safety. "Let me talk to Trey."

"Here." A scuffle sounded on the other end of the phone as the kidnapper said something, and then there was a thump. Trey's voice cried out in pain from the other end of the line—I recognized it from earlier that evening when I'd spoken briefly with him in the car. When the kidnapper came back on the line, he sounded smug. "There. Happy?"

"No. See, we didn't talk to the cops. They came to ask us about Fat Jim's murder and—"

"Lola, Lola, Lola," the kidnapper said. "I have one more instruction for you tonight."

My heart thumped so loudly I was sure he could hear it in the silence. "What?"

"Run."

My mind barely had time to process the demand before the world exploded with a flash, a bang, and smoke. I think there was smoke—it was hard to tell because I couldn't see. I couldn't hear.

The kidnapper's vague instructions to run pelted through my brain, but I couldn't even do that. I stumbled away, dropping the phone in the process before tripping over the bike. I blinked my eyes but couldn't see anything beyond blackness.

Cursing, I untangled myself from the bike, feeling something sharp digging into my leg. An excruciating pain and the wet metallic scent of blood hit me at once. I might have cried out, but I couldn't remember. I crawled away, dragging myself until I could regain enough balance to stand, but even then, I wobbled at best.

In the distance, I might have heard an echo. Maybe my name. A shuffle of movement came from the smoke, and then nothing.

I wandered, stumbling until I couldn't go any further. Out of pure exhaustion, I crumbled to the ground, curled into the grass, and waited. I felt dizzy and nauseous, as if someone had punched me straight in the head. My vision came back first, which wasn't all that useful seeing as it was pitch black outside. My ears rung like a cowbell and my head felt like it'd been cracked in half.

It felt like I laid on the side of the path for years.

Later, Dane told me later it was the worst ten minutes of his life.

"Lola!" Dane's voice finally made it through to me, though it sounded like he was speaking into a vat of Jell-O, and I was hearing the resulted garble from the bottom. "Are you okay?"

"What?" It sounded like he was speaking in slow-motion. "I can barely see. Where are you?"

I struggled to a sitting position with Dane's help, and as my fingers drank in the feel of him, I slipped my hands around his expensive shirt and felt the ripple of firm abs underneath.

"Yep, that's you," I said, though I could hardly hear myself. "Dane Clark, alright."

"What happened?" Dane asked. "Are you hurt? Where's Trey? Why did you run off without warning us?"

"My head is killing me," I said. "Can we finish this conversation later? I feel like my ears have broken."

"Come on, we have to get you to the hospital," Dane said, scooping me into his arms. "God, you scared me, Lola. Don't ever do that again."

He set off, carrying me against his chest, and I sunk into his embrace and enjoyed it. Sometimes, a girl wanted her independence. Sometimes, she wanted to be a badass and fight criminals. And sometimes, she wanted to be taken care of by her man. I was firmly in camp three for the moment.

Dane marched me out of the woods and straight past a few looky-loos from the nearby condos that must have heard or seen the flashbang sort of device that the kidnapper had used against me. Without speaking, he placed me in the SUV, got into the driver's seat, and aimed the car straight toward the hospital.

"Where's Semi?" I asked, struggling to stand on my own two feet. "You can't leave him behind!"

"Semi is otherwise occupied." Dane hesitated, glancing my way. "He went after the kidnapper. He said he'd find his way home; I'll call him from the hospital."

"About that—I really don't need a doctor, Dane. We can't go in there; we'd have to explain. We can't call the cops. The kidnapper knew that they came to Castlewood this afternoon."

"That *who* came to Castlewood?"

"The detectives," I gasped. "He said this isn't over yet and that we'd have to pay for our mistakes. That the million dollars was just the start of it."

Dane's lips went into a grim line. "We'll get to that later. First, we have to make sure you're okay. You're bleeding, Lola. What were you thinking?"

The car ride was tense and mostly silent. When we finally reached the hospital, I slunk into the waiting room behind Dane as he checked us in. When I took a seat next to him on the hard metal chairs, I leaned my head against his shoulder.

"I was just thinking about Trey," I murmured. "We didn't have time or options, and I did what I thought was best."

Dane clasped me to his chest. "I know, but dammit—my heart almost stopped when you disappeared into the woods. We chased after you at a distance, but we were still too far away to see what was happening. Then he tossed a stun grenade, and..." He blinked, shuddered. "I wish you hadn't done that."

"It's okay, I'm here now."

"Yes, but what if you weren't?" His voice had an angry edge to it. "What if you hadn't come back? Then what? We wouldn't have you and we wouldn't have Trey."

"I know, Dane, I'm sorry. I didn't mean to scare you—"

"Scare me? You almost killed me."

For the first time since my world had imploded at the drop site, I noticed the absolute paleness of Dane's skin, the clammy coolness of his hands. His jaw was clenched tight enough to give the man an aneurism, and his entire body seemed to tremble with rage.

For a moment, I thought he was angry at me—until I realized the symptoms for what they truly were: Dane had been scared out of his mind. Terrified in a way that no business venture or monetary risk had ever frightened him.

I decided that, just for now, I'd let go of my arguments. We could have the talk about me being all feminist later. For now, he just needed to know that I was okay.

"Come here," I whispered, dragging him into an unused corner of the waiting room. "I'm fine. You're fine. Trey's alive. Everything is going to be fine. Can I rest my head in your lap while we wait? This headache is worse than a tequila hangover."

Dane gave a thin smile and sat on the worn, bland old couch, then pulled me next to him. I tipped to the side and rested my head over his lap, smelling the faint scent of woodsy foliage and pine nettles, and closed my eyes. Dane's fingers ran through my hair, lulling me into a trance-like state. Over, and over, and over, seeping his anxiety into every motion, touching my cheek now and again as if to make sure I was real. That I was alive and safe and warm.

"I love you," he said, bowing his head to kiss my hair.

"I love you, too," I said, and then gave him a smile. "Maybe I wouldn't have had to go into the woods if you weren't terrified of bicycles. Maybe he would've asked you to go in, then. I'm just saying—it's a good incentive for you to learn how to ride a bike."

Dane started, his fingers tensing, then relaxed. "A joke?"

"Yes, Dane," I said, pulling his palm to my lips for a quick kiss. "A joke."

Chapter 12

The doctors checked me out—a quick catch and release that didn't tell me anything I didn't already know. I had a mild concussion, and I'd suffer from the incessant ringing in my ears for another hour or two at the minimum. My vision was back entirely, and my scrapes and bruises would all heal on their own. I popped an extra strength Tylenol on the way out the doors for the headache, and that was the end of it.

We made it back to the castle before it hit me that we were still missing a party from our triangle of crime fighters. "Have you heard from Semi?" I asked anxiously. "Did he catch up with the kidnapper?"

"No." Dane glanced toward his feet. "He found remnants of a flash-bang as we thought and a cell phone—a burner, likely a dead end. It was wiped clean. He also identified a few markings that would indicate the kidnapper parked a car on the other side of the clearing. Near there, Semi turned up a few scuffed footprints, but I doubt that will lead us anywhere. He grabbed photos, but it's impossible to determine a true shoe size."

"That doesn't leave us with much," I said, running a tongue over my teeth as I replayed what I could remember in my head. "So, our kidnapper must have watched from his vantage point to make sure it was only me going into the woods. Once he confirmed that much, he gave me a call and let me hear Trey's voice. I'm guessing Trey was handcuffed and locked in the car."

"I think we need to consider the fact that the kidnapper might have an accomplice," Dane said. "Someone who stayed back with Trey."

"It's possible," I agreed. "But I don't think necessary. Once I heard Trey, the kidnapper gave me the instructions to run, launched his grenade, and picked up the money. He was gone before either you or Semi arrived."

"That sounds about right," Dane said. His gaze flicked down at his phone. "Semi has confirmed he's here at Castlewood—he'll be spending the night in the guest wing. We'll want him close in case there are any developments."

"I suppose," I said slowly as Dane and I climbed the front steps to the castle, "that all we can do is wait. I'm sure we'll have further instructions soon enough."

"I imagine so."

"If there's a silver lining, it's that we know Trey will be safe awhile longer," I pointed out. "As long as the killer wants something, he needs Trey alive. If he were to get rid of Trey, the game's over."

"No," Dane said darkly. "If he kills Trey, the hunt begins."

On that eerie note, Dane and I fell silent, weaving our way through the castle and making an effort to avoid the staff. It was easy, seeing as the hour was nearly three in the morning and not many people aside from a few of the security staff members were wandering around.

We passed by the kitchen, but I wasn't all that hungry—a sign that the flashbang probably had more of a lingering effect than I'd thought, seeing as my appetite had never before been an issue. Foregoing food, Dane and I climbed into the jacuzzi to relax and soak our weary muscles.

The day had been long. It was hard to believe that barely forty-eight hours before I'd been relishing under the grapevines with a glass of bubbly in hand before watching the sunset and wondering how I'd gotten such a lush and spoiled life.

It didn't feel so spoiled today. It felt a little bumpy and risky, if I was honest, but despite all the unease and uncertainty that went alongside the kidnapping, there was a contentment as well. All I had to do to find it was look at Dane, and I knew I was home.

Feeling a surge of love for the man, I floated across the whirlpool and eased myself onto his lap, wrapping my legs and arms around him until I held him as tight as physically possible.

"Lola, what are you doing?" His jaw was still tight, as if someone had turned the screws a little too hard on its hinge. "You're hurt. You need to rest."

"Maybe I need rest, but I'm not all that hurt," I said, letting my lips slip to his ear so my breath tickled across his neck just how he liked. "I am in love, however."

"Me too."

I rested my head on his shoulder and just floated, the warmth of the water hugging us together, bringing us closer while the crispness of the early morning air and the starry night above painted us straight into a picture. The beat of our hearts seemed to sync up, linking us together in a deeper, more certain way than ever before.

When I pulled back to study Dane's face, I saw a shine in his eyes that I hadn't seen ever before. "Dane?"

"I couldn't live without you," he said, his voice hoarse. "Never ever do that to me again. At least let us go together if you risk your life like you did tonight—I would rather die together than live alone."

"That's a little morbid."

"It's true."

"Kiss me, will you?"

"That wasn't a promise." Dane held fast in his position, his eyes darkening. "Promise me."

"I will never run straight into the arms of a kidnapper again," I said, making the most specific promise I could muster. "Does that work?"

He gave the thinnest of smiles. "It's a start."

I pulled tighter and tighter against him until I felt Dane's shoulders begin to relax, his hands begin to respond, his breath begin to quicken. Then, with the zing of a shooting star, Dane took my face in his hands, clasped my cheeks between his palms, and held me close as we dove together into a kiss. We stayed that way, together, for so long I couldn't say where Dane ended and I began.

When our skin pruned, we moved to the showers where we stood together under the stream, admiring one another. His arms kept me close, my fingernails digging into his shoulder as he held me tightly, promising to never let me go. And when the shower grew cold, we moved to the bedroom where we lay naked, wrapped around one another until we were too exhausted to speak.

Dane drifted off to sleep before me, a rarity in our lives. Normally I slipped into dreams the second my head hit the pillow while Dane held me close. The poor man was exhausted.

On the other hand, I was wired. It seemed the flashbang had finally worn off and most of my bruises and scrapes had been soothed by the jacuzzi, turning the initial sting of pain to a dull ache. The realization of how dangerous my actions had been this evening was starting to truly hit me, and with it, the burst of adrenaline that I could've used four hours before.

Combined with the electric feelings leftover from an intensely emotional evening with Dane, it suddenly felt as if every touch on my skin was heightened. Every breath of air on my cheek a sharp prick, the rustle of soft sheets against my back a tingling sensation. I lay there in silence for a long while, listening to my heartbeat, counting Dane's breaths.

Until finally, my stomach growled. A sure sign I was beginning to feel better. My appetite had returned, and so had my thirst for answers. As Dane slept, I slipped from bed and put on a huge, fluffy pink robe softer than a wisp of fresh cotton, and gigantic slippers to match, and padded down to the kitchen.

Nobody was around, which was all the better. It wasn't often I had open reign in the Clark kitchen—a surprising fact that I missed about living in my apartment. At Dotty's place—my former home—I could walk over to the refrigerator and open it as many times as I liked, hoping it would magically change contents every five minutes. If I did that same thing at Castlewood, I looked like an idiot.

I thought fondly of Shades of Pink—my little storefront on the Sunshine Shore—as I moved through the kitchen. It'd been nearly a week since I'd been there last to see the updates with my own eyes. I could hardly believe I'd let so much time lapse between visits, but I'd been assured by Dane Clark himself that the renovations were being handled by none other than the best, and that my being there in person would only slow things down.

The opening date I'd tentatively scheduled in my head was looming sooner than ever before, and still, Dane continued to promise me the work would be done in time. Despite my faith in Dane, I had my doubts. I knew how these things went.

But for now, it was best if I didn't think about things that couldn't be helped—and instead, focus on things that could. Like getting Trey back alive.

Humming a happy little ditty to myself, I luxuriously threw open all the cabinets and did an excited little tap dance between them. I pulled out a variety of mismatched items: Peanut butter and saltines, Pop-Tarts, pasta sauce, Nutella, ice cream, and a slew of leftovers in Tupperware containers. I moved it all to the grand dining room table and spread the mess out before me.

There was something utterly satisfying about the hodgepodge of my four in the morning snack. Though Mrs. Dulcet and her staff prepared enough fine dining options to keep me full for years, sometimes a gal wanted to eat Nutella with a spoon and dunk it in a pint of ice cream.

While I launched into my mess of food—which would also have given Dane Clark a heart attack had he witnessed the chaos—I pulled out my phone and began tapping away and reading to my heart's content.

I first researched Fat Jim's murder, but there wasn't much on the internet except stories and wild-theories, none of which rang true to me. Half of the stories didn't even have the details correct, and the other half tried to tie Dane Clark's name to the murder, never mind the fact that we both had a solid alibi.

For now, unless I could figure out what Fat Jim had been trying to tell Dane, he was a dead end. I winced, realizing my poor choice of words, and decided to try a new subject: Stacey from Warehouse 5.

It didn't take long to pull up her name since she'd been featured in several articles about the Clark Company in the latest PR wave on women in technology industries. The confidential nature of her work wasn't included in the articles, but the media had latched onto Stacey as a successful woman in a male-dominated industry, making my research on her quite easy to follow from one article to the next.

Her full name was Stacey Romano. Her smiling face beamed back at me from a variety of websites, niggling something in my brain as I stuck the spoon back in the ice cream, launched another bite into my mouth, and dug deeper. I couldn't put my finger on why, but something felt off about her. Something...intangible.

Half an hour and a melted pint of ice cream later, I gasped. I'd finally found my connection. Scurrying, I gathered my food assortment and returned the items to their rightful place. I rinsed my dishes, shoved them in the washer, and then rushed back to my phone for a second look.

Stacey Romano wasn't actually Stacey Romano.

Her real name was Stasia Romanov. At least, that's what it looked like, seeing as there was an article about her at her old company—the Russian version of the Clark Company from what I could tell—with the same smiling face on it. I stared at the article, feeling lucky I'd clicked on it. I'd taken a chance on one of Google's suggested reads that appeared not to be related... and discovered the two articles were perfectly related after all.

Stacey Romano had worked for one of Dane's biggest competitors under a different name.

Was corporate espionage the name of the game? And had Trey Hampton caught on to our friend's true interest in working for the Clark Company?

I debated going back to bed to wake Dane, but he needed his rest. While I needed rest, too, I was antsy with excitement and a full-on sugar rush. It was still dark outside, but we were nearing the early morning hours when it would be acceptable to be awake.

With a start, I recalled Stacey's voice telling me that most people worked round the clock—or close to it—when they were employed by the Clark Company. Maybe she'd already be in for the day. It certainly couldn't hurt to check.

I felt a slight twinge of guilt at the thought of not waking Dane, but he'd specifically told me to make myself at home around Castlewood. Warehouse 5 was part of Castlewood, and I now had an all access pass to get to wherever I needed to go. My promise to him had been to not run straight into the waiting arms of a kidnapper. While I might have my suspicions about Stacey's motives, she most certainly wouldn't do anything risky on Castlewood grounds—that would be stupid, and as I'd already covered, the kidnapper wasn't stupid.

I poked my head out the back entrance to the castle and saw a minimum of four security guards patrolling the quad. Heaving a sigh of relief, I also saw a few other early morning folks walking with their heads down, coffee cups held high, though the grasses wet with dew. The Clark Company was already up and at 'em.

I stopped by my old room to slip into jeans and a sweatshirt to battle the early morning chill and was back outside in ten minutes. I was just one of the gang, I convinced myself as I stepped onto the train and flashed my badge for Warehouse 5. The soon-to-be Mrs. Clark out on the town.

Agent Clark, reporting for duty.

THE TRAIN PULLED UP to station five, and I exited onto the platform, taking a second's hesitation to scan the surrounding area. As I'd noted earlier, there were at least four security guards prowling the premises in addition to a handful of nerds. I didn't exactly fit in with my fluffy sweatshirt and jeans and the hefty bags under my eyes from a sleepless night.

As I let myself into Warehouse 5, I realized that I didn't look as far out of place as I'd thought, despite my somewhat bedraggled and exhausted appearance. One man—probably an engineer of some sort—was looking especially harried as he leaned up to a computer that spewed LED images mid-air before him. He wore a wrinkled old sweatshirt and a pair of track pants from the 80's. On his feet were black socks and flip flops. Obviously, Dane Clark did not hire on style.

"You'll have to excuse Martin," a smooth voice said from beside me. "He worked all night long. Boss's orders don't require him to wear a suit unless he's got meetings, and you'd better believe Martin appreciates that clause in his contract. He's brilliant, though."

The voice registered almost at once. I turned as Stacey spoke, finding her dressed in a neat black pencil skirt with a starched white blouse. She looked comfortable in that outfit, which was impressive. I'd never worn a pencil skirt and high heels and felt truly comfortable. She earned bonus points for style, even if it wasn't my sort of style.

I gave her a thin smile. "I wondered if I might find you here. You implied you worked very long hours."

"I enjoy my career."

"I was trying to enjoy my sleep but was unsuccessful." My grin turned wry. "Can we chat for a few minutes?"

"I wondered when you would come," she said faintly, as if this were all part of her master plan. "Would you like coffee? Mr. Clark makes sure we have the best."

"Oh, I would love some!" As Stacey led me across the mostly empty floor of Warehouse 5, I leaned in like a conspiratorial girlfriend—hoping it'd help when I asked the harder hitting questions. "Living in the castle is incredible, of course, but to be honest—I haven't found the coffee machine yet. If Mrs. Dulcet isn't around, I'm out of luck."

Stacey gave a tinkling laugh. "Yes, well, First World problem, don't you think?"

There was a biting edge to her sentiment that caused me to shut up immediately. We passed two more engineers—one dressed in rumpled clothes from the day before, the other dressed in a crisp button-up shirt and jeans that looked fresh. I began to understand that working for the Clark Company wasn't a nine-to-five job. It was a cycle here, constantly revolving, ever tuned to a desire to change the world one piece of technology at a time.

Stacey led me into a long, modern kitchen with all black cabinets, marble countertops, and anything one might need to prepare a gourmet meal, including all top-of-the-line appliances. A few table and chair arrangements provided a plethora of seating options.

"Wow, this is nicer than my kitchen at home," I said, eyeing the amenities. "I'm finally just getting a decent dishwasher with my renovations."

"Shades of Pink, isn't it?" Stacey asked, pulling two dainty mugs from a cupboard and hooking them into some sort of fancy cappuccino maker. "Do you like yours sweetened?"

"Uh, yes," I said, struggling to keep up with her quick-changing choice of subjects. "Highest sweet setting, please."

Her smile told me my answer was cute. She probably drank classy, Italian-bitter espresso out of a cup the size of a thimble. A tradition I'd never quite understood because it seemed impossible to enjoy a coffee when it was gone in a gulp.

But I wasn't here to debate our caffeine habits, and Stacey knew that. In fact, she'd seemed ready for me, which meant this whole song and dance between us so far was a stalling tactic for the main event.

There was a hum and a hiss and several gurgles as the machine spit out two caffeinated beverages. Stacey removed one and handed it to me, then glanced into hers with a slight frown. She reached for a stirstick from the nearby compartment and dunked it in, whirling it slowly in circles, as if it helped her think.

"Stacey—" I began, at the same time she looked up.

"What brings you here?" She talked louder and longer than me, so it was her question that became the priority. "What could possibly be keeping you up at night?"

The tone of her voice had turned slightly hostile, and I was suddenly glad for sloppy Martin out there, working along in his track pants. Add the other two engineers and the fact that morning was rapidly appearing, and I felt safer knowing I wasn't alone.

"I thought you'd come to bring the sample back that you'd stolen from the lab," she said, "but that wouldn't require a cup of coffee and you chattering with nerves."

"Um, one second," I said, holding up a finger. "I didn't steal anything; I just forgot the demo thing was on my ear and walked out with it. Dane's going to bring it back—I just forgot about it."

"Mmm."

"Second, I'm not chattering with nerves," I said, ignoring the clink of the spoon in my coffee. I'd followed Stacey's line of thinking, trying to look sophisticated and suave as I'd grabbed a spoon from the drawer and thoughtfully twirled it around my glass, but it didn't work. My hand was trembling so hard it sounded like I was playing a set of fine china bongo drums. I quickly removed the spoon and tossed it in the sink. "That wasn't nerves—I'm just really tired."

"Mmm."

Stacey had mastered the art of murmuring something unintelligible, almost as if she was enjoying a decadent dessert and couldn't be bothered to say 'yum'. It had the added effect of drawing out awkward silences and giving me the urge for verbal diarrhea. Words started spewing out just to make up for the lack of Stacey's portion in the conversation.

"Look, I'm getting the vibe you don't like me." I rested one hip against the counter and took a fortifying sip of coffee. "That's fine—you don't have to like me, but I did find something a little interesting in your records that I need to clarify."

"Mmm."

I rolled my eyes this time. "Your real name isn't Stacey."

Surprisingly, she barely flinched. "No, it isn't."

"It's Stasia Romanov, and you're originally from Russia, aren't you?" I asked. "There, you worked for a competitor of the Clark Company."

"Very good," she said. "You've read my resume."

"But—"

"But I don't make it obvious? No, of course not. When I moved to the country, I Americanized my name and practiced the correct, non-distinct accent for hours. I didn't like being different. I'm not sure you understand, seeing as you're..." She hesitated, scanning me from head to toe. "Blissfully unique."

Her words seemed like a compliment, but her tone of voice told me she meant it as a negative. As if being unique was a poison, something that could spread and contaminate the water and make her different, too.

"Okay," I said, for lack of something better to add to the conversation. "What would Dane say if I told him that you formerly worked for one of his largest competitors in the world?"

She shrugged. "I imagine he'd say 'okay' or something similar. He knows already."

As I digested that information, Martin stormed angrily into the kitchen. He was muttering to himself and seemingly lost in his own world; he neither offered us a hello nor a wave. I wasn't even convinced he knew we existed in the same universe as him.

"I think we need to chat somewhere more private," Stacey said. "I know the place."

My heart thumped. I'd tossed my cards on the table, and now Stacey knew exactly what I suspected her of doing. I'd been stupid to come here. I should have climbed back in bed after my Nutella snack break. But no, I'd put on my Agent Pink shades and taken to Warehouse 5.

My mood lifted considerably as Stacey wound her way through the warehouse toward the front doors. I'd already decided that if she led me somewhere unsavory—a dank dungeon or dim corridor—I'd turn and run. I'd left my purse and cell in the house, and I wasn't going to walk into a trap. So, when Stacey pressed the front doors open and asked if I minded a chat in the quad, my heart positively leapt for joy.

"Sure," I said. "How about over there?"

She followed my gesture to a small bench in the center of the green commune. The most public place possible and visible from all angles. Nothing unsavory would go down out here in the middle of manicured lawns, stunning goldfish ponds, and leaping fountains. Even the hedges obeyed orders, growing in neat little rows, and the flowers seemed to bloom on command.

As we sat, the light changed from a pre-dawn haze to the glow of a new day. I loved sunshine. All shades of it—the bright yellow, the subtle orange, the last glimmers of pink before dusk fell. With darkness came terrors of the night, and with sunlight came hope.

This daybreak would bring about the end of my night in the woods—unsuccessfully attempting the recovery of Trey Hampton. Hopefully, it would also bring about answers.

With that, I took a shuddering breath. "You're not who you say you are."

"I am Stacey Romano now," she said. "My name is changed legally, so yes, I am exactly who I say I am, and Mr. Clark knows my history."

"You worked for Dane's competition before you left Russia," I said carefully. "Does Dane often hire his competition?"

"Not usually." She said this with a soft smile. "But he hired me. Like I said, he only hires the best."

"Did he know your real identity when he hired you?"

She shrugged. "I got hired; that's all I cared about. That and my work, of course. That's really why anyone works for Dane Clark, isn't it? He provides the freedom and resources to let the rest of us do work that changes the world. He provides a safe and healthy working environment. What more can someone ask out of a career?"

"I suppose that makes sense." I clasped my coffee mug tighter as I asked my next question. "Are you in communication with any of your friends from your previous company in Russia?"

"Of course not," she snapped, her eyes flashing as she looked me over from head to toe. "I wouldn't go back to him."

"Back to who?"

"Artur, of course—that's who you think this is about, isn't it?" She glared up at me, the first sign of real emotion I'd seen from her. "Of course it is—it always comes back to him. Will he never cease to haunt me?"

"Who is Artur?"

Stacey blinked. "You didn't get very far in your Googling if you didn't find his name attached to mine."

"No," I agreed. "I got a little overexcited and came out here to talk to you first. I figured it was better to get the full story from you than it would be to read about it in old articles."

She gave me the briefest of smiles. "Artur owns the company I used to work for. He was also my former fiancé."

I blinked, obviously speechless.

"I guess Dane hasn't told you the full story about me," Stacey said carefully. "If you want to hear it, sit down. I have ten minutes before I need to get back to work."

I returned to the bench and sat. "Start at the beginning."

"No. I'll start where it's relevant." She took a careful sip of her espresso—though how she had anything left in that tiny mug was a ridiculous feat. She'd been sipping it for almost ten minutes already. "I'll start with my former career, which was a corporate spy."

"Excuse me?"

"I have certain...assets if you will. I speak five languages, and I have the ability to make men..." She paused for a self-indulgent smile. "To make men trust me implicitly."

"Your former boss hired you as a spy?"

"Of course not," she snapped. "I was hired on as an engineer. I thought that I'd found the job, gotten it on my own merit, been hired for my intelligence, but I was wrong. Artur had had his eye on me the whole time, guiding me until he had me right where he wanted me."

"Guiding you to fall in love with him?"

She gave a quick nod. "At first, we flamed hot, bright, and he began easing me into small roles. A quick consulting job to gain internal secrets from a vendor. A meeting with a harmless little side-mission attached to gain intel. Until these little side missions grew and grew into something I could no longer control. My longest assignment up until the Clark Company lasted three years in Germany. I speak German," she added unnecessarily. "I wasn't ever caught. My presence there earned Artur millions."

"But..." I hesitated. "You didn't like the work?"

"I loved it," she said, seeming to surprise herself as well as me. "I didn't have any moral dilemma with my work whatsoever. Yes, Artur was using me—I knew that—but he also loved me. I was fine with our arrangement. As for the espionage...I was only spying on huge, multibillion-dollar companies. Pharmacies, tech companies, you name it—all of them are corrupt anyway. What did it matter if Artur was the corrupt asshole or some German schmuck?"

I cleared my throat. "Your next target was the Clark Company?"

"Oh, yes," she said. "Dane Clark was the elephant in the room. The pie in the sky, the golden goose. Artur had talked about going after him for years—lovingly, almost. It was odd. He was obsessive about Dane and that—" She broke off, looking down at her hands. Her fingers trembled in her lap, but she forced herself to continue with a blank, emotionless stare. "It was our ruin."

"I'm not sure I understand," I said. "You got hired on here as an engineer and Dane didn't suspect a thing? How is that possible?"

"I thought so, too," she said. "But Artur is very smart, and my back story was solid. I had adopted a different identity, a new social security number, an entire history. There was no reason for Dane to even suspect I'd stepped foot in Russia, let alone was engaged to his competition."

"Yet something happened."

"Nothing was ever quite right," she said. "I suspected from the first week that Dane knew more than he let on. He was ever the professional and always kind to me, but it was just that gut feeling, you know? It wasn't right. I always trusted my gut. I told Artur we needed to pull out—that his plan wasn't working."

"He didn't like that idea."

She shook her head. "He'd been going after Mr. Clark forever, and he'd been grooming me to do it for years. There was no way he was backing down."

"But something happened," I said. "Otherwise, you'd probably be hiding the fact that you're a spy. Just a wild guess."

She gave a flimsy smile. "I confessed to Mr. Clark after a month here. I'd begun to realize that Artur didn't love me at all—that our entire relationship, that most of my *life* had been a game to him. He'd been controlling me like a character in a video game, pulling the strings of my heart to make me jump like a puppet for him."

"I'm sorry, Stacey," I said, finding I meant it. "Or Stasia?"

"I'm Stacey," she said firmly. "I do not associate with my former identity."

"Stacey," I said in agreement. "Why did you confess to Dane?"

"I have never been quite sure," she said finally. "Something told me that he was my only option to get out alive. The only way to shed my old skin and move on with my life. I was sure he'd fire me, if not worse, but..." Her eyes flicked to me with the intensity of a snake's gaze. "You know him well. He's honest, and he didn't deserve what Artur and I were doing to him. Mr. Clark has never confirmed it, but something tells me he knew the whole time. He knew from the second he hired me that I wasn't up to anything good, and yet I still can't help thinking he saw something in me. I don't know, maybe it's wishful thinking."

"You're still here, aren't you?"

"Yes, true," she said. "He appreciated my confession and offered to keep me with no stipulations, no warnings, nothing. It seemed that once I told him everything, he listened, accepted it, and moved on without another thought."

"He's a good man, Stacey. He is the best kind of person."

"I know," she said softly. "I realize now that I could never have made him fall for me in the way that Artur wanted me to—he wanted me to use my, ah, feminine charms, but Mr. Clark would not have been hooked. I just know it. Female intuition."

"Dane has peculiar taste in women," I said with a shy smile. "I'm not sure there's any rhyme or reason to it."

"There is." She gave a firm nod. "For years I wondered where I'd failed, where I'd gone wrong. If maybe Dane Clark could have fallen for me if I'd just said the right things, wore the right clothes, acted the right way, but now that he's found you, I see why I was never meant to be with him—even in a false capacity."

Despite Stacey's change of heart, she still saw herself as a tool. It was startling to me, and I felt a rush of sympathy for what that man had put her through to scar her in such a way. "Stacey—"

"When I first heard Dane Clark was engaged, I wondered what this fiancé had that I didn't," she said, speaking more to herself than to me. "Is she prettier than me, smarter, sexier, more elegant, wild...more perfect than me?"

I cleared my throat. "Clearly the answer to all of those questions is no."

Her eyes flicked to me, and while she didn't disagree, she gave a questioning tilt of her head. "The answer is much simpler. He just *likes* you, Lola, plain and simple. Because you're you. Do you know how strange that is to me? For years, I've been loved because I'm something: intelligent, sexy, multi-lingual, you name it." She gave a hard, caustic laugh. "I was trained to be a Barbie with a resume. To conform to whatever character I needed to be in order to get the job done. That's what you have that I will never have, Lola."

"Which part? The lack of intelligence or the lack of sexiness?" I asked dryly. "I couldn't keep up with your resume."

"Dane Clark loves you because..." She hesitated, widened her hands with a look of mystification. "Because you're Lola Pink."

I nodded, looked down at my hands. I felt the same way toward Dane, and my throat tightened just thinking about him. About how fortunate it was that we'd found one another.

Stacey recognized my discomfort and stood, brushing imaginary lint off her skirt. "Well, I must get back to work. This was a fun chat."

"Wait! We didn't—you didn't really tell me anything," I said, standing too, though Stacey stood several inches higher than me on heels. "Why did you stay?"

"I didn't realize good men—let alone good businessmen—existed in this world. When I found one, I didn't want to leave. I enjoy working hard, and I have discovered that I enjoy working for the right reasons. Until Mr. Clark asks me to tender my resignation, I plan to stay here forever."

"I, ah—I hope you do," I found myself admitting, even as she took a step back toward Warehouse 5. "And Stacey—"

She turned, raised an eyebrow in my direction. "Yes? If you're asking the unasked question—no, I am not in touch with Artur, and I would never dream of turning on Mr. Clark. I will swear that to you in blood."

"I believe you," I said. "But I need to know if you can tell me anything about Trey. When I found your name linked to Dane's competition, I had to wonder if you'd...done something with Trey."

Her gaze flitted nervously over my head toward the house. "Don't be ridiculous. I just told you my story, and you said you believed me. I have no more to say on the subject. Trey was a friend."

"Hold on—" I was desperately trying to interpret Stacey's nervous glance over my shoulder. I stepped closer to her. "Wednesday nights: Where did he go?"

"I don't know."

"I'm sorry, but I don't think that's true."

"I don't know where he went," she said, exasperated. "Okay? Just leave me out of this—I didn't have anything to do with him disappearing."

"You knew he was in trouble—why? Is Artur after him?" I asked. "Does he want the translation tech in order to get back at Dane for keeping you?"

"I believe our meeting has come to an end," she said. "Have a good day, Lola."

"Stacey!" I took a few steps after her and stopped in front of her. "You are going to find someone who loves you for you someday—don't give up."

"I am not you, Lola. I don't have this defined, cute little personality," she said, her voice taking on a harsh edge. "I'm a piece of Play-Doh, and I mold to what men want me to be. Do you see the problem with that? How can I be myself when I don't know who the hell I am?"

"You do, Stacey—and if you just tell me about Trey, that'll be the first step," I said. "Who was he meeting? Is it Artur? Why are you covering for him?"

"This is over, Lola," she said. "If you continue to push me, I will quit. I told you I'd stay here forever, but not at the expense of my integrity. Either you believe me or you don't, and that is final."

Chapter 13

I watched Stacey return to Warehouse 5, sensing my following her at this point would do no good. She was angry and determined, and she was hiding something. I was certain of it. But *what*?

As I turned back to the castle, I realized I had a problem. Or rather, several problems. My first order of business was that I needed to climb back in bed before Dane woke. Then, I had to find a way to confess I'd been running about the quad in the early morning hours, poking at old wounds and causing his employees to consider quitting, while learning absolutely nothing pertinent to Trey's kidnapping.

On days like today, I really did wonder why Dane Clark liked me. Sometimes it felt like all I did was make problems worse, even when my only intentions were to be useful. I hadn't really gleaned anything helpful from my work this morning—nothing Dane didn't already know. While I could blame an incredible lack of sleep or a near-concussion after the flashbang, I knew in my heart those weren't the causes for my actions. The reason I'd gone after Stacey was plain old-fashioned nosiness. If curiosity really did kill the cat, I could understand why.

I was nearly back to the castle, lost in my thoughts as I pictured various ways to break the news to Dane. I could slide into my sexiest little nightgown and hope my femininity distracted him, or I could go for broke and just climb in bed naked. Even as the thought crossed my mind, I knew that wouldn't be right. I was calculating whether serving Dane breakfast in bed while I relayed the news of my morning adventure would help diffuse the situation.

"Lola!" The hiss came from bushes near the back entrance to the castle, and I did a double take at the sound.

"Who's there?"

My pause gave the mystery guest just enough time to leap from their hiding place and nearly tackle me to the ground with wide-eyed fear. "Lola, you have to help me."

"Annalise?" I blinked, shaking my head. "Why are you hiding in Dane's bushes?"

"I'm not—I didn't mean to," she said. "I was looking for something, er—someone, and, well, it's embarrassing."

While I felt bad for Annalise, I had to admit the distraction was a welcome one. Obviously, something had Annalise spooked, and I had to help her out. A nice little excuse to put off telling Dane about Stacey for just a few more minutes. I knew the problem wouldn't disappear if I ignored it, but a gal could dream.

"What are you doing here?" I asked Annalise again. "I am not sure there's anything left for you to be embarrassed about. I've known you almost your whole life, and I just caught you hiding in my almost-husband's bushes. That's weird."

"I haven't told you why," she argued. "I was looking for Semi."

"Annalise!" My voice took on an urgent tone. "Are you stalking him? Did your breakup turn you into a stalker?"

"No! I mean, maybe an accidental one." She raised dainty little fingernails to her mouth. "Oh, my stars, Lola. I'm a stalker."

"You're not! You're not. Just tell me what happened."

"I wanted to talk to Semi like you suggested. You know, to make sure that we hadn't broken up because of some stupid misunderstanding," she said, thus far sounding logical. "I went to his house—you know, at the back of the Castlewood grounds. The guards know me, so they let me right in, and I knocked on his door. And I waited. And waited."

"He wasn't home," I said, the problem dawning on me. "And you panicked."

"Panicked?! I almost died. What if he's already got another girl-friend?" Annalise's eyes watered. "What if he—what if he's over me? What if I'm the only one hung up on this thing, and..."

"Annalise," I said. "Stop. Semi spent the night at the castle."

"With another woman?" She glanced around. "Is it someone who works here?"

"No, he was on duty," I said. "Dane asked him to stick close for business reasons."

"Oh, what a relief!" she said, and then at once she stiffened. "You've been holding out on us. There's something happening here, isn't there?"

"What are you talking about?"

"Why do you need extra security at Castlewood? That's the only reason Dane would need to keep Semi close." She lowered her voice and stuck out an accusatory finger. "What's wrong?"

"Says the stalker."

"I'm an accidental stalker," she said. "It's not like I'm going to keep doing it."

"Did you sit outside of his house all night?"

"Shut up!" She huffed, crossing her arms. "You're lucky I was there, as a matter of fact. Dane should be thanking me."

"Because you're an extra security guard?" I glanced at her slender arms. "With muscles like that, watch out baddies."

"It's true!" Annalise jabbed a finger in my direction. "I scared away some punk who was heading onto Dane's property."

"Hold on, what? What sort of punk are you talking about?"

"The sketchy variety who didn't look like he belonged," she said, her cheeks flaming red in embarrassment. "If I tell you more, you have to stop making fun of me."

"Deal. How did you scare this guy off?"

"Well, Semi lives in a small house at the very back of the Clark Company properties."

"I know—a bunch of employees live in the residential section."

She shook her head. "He lives elsewhere. You see those trees?"

I nodded, following the line of her finger down toward the cable car structure that hadn't been used for years—supposedly leading to the mystical Warehouse 11.

"There's a windy road that takes you back to Semi's place, which is sort of secluded in the woods. It'd be creepy if Semi wasn't strong enough to scare away most humans."

"Have you seen Warehouse 11?" I asked, stepping closer. "Dane hasn't even told me what's in there. He keeps promising to tell me when the time is right, but I have no clue what that means."

"I've only seen a tiny tip of the roof," she said. "Semi was very strict about making sure I never got a glimpse of it—it's a hike from his place anyway, and I have to imagine it's locked or protected somehow. I mean, if I know Dane, he's got that under control."

"Tell me more about this guy," I said. "Did you tell anyone else about him?"

She shook her head. "I didn't catch a good look at him. He had a hoodie pulled high and dark sweatpants on. Honestly, I thought he was some high school kid being dared to pull a prank. The second my head-lights hit him, he ran."

"Where exactly were you?" I asked. "Was he alone? Carrying anything?"

"I was rounding the second curve in the road—Semi or Dane will know what I mean. It's this blind turn, so he wouldn't have gotten much warning in the way of my headlights. He was just starting to cross the road when my lights swept over him. He pretty much turned and ran at the sight of me."

"That's so strange. I wonder why he was coming from the back."

"Do you know who it is?" Annalise's eyes bugged out. "What was he doing on Dane's property? Was he trying to steal something?"

I grabbed Annalise by the wrist and pulled her into the shadow of a neatly trimmed hedge that shielded us from view of the quad. "You have to trust me when I tell you that I can't give you the full truth."

"Why not?! I'm not going to tell anyone."

"It's not really my news to share."

"It's something to do with Semi, isn't it? That's why he didn't come home last night. Something is wrong—someone's after him!"

"Not exactly, but someone is after someone he cares about." As soon as I spoke, Annalise's eyes darkened. I shook my head, resting my hands on her shoulders. "It's not another woman, Annalise—I promise you that it's nothing romantic. But we are in the middle of something big, and you have to give Semi a little space. At least until we get to the bottom of this."

"I don't—" Her lip trembled as she broke off. "I'm beginning to think I didn't know him very well. Aside from Dane and a few employees, I didn't even know Semi had friends. Or is it family? Does Semi have a family he didn't bother to tell me about?"

"Annalise, listen to me—that's all between you and Semi. I'm asking as a friend—and because I care about you—to give him a few days. Back off for a bit. Once this mess is cleared up, you can stalk him as much as you want. In the meantime, it's not safe for you to be near him."

Her brow furrowed. "That's exactly the reason I should be around. I should be helping him. I still love him!"

At that very moment, Dane appeared on the platform at the back of the mansion, his eyes swiveling to our not-so-secret hiding place near the bushes.

He masked his confusion well. "I suppose I'll come back."

"No, Dane—wait." I gestured for him to stop, and then turned back to Annalise with a pleading expression. "It's too dangerous. You've waited this long, just give it a few days. I promise I'll update you with more information as soon as I can."

Annalise stared at me, her face broken, her lip trembling. And then even the tremble stopped, and she merely froze. Then she gave a jerky nod before spinning away on her heel and marching off without a response.

I was too tired to chase after her, and I doubted she wanted to see more of me anyway, so I let her go.

Dane raised his eyebrow as I turned to face him. "You've had a busy morning."

"You have no idea," I breathed. "I'm sorry."

"For what?"

"Everything."

"I don't understand," he said cautiously. "Why don't you start from the beginning?"

"Okay," I said.

And then I burst into tears.

I CRIED FOR THE BETTER part of five minutes. It wasn't a long cry, but it was the really nasty, explosive kind that came due to severe overtiredness mixed with fear and frustration. And plenty of other things that I was too tired to name.

A bewildered Dane led me into the castle and to the breakfast table. He was very confused when I waved away the offer of my favorite biscotti, and I didn't have the heart to tell him I'd overdosed on Nutella like a compulsive, sleepwalking binge eater. None of those were very attractive qualities in a mate, and I wanted Dane to still marry me—even after I told him about my morning adventures.

Dane pulled my chair closer as we sat side by side at the dining room table. "You're out of bed at the crack of dawn, you're so worried about something you're crying, and you are passing on the biscotti? What's wrong?"

I wailed. "I'm a mess!"

He eyed my clothes, the bags under my eyes. "You had a long night, but I wouldn't call you a mess. Did you get any sleep?"

Dane was dressed in perfect suit number 43, looking as if he'd spent the prior evening cocooned in spa treatments that softened his skin, made him glow, and gave him a perfect night's rest. He certainly didn't look like he'd scrounged through a forest for his mess of a fiancé and barely logged two and a half hours of shut eye.

The hour was just barely six a.m., and the sky was beginning to show the haziness of the incoming morning. The whole thing was new to me, seeing as six a.m. was usually the hour where I ramped up the REM and slipped deeper into sleep after Dane crawled out of bed.

"Please explain," he said simply. "I've run out of questions to ask."

"Can we take a drive?" My tears had thankfully come to a stop, and my tiredness was almost disappearing, reaching the point of a generous second wind. I was in a trancelike daze, but the caffeine was beginning to kick in, and the adrenaline to see this kidnapping mess through to a conclusion was driving me to stay awake. "I will explain on the way."

"Gerard," Dane called. "Keys to the..." He turned to me. "Where are we going?"

"Semi's place," I said. "Around back. Sort of near Warehouse 11."

Dane's cunning gaze landed on mine. He could tell I was fishing for more information, but he was too smart to lean into it. "We'll take the Jeep, Gerard."

Gerard popped out from the kitchen, a shiny apple once again in hand—I was beginning to think that was all the man ate—and gave a good-natured nod like a Labrador agreeing to play fetch. "Sure thing. Morning, Lola."

I gave a half-hearted wave. "Mind if I shower and change, quick?"

"Lola—" Dane grabbed me by the waistband and spun me back to him as I tried to leave. "Do you need company?"

I flashed him a tender smile. "Unfortunately, I don't think there's time. Plus, aren't you exhausted from last night?"

He blinked in confusion. "That was yesterday. I had a full night's rest."

"God, to have your energy," I said on a whine. "That was two hours ago!"

With that, I stormed my human-self off for a shower while Dane used his robotic levels of focus to jump on a phone call to Germany.

A shower did a world of good for me. I paired fresh jeans with a white tank top that had cute lace patterns dotted across the top, along with a gauzy white shawl over my shoulders. It felt very bridal, and in the event I had to go straight to the flower shop, this would do better than a fluffy pink robe or day-old jeans. At the last second, I added some heavy-duty aviator shades that would block the world from seeing my bleary eyes.

We climbed into the Jeep, and I instructed Dane to drive toward Semi's house and stop after the second bend in the road. He didn't ask for clarification so I assumed he knew exactly where I meant.

"You smell great," Dane said as we took off. "I missed you in bed this morning. I hate waking up without you."

"Is that why you always change back into pajamas and sneak into bed with me around eight?" I asked, giving his hand a squeeze. "So I don't have to experience waking up alone?"

"That," Dane said with a secretive smile, "and other reasons."

I had a pretty good idea of several things on his secret list, but unfortunately, we didn't have time to review the fun flash cards. Instead, I launched into my morning's tale.

"It all started because of great sex," I said. "Please keep that in mind as I continue. If you hadn't got me all riled up, then I would have just fallen asleep and none of this would have happened."

"Noted," he said seriously. "I will take full responsibility."

I laughed, appreciating his attempt at lightness. Because I'd run out of time to stall, I launched into my initial search through the castle for food. That resulted in my Googling Stacey's name out of suspicious boredom, and the eventual discovery of her true identity. My morning had been very *If You Give A Mouse A Cookie*.

"Did you know Stacey was a spy?" I asked. "Probably a dumb question."

"There are no dumb questions, but yes, I knew she was probably trying to extract information for Artur."

"Did you know that when you hired her?"

"Yes."

"Yet you hired her anyway?" I gave him a suspicious glance. "Did her charms work on you?"

"It wasn't so much her charm as what she had to offer."

My heart nearly stopped, and my voice came out all tinny and hollow. "Exactly what did she offer you?"

"Why do you sound funny?" Dane asked. "What's wrong?"

"It's just—I know Stacey tended to use her, ah, feminine wiles on the men she was trying to rope into giving her information." I gave a shrug. "She's very beautiful, and I just wondered if—"

"No. Never."

"Never?"

He shook his head. "She was good at molding herself into someone she thought I could love, but it wasn't enough. She wasn't the real thing."

I blinked, unsure where Dane was heading.

"Lola, I firmly believe you're the only person who could've knocked me off my feet, as the saying goes," Dane said. "I intended to remain single all my life."

"And what, live celibate in your castle?"

"Er—no, but—"

"You've never told me about any girlfriends," I said suddenly. "There were, ah, ex-girlfriends, weren't there?"

"You haven't mentioned ex-boyfriends."

"Eh," I said. "There aren't any worth mentioning."

"I feel the same way."

"How long was your longest relationship?"

"Four months." He glanced at me. "What are you avoiding telling me?"

"Eight months for me," I said, and then sighed. "Stacey threatened to quit."

"Excuse me?"

"She threatened to quit her job," I said, and winced as Dane jerked the wheel in reaction to my news and then overcompensated to steady it. "I thought she was hiding something, and I tried to get it out of her. I must have pushed too hard."

Dane looked extremely unbothered by the news after having a second to digest it. "Alright."

"That's it?" I swiveled my gaze to him. "*Alright*?! I just shook down one of your best engineers in the middle of a huge project, and you are saying alright?"

"You didn't force her to quit, did you?" Dane asked. When I shook my head, he continued. "Then it's her choice. I don't force anyone to work here, and while it's inconvenient to replace people, I don't have to do it often. Most people I hire never leave. I would prefer someone quits if they don't want to be here. Staying when someone doesn't want to be here only breeds unrest, unhappiness, and it is not productive for anyone. But, I'll talk to her before she makes a rash decision."

"That is very..." I hesitated. "Logical."

Dane crooked an eyebrow. "So, is she hiding something?"

"Yes." I tapped my fingers nervously against my leg. "At least, I think so. She told me her story about Artur and how you changed her mind to stay. By the way, you still haven't told me about your decision to hire Stacey even when you knew her real identity off the bat."

"A window goes both ways," Dane said. "Artur and Stasia had gone through a lot of work to create a new identity for her. Most employers wouldn't have found her real identity."

"Unless it's tinted."

"What?"

"I mean, it's really hard to see into a tinted window," I said with a shrug. "I'm not trying to ruin your analogy, I'm just saying. Tinted windows only go one way."

He barked out a laugh, clicking the turn signal on as he pulled onto a side road near the back of Castlewood grounds and buzzed through the residential section created specifically for employees of the Clark Company. "I suppose in this case, I am the tint."

"Because you didn't let on that you knew who she was," I said with a nod. "And you were planning to let her try to extract information—possibly false information—or use her as a window back to Artur?"

"Exactly," Dane said. "Also, I had the feeling Stacey was no longer fond of Artur and needed a way out. The only way out I could give her was the chance to find safety in a new country, and that is what I did. I couldn't be her conscience, but I could let her conscience catch up with her."

"For being awkward with social skills, sometimes you're very intuitive."

"To me, it's strategy when it's business," Dane said. "Either way, the outcome would have worked for me. If Stasia stayed with Artur, I could have fed him false information. If Stacey decided a transformation was in order, I would have a very skilled engineer who enjoyed working for the Clark Company and would never wonder if the grass was greener. Because the grass in her home country would be dry and dead, and I would have her full loyalty for the rest of our lives."

"My, that's morbid," I said, "but I suppose accurate."

"What do you think she's hiding?"

"I think she knows something about what happened with Trey—at least, where he was going on Wednesday nights," I said. "But she wouldn't tell me. It's odd—I get the feeling she's still loyal to you in her own way, but something is holding her back from being completely honest."

Dane gave a shake of his head. "We'll find out. Sooner or later."

"Do you think Artur could have something to do with Trey's disappearance?" I asked. "Has anyone been asking around about the translation software? A buyer, an investor, something that might lead Artur to need your secret sauce?"

Dane's face went passive as he thought. "I've entertained a few private offers for the software recently. None I've accepted."

"What if Artur's plan is to steal the software out from under your nose and sell it quickly to the highest bidder?"

Dane's lips tightened. "It's possible, though I doubt he'd bother himself with it."

"I don't know. It sounded like he was pretty obsessed with you from what Stacey said. She told me that he was willing to give her up to get to you," I said. "Maybe he really did love Stasia and is after revenge. Maybe he thinks you stole his girl."

"But I didn't. I didn't steal anyone—he sent her here."

"She saw you, and she decided you were better," I said. "That's got to sting a man's ego."

Dane cocked his head to one side as if he couldn't be bothered by such a trivial thing as someone's ego. "None of that explains where we're going now."

"On my way back from talking to Stacey, I ran into Annalise—"

"How does one run into Annalise at 6 a.m. in the morning on our property?"

I felt a little bubble of warmth at how quickly and easily Dane had adopted the words *our* and *we* into normal conversation. Of course, I knew the company was his and always would be, but the show of togetherness never ceased to make me appreciate his thoughtfulness.

"Well, she was..." I coughed. "Visiting Semi. Or rather, trying to."

"He wasn't at home."

"Yeah, she realized that," I said dryly. "Anyway, the important bit is that she scared someone away—someone she thought was trespassing onto your property."

"And that's where we're headed," Dane said. "Though I have to say, it doesn't make sense. If she scared this person away, I highly doubt he or she is still hanging around."

"No, but if he was in a hurry, maybe he left something behind. She didn't get a good look at any of his features, but maybe he left a footprint or his clothing was torn or something."

"Sure," Dane said with a thin smile. "I'll have my lab get right on the DNA samples."

I gave him a light smack to the arm at his sarcasm. "Come on! It's worth a shot. Plus, you're Dane Clark. I don't doubt you could get blood spatter analysis done on a dime."

"Who said anything about blood?"

"Stop! This is it," I announced as Dane came to a halt at the second bend in the road. "She said it was somewhere around here. Give it ten minutes, and if we don't find anything, we can head home."

For the next nine minutes I prayed we'd find something. A hint of something, anything that might lead us to the kidnapper's identity. With each passing hour, the time until the kidnapper called us again grew shorter and shorter. And we had even less of a plan this time around, which wasn't saying much. I feared that if we didn't find something on this guy fast, we weren't going to see Dane's money ever again, or worse, that Trey would die despite our best efforts.

As I kicked through grass, my efforts feeling more futile with each passing minute, I found my eyes lifting toward the skies in search of the elusive Warehouse 11. There on the horizon was a small triangle of slate gray just as Annalise had claimed. It sparkled at me, dancing mercilessly in the distance, shining a spotlight to tease me.

"Dane." I whirled on him more seriously than I intended. "There's nothing in Warehouse 11 that is illegal, right? You promised me. Nothing that Artur might want? Nothing that might be the reason Trey was kidnapped, right?"

Dane's eyes went blank. "I promised you, Lola."

"I know, I'm sorry. I'm just so tired, and after my failure last night, I'm on edge."

"You didn't fail, Lola! Is that what you think?"

"There!"

I dodged Dane's outstretched arms in exchange for a shiny new thing on the horizon—this one in the middle of the road near the Jeep. So near to the rear wheel that I'd almost missed it. I picked up the glinting metallic object and returned to Dane's side, wriggling under his open arms for a half-hug as we examined the object together.

"It's a key," I said, my brows furrowed. "An old looking key. Do you think it's been here a long while?"

Dane shook his head. "No, it's not grimy enough. Look how shiny this is—I'd bet it's from last night's intruder."

"Where were they trying to get with this?" I asked. "The Warehouses? You have way more security than a little keyhole on all of those. Either the person is an amateur, or this—"

"The garage."

"What?"

"This is a shanked key," Dane said easily, and then ran his finger over the edges. "It's been filed down."

"What good does a filed down key do?"

"It's one of the top five tools used to steal cars," Dane said with a wry smile. "A shanked key can get some older models to start if used correctly. Maybe this wasn't meant to be used on the break-in last night; maybe it was just something the intruder had on his or her figure."

My breath accelerated while my blood seemed to freeze. "And we know who steals cars."

Chapter 14

Darius wasn't in his usual spot on the beach.
Either it was too early for him, or he'd gotten spooked after his jaunt into Castlewood grounds in the wee hours of the morning and decided to blow town. I hoped it wasn't the latter because it'd be near impossible to chase after him with everything we had going on at the castle, and we couldn't risk calling the police. The police's inadvertent arrival had already ticked off the kidnapper once; I certainly didn't want to take any chances in delaying Trey's safe return.

Despite our thorough scouring, Darius was nowhere to be seen. No cars had been reported stolen for the last few days, and the tourists resting on beach towels hadn't been harassed by anyone selling random crap. Apparently, Darius had taken the day off. We just had to determine if his absence was voluntary.

Coming to a stop at one end of the beach, I folded my arms over my white lace tank top, my gauzy shawl hanging over one shoulder. The sun was warm, and if I'd accomplished nothing else in looking for Darius, at the very least I'd soaked up some Vitamin D at the beach.

"Do you think we should try the casino next?" I asked Dane as Semi wandered some ways away from us down the path, eyes peeled for our guy. "We haven't been back since you schooled Fat Jim and then he died."

Dane looked a little surprised at my wording.

"I didn't mean *you* killed him," I revised. "I just meant the chain of events. Anyway, we should ask around and see if anyone saw Darius there, maybe talking to Fat Jim or something."

"You think they could've been working together on this thing?"

"Probably not, but I honestly don't know what to think. I believe Fat Jim was killed due to his involvement, so I'm just trying to piece together our connections. We have Darius on your property the day after Fat Jim dies, which is coincidentally the day after we introduced ourselves to him, and also the day after we interacted with the kidnapper. There are too many oddities for that to be an accident."

"It could explain why we haven't heard from the kidnapper yet," Dane agreed. "Because he's been busy sneaking onto my property. There's only one problem with this whole thing."

"I believe I know what you're thinking," I said. "Darius doesn't seem smart enough to lure Trey away. Even if Trey did let himself get kidnapped—say they were friends and Trey trusted him—Darius isn't clever enough to keep him there. If Trey is anything like your other employees, he's a near genius."

"Yes," Dane said simply. "Let's find Semi."

After driving us to the beach, Semi had wandered off in another direction. He didn't blend in easily, seeing as he was the size of a refrigerator. Dane and I could stroll hand in hand down the beach and, save for the fact he was dressed in perfect suit #44, we could be just any couple for a walk by the water.

I held his hand tighter as we walked back, feeling secure at least in the knowledge that we were in this together. We'd be in everything together from here on out, and that was a breath of fresh air when your life partner revealed himself to be Dane Clark.

"Nothing?" Semi asked when we reunited at the car.

"Nothing," I confirmed. "Let's head to the casino and see if we can connect Darius and Fat Jim—or anyone else. Let's include Stacey in the mix when we ask around. Just in case."

Dane hadn't seemed to give much weight to the Artur theory, but every time it was mentioned, the lines beside his eyes tightened ever so slightly, just enough to tell me that even if Dane didn't let himself look worried about it, his concern hadn't disappeared.

Artur was just as viable as a suspect—if not more so—than Darius. I just didn't know where to start looking for him. Especially since I'd pushed Stacey away. I doubted she'd be in the mood to cooperate with me.

"I need to talk to Stacey again when we get back," I murmured to Dane. "I'd feel really bad if she ended up giving her notice because of the things I said."

"It's not your fault," Dane said. "She's a grown adult and a capable woman—she can do as she likes."

"It doesn't bother you that she might quit? Or that I made her do it?"

"Lola—"

"Fine, I didn't *make* her, but sheesh. I led the horse to water, and she's drinking it. She's slurping up that water. What if she's already gone by the time we get back, and I don't get a chance to set things right? I think she knows more about this Trey thing than she's letting on."

Dane picked up his phone and set to typing.

"There," he said a few moments later, slipping the sleek, not-yet-on-the-market gadget back into his pocket. "Human resources scheduled an interview with her at one. She'll be there until we get back at least."

I exhaled. "Thank you. Do you think she's involved?"

"No."

"That's very certain of you."

"You asked my opinion, and I gave it," he said. "I don't believe she's involved. She might know something, but I don't believe she was responsible for the kidnapping. She was clocked into the system last night at midnight—if she was here, she couldn't have been in the forest."

"So, you were suspicious, too," I said with a smile. "You checked up on her."

"I check up on everyone," Dane said simply. "Standard procedure."

"Yikes."

He winked.

"Here we are," Semi said. "Let me grab the door for you, Miss Pink."

Semi had the habit of opening and closing doors for me—and other ladies—whenever he could get to it first. It'd become somewhat of a game for me to try and slide out and close the door before Semi had a chance to get around the car. I appreciated his chivalry, but we weren't on a date, and I wasn't an invalid.

This time, however, I let him open the door for me. I could sense that Semi's desperation was growing, and he needed a win. I smiled broadly and thanked him profusely while I slid out.

Our first stop was to the man parked out front of the casino. The same man Dane had given a pile of cash at our last visit.

"Hi there," I greeted him. "You might not remember me, but—"

The man raised a hand and stared right past me, waving at Dane over my shoulder.

"Ah, you remember *him*." I stepped out of the way. "Dane?"

Dane approached looking quite marvelous in Suit #44 and crouched to his knees to go eye to eye with the man. "Sir," he said, "have you happened to see a man just shorter than her height—African American, gap between his front teeth around here?"

"You mean Darius?" The guy cackled. "Sure, he's inside. Good kid."

"That's to be determined," I muttered. "Thanks. Do you know if he ever talked to Fat Jim? Does Darius come around here a lot?"

The man thought for a second and then nodded. "He was here yesterday morning. I don't know if he talked to Fat Jim, but I'm sure they were familiar with one another. It's a small enough casino."

The casino didn't feel small as we walked inside, but I noticed some of the same crowd hanging out at the tables from our previous visit. One grandma in a loud purple sweat suit didn't look like she'd moved, let alone showered or changed in the last few days. I briefly wondered about bathroom habits, or if she was able to subsist solely on casino smoke.

"You do realize," I murmured to Dane as we scoured the floor for Darius, "that our friend out here is placing Darius at the scene of the crime. At the correct time. Fat Jim was murdered in his car. If Darius was hanging around, that means he doesn't have an alibi."

"I know," Dane said. "I suppose I could be wrong about Darius, but I hate to think he's responsible."

"It doesn't feel right," I agreed. "So, was he in the wrong place at the wrong time?"

"Boss—" Semi interrupted. "Found him. I think you should come on back this way. Bring your cash."

Darius looked like a misguided rapper sitting at a low-stakes black-jack table. He had three ladies hanging on his arms wearing little more than tinsel over their privates, though his crowning glory was a cheap, party-favor tiara perched on his head. Darius wore an oversized basket-ball jersey and shorts that he could swim laps in, but as usual, he had a huge grin on his face.

Maybe it was the grin or maybe it was his sunny disposition, but I just didn't see the guy as a killer. Unless he was a complete and utter psy-chopath, I suspected someone was setting him up to take the fall—and he wasn't aware in the slightest.

"Darius," I said as Dane and I took seats at the table. "How's it go-ing?"

"Dude," he said, grinning with a hundred-watt smile at me. "Look at these chicks! I've got three of them hanging on me. Things are going great."

"How much are you up?" Dane asked, nodding to the pile of chips.

"Thirty-two bucks," he said smugly. "Big money. You know, because usually I lose."

"Ah," Dane said. "I'll donate triple that to your funds if you answer a few questions for us."

"Dude, I told you everything I know already," he said, but he lied badly. His eyes flickered back and forth between the ladies and the dealer. "I'll take the money for spilling my guts, but I don't know any-thing else."

"Then I assume you don't know about this," I said, pulling my purse close to me and flipping out the shanked key we'd found on the ground. I slid it across the table to Darius. "You wouldn't have seen this before?"

Darius froze. "Ergh, I need a soda. Ladies, get me a soda, will you? Mr. Clark, pretty lady, come with me."

The Clark trio trailed Darius to a small sitting area in the corner of the room. Darius plopped down in the chair, locked his fingers in front of his body. He was trembling when he looked up at Dane.

"I didn't mean to actually take anything," he said. "In fact, I screwed it all up."

"What'd you screw up?" I asked. "What was the plan?"

"I was supposed to sneak near your garage and drop the key there," he said easily. "You know, as if I was trying to steal Mr. Clark's old cars and shit. It's not a surprise that he's got a sweet-ass collection of them."

"Thanks," Dane said with a hint of pride. "I enjoy them."

"Dude, I know," Darius said, shaking his head in awe. "I saw that latest article with all the photos—the self-driving car chip. That new design is sweet!"

"Yeah, hey—cool cars, we can discuss them later." I tapped my arm impatiently. "What do you mean you were supposed to sneak near the garage? You weren't actually trying to steal Dane's cars?"

"Dudes." Darius gave a patronizing shake of his head, as if I was being slow. "Of course not. I'm not smart enough to deal with all those fancy gadgets Mr. Clark has. I can lift a car off the street in under two seconds—seriously, I'm thinking of having that printed on my business card—but when it comes to complex computer locks and gauges and alarms and whatnot, I'm out. I'm old school and dumb."

"You're not dumb," I said. "You just have a different skillset."

"Yeah, true," Darius said. "You're a real motivational speaker, Miss Pink. Anyway, you've gotta believe me. I respect Mr. Clark here, and I'd never steal his cars. They're his babies, even I can see that. I got a code of honor, you know?"

"Oh, um, sure," I said, "except that doesn't make sense. Why were you on Clark Company property last night?"

"I screwed up bigtime," he said. "I hope the dude who hired me doesn't notice. I mean, you found the key—so technically I accomplished my mission. Maybe you just pretend you found that key near the garage? That'd do me a real solid."

"Darius, are you saying someone hired you to fake-break into Dane's car collection?"

"Yeah, except I didn't even have to break in," he said, shrugging his skinny shoulders. "I just had to tip toe onto the property, make sure I was seen, and drop the key."

"And you were seen," I said, "but on accident by Annalise."

"Yep—dropped the key on accident, too," he said. "I meant to sneak round from the back because the front gates are impossible to get through. I didn't make it."

"Obviously not," I said. "Who hired you?"

"I dunno."

"Sorry, try again," I said. "We don't like that answer."

"Seriously," Darius said. "I don't know. I was hassling the tourists like I always do yesterday, and one of them offered me the gig. I'm sure he was just a messenger for whoever *actually* hired me. I've never seen the guy before in my life. He looked all nerdy—white socks with those huge-ass sandals. Fanny pack. Camera. Big-ass sunglasses. Wide-ass hat."

"Your descriptions are impeccable," I said dryly. Ironically, I really could see the type of person Darius meant through his very colorfully painted picture. "So, they got someone to deliver you a message who looked like a tourist. And you have no idea who was behind it? How much did they pay you?"

"It's rude to ask about finances," Darius said. Then he tipped his head to the side and gave me a cheeky smile. "Okay, he paid me five hundred bucks."

I turned to Dane. "Wild goose chase."

He gave a slight nod and pulled me to the side while Semi stood guard over Darius. "The kidnapper is playing with us. He's trying to keep us occupied, too busy to come up with a plan of attack."

"All while he comes up with the next step," I said. "We've been wasting our time."

"It might not be wasted," Dane said. "If we could find the messenger..."

"Not a chance," I said. "This kidnapper has been so thorough he might have three layers of messengers to work through. Even if we start cracking that chain of command, it'll be too late before we find the man—or woman—behind it all."

"We can't sit around and do nothing." Dane flicked a glance at his watch and frowned. "But I do have a meeting with Germany that I absolutely can't reschedule in half an hour. I'm so sorry."

"Hey, it's fine—better to stay busy." I rested my hand on his arm and rubbed my thumb gently over his skin until his shoulders relaxed just the slightest amount. "We can't do much more until we hear from the kidnapper."

Dane gave a succinct nod. "Fine."

"In the meantime, I'd like to talk to Stacey if that's alright with you," I said. "I just—I want to clarify a few things."

"Like what?"

"Things we spoke about this morning," I said vaguely. "I need another chance."

"I have a meeting with her this afternoon after she finishes her HR meeting," Dane said. "You have until then. In the event that she does give formal notice, we will begin the process of locking her systematically out of accounts as well as the physical grounds of Castlewood. Security procedure of course—you will not easily have access to her after that."

"Understood, and thank you," I said, squeezing his arm. Before letting go, I tilted my gaze up to face his. "There's one more thing."

"What?"

I gestured my head and moved us a few feet further from Semi. "I've been thinking a lot about the people you hire. Most of them are at the top of their field, wouldn't you say?"

Dane nodded, at the same time waving off the offerings of a server with a tray full of drinks. "That's safe to say, though it's not a requirement."

"Trey was intelligent—is intelligent," I corrected. "Everyone seems to agree with that."

"Yes, even before he worked for me, he had raw common sense and understood things that most people of his background had no real business understanding. Complex topics, advanced mathematics, statistical models—things click for him."

"Right. So, don't you think it's odd that everyone who seems to be involved in this thing is from Trey's former life?" I asked. "Yet none of them seem individually capable of kidnapping him? I mean, Fat Jim is dead now, but he wasn't the brightest bulb. He ruled with sheer brawn and intimidation. Darius? I actually like the kid for some odd reason, but he's the first to tell you he's not up for kidnapping a Clark Company employee."

"Are you referring to Stacey?" Dane asked. "Yes, she'd have the capacity to pull this off, but you've already asked my opinion, and I've told you I don't believe it's her. I suppose your theory is that she's working with Artur."

"Yes, that's one theory," I said, "but my other theory is that Trey hasn't been kidnapped."

Dane blinked. By the time he came out of his silence, he'd followed the same train of thought that I had to reach a very similar conclusion.

"You believe Trey falsified his kidnapping and is using that to extort money from the Clark Company," Dane said. "He would be intelligent enough to pull it off, nobody gets hurt, and at any time, he might show up to work and claim he's disorientated...and we would likely believe him."

"It's the perfect crime," I said. "Maybe he's in trouble, needs the money. Or he just saw how much you have, and he got greedy. He gets a huge payout *and* gets to keep his job. Plus a few vacation days."

Dane laughed wryly. "I wouldn't call them vacation days. He's put in a lot of work if this is the case."

"Okay, you can admire the kidnapper later," I said blithely. "Let's think about it. At first, Semi was hesitant to even tell you that Trey was gone because of his past. We know he's not Mr. Squeaky Clean. Is it possible he's reverted to manipulating his old friends like pieces of a monopoly game? He might have been playing with us the whole time, setting up Fat Jim, Darius, Billy—the whole lot."

"I don't know," he said finally. "I don't think so, but I don't know him well enough to say."

"You know Stacey well enough to say," I said. "Why's that?"

Dane eyed me carefully. "Because I do."

"Ah."

"After Stacey confessed her true identity to me, it was easy enough to see that she had no desire to go back to Artur or that way of life. It was painful and torturous for her to even think about it. However, with Trey, I'm not sure that's the case."

"Why do you say that?"

"The allure of the *good old days*," Dane said. "Even after Trey began working for the Clark Company, he didn't...hate his time before it. While he was grateful for a fresh start, and while I trusted him implicitly with company secrets, I never knew what was going through his head. I'm not saying he's done this, or that I don't trust him, but I have to admit he's capable of pulling it off."

"But this isn't reverting to old ways, not really," I said. "This is a whole new level of the game, and there might be an appeal in that. I'll bet he's competitive and likes a challenge."

"Yes." Dane's lips went to a thin line. "That's the reason he excelled in learning programming languages in the first place. He hated not understanding, not being the best. And eventually he became one of the best."

"It still doesn't explain where he went Wednesday nights," I mused. "I don't know, Dane. I'm stumped. It could be Stacey, Artur, Trey, Darius, or someone we haven't even considered yet."

Dane's eyes flicked back to his watch. "You'll talk to Stacey, and then together we can look into Trey's—"

I held up a finger. "After my chat with Stacey, I'm off to pick flowers with your mother."

Dane winced. "I agreed to go to that, didn't I?"

"Stay at the castle," I said firmly. "I'll get Babs to go with me. Between all the kidnapping stuff, Stacey possibly quitting, and whatever your business with Germany is—you have things to take care of at the office."

"But—"

"I swear it," I said. "You can even send Semi with us if that would make you feel better."

He smiled. "Are you sure?"

"Yes. It'll be good for me to, ah, see your mother by myself," I said. "Mrs. Dulcet is coming, too. It'll already be a full car, so unless you want to spend the afternoon surrounded by a pack of females..."

"I have a lot of meetings," Dane said hurriedly, "and we need someone staying behind at the castle to wait for the kidnapper's next instructions."

"Yeah," I said with a wink. "That's what I thought."

We returned to the seating area and Dane tossed a hundred-dollar bill on the table in front of Darius. "Have fun," he said, and then gestured for me and Semi to follow him.

Darius was grinning like the king of the world when we left. As I glanced back over my shoulder, he was straightening his tiara and beckoning for the ladies to return to his side.

"That man is something else," I said. "Why do we like him?"

"Nice smile," Semi said.

I laughed, sliding next to Dane as we reached the SUV. Semi beat me in our game this time and opened the door before I could reach for the handle. Dane and I slid in first while Semi circled the vehicle, doing the little checks he performed regularly.

"One more thing," I whispered to Dane, "I don't think we should mention that last theory to Semi yet. Just in case."

"In case of what?"

"In case we're wrong," I said. "I don't want to worry Semi if we don't have to."

"He's already thought about it," Dane said. "I'm sure of it."

"Let's just keep that between you and me for now, okay?" I leaned over and kissed his lips, sealing off any argument. Then Semi slid in, and it was too late for Dane to retort.

"You did that on purpose," Dane muttered.

I shrugged, glanced out the window. "You got a problem with it?"

He reached for my hand and squeezed, and I took that to be a no.

Chapter 15

The ride back was a quiet one. When Semi parked outside of the castle, I announced that they could find me back in Warehouse 5 in the event they needed anything. Dane nodded, too distracted to argue with much of anything. I'd rarely seen him this agitated over a work meeting, so on second thought, I decided to walk him inside.

"Hey," I said, tugging him to a private corner in the entryway. "Is everything okay with the company? You usually don't look this worried over one little meeting."

"It's the Germans," he said, as if that explained everything. "We're at an impasse—they don't understand me, and I don't understand them."

"Language barrier?"

He massaged his forehead looking stressed. "I'm a little rusty on my German, but it's more of a cultural thing. Neither of us are budging, but neither of us can walk away. Negotiations are tense."

"I'm sorry—I wish I could help you, but I don't understand German, and I have no clue what you're negotiating."

Dane kissed me on the forehead. "I'll see you—when?"

"I've got flower shopping at two," I said. "So sometime after that. Probably around four p.m.?"

Dane again glanced at his watch and gave a quick nod. "Be careful and don't ditch Semi."

With that, he was gone.

I pondered on Dane's work frustrations as I headed out back to the platform and used my all-access pass for a quick swipe to Warehouse 5. It felt good showing myself around the grounds—as if I belonged here and wasn't just the little puppy dog trailing after Dane. Making my own decisions, poking my nose into the business, trying to learn—all of that was new and fresh and exciting.

I buzzed quickly through the doors to Warehouse 5 and found Martin at work in the same clothes as before. It was hard to say if he'd worn them yesterday or if they'd just come wrinkled out of the laundry, but I stayed far enough away to not smell him either way.

"Is Stacey here?" I asked. "I have a few questions to ask her."

"She's packing up shop," Martin said. "Somewhere over there."

Martin nodded in a way that encompassed the rest of the warehouse and was entirely unhelpful. But he was already engrossed back in his work, and since I didn't want to tick him off, too, I opted to look for Stacey myself.

I found her at the coffee machine. "Mind if I grab one of those with you?"

The only sign of her surprise was a quick straightening of her shoulders. "You're back."

"Yes, looking for you."

Stacey took her time whipping up a tiny little espresso for herself, and obligingly pressing the button for a latte that she eventually handed to me. "Happy?"

"Look, I really didn't mean to upset you. I hope you're not actually considering quitting. I'm here to apologize if I pushed you too far. We've been under a lot of stress lately what with..." I hesitated and cleared my throat. "You know, wedding planning."

"You mean Trey."

"That too," I said. "And wedding planning."

"Mmm," she said, not convinced. "I appreciate your apology, Miss Pink."

"It's Lola, please." I stepped toward her, hugging my mug to my chest. "Dane thinks really highly of you, and I would hate it if you left the company because of me. Can we talk somewhere for just a few minutes?"

Stacey led me to a small conference room and sat. "No recording devices or cameras," she said as she sat down. "Let's make this quick. I have meetings this afternoon."

"Earlier today, I brought up a theory to Dane. Trey is kidnapped," I said, opting to hold nothing back. I imagined that, like Dane, she valued honesty. "I suggested you might be one option as to who had taken him."

"Because of my connection to Artur."

"That, and because you're smart," I said. "Not everyone has the intelligence or the guts to pull off a heist on the Clark Company."

"I had nothing to do with it."

"I know that," I said. "You and I just met, but Dane trusts you and that's good enough for me."

"Frankly, Miss Pink, I don't give a damn about who you trust and who you don't."

"Then why did you threaten to quit when I spoke to you this morning?"

"Because I refuse to compromise my loyalties."

"What loyalties? To Artur?"

She scowled. "To Trey."

Her news hit me like a blast of icy air. My eyes did a long, slow blink as if them shutting and opening them would reset the situation. "What loyalty is that?"

Stacey raised her espresso to her lips and took a sip. Her lips puckered at the hit of bitterness. "I know where Trey goes Wednesday evenings. But I would rather quit my job than betray my friend's trust. I promised Trey I wouldn't tell anyone."

"I understand," I said slowly. Her loyalty was a double-edged sword—while I respected her for it, her stubbornness was potentially hindering our chances of bringing Trey back alive. "I think that's very noble of you. But Trey's life is in danger. If he's dead, it's not going to matter what he was doing anyway. Can you at least tell me if it was personal? Was he seeing someone at the company? Were you in love with Trey?"

"No, no—of course not," she said. "Though we are good friends. Trey was one of my first friends at the company. I think—well, we both have rough histories. It was a point of bonding between us."

"And you're loyal to a fault."

She cocked her head to the side. "Like you said, I have compromised my morals enough with my work for Artur. Trey is a good man, and he is my friend. If I shared the information about him that I'd discovered accidentally, it would hurt him—potentially damage his career."

"But we're beyond caring about careers now," I said. "This is about his life."

She bit her lip, her eyes watering. "I know."

I could see the care she had for her friend and co-worker, and the battle that waged there. More than ever, I had to tiptoe carefully in the conversation—I couldn't afford to spook Stacey back into silence.

"Trey directly disobeyed protocol for the Clark Company. I don't know what to do, Miss Pink." She shook her head, her gaze focused on the distance. "He wasn't intentionally hurting the company. But if I turned him in, he would have lost his job and possibly reverted to his old lifestyle."

I sensed Stacey needed some space to formulate her thoughts, so I lapsed into silence and focused on my latte. I sipped the frothy beverage as I felt myself beginning to fade. With hardly any sleep the night before, I was holding on by a thread.

A part of me hoped the kidnapper would just calm the heck down and wait until tomorrow to get in touch with us so that I could pick out wedding flowers and go to sleep. My eyes felt like sandbags, and I was sure I looked like a real treasure with bags under my eyes the size of oversized suitcases.

Finally, Stacey exhaled a shuddery sigh. "He met a friend every Wednesday night. I don't know if the friend is male or female. I didn't see the other person; I only saw Trey."

"Where did you find him?"

"The Lost Leprechaun," she said. "You know, that weird little Irish pub on the outskirts of town? Not very popular with the locals."

"I know the one," I said. "I know Big Richard and Little Richard quite well." At her confused expression, I hurried to explain. "The names of the owners. Never mind. What was he doing there?"

"He was sitting at the bar waiting for someone. He looked a little nervous; I guess it was the first time he was meeting this friend. It was the first Wednesday he left work early."

"How long ago?"

"Oh, I don't know. Six months?" She counted back in her head. "Yes, around then. I was at the bar for a first date. My date never showed, so I was sitting at the bar alone. Hence the embarrassment for both of us."

"Did you two talk?"

She nodded. "Like I said, we were friendly from work—we recognized that we had similar situations. Neither of us liked to talk about the past much, so we focused on business."

"I understand," I said. "What was so odd about that night?"

"Aside from the fact that neither of us ever left work early—that was the biggest thing, actually—is the fact that he had a...*ah*, diagram of the translator device we were working on."

"You mean, the one you showed me yesterday?"

"The one you still haven't returned to the lab?" she retorted stiffly. "Yes, that one."

"Point for you," I said. "Why was it there?"

"That's the question I've been asking myself," she said. "He covered it up quickly, and I sort of asked a few probing questions. He must have known I saw it."

"Did he say anything about it after the fact?"

"Sort of—I think in a way he was trying to explain to me." She glanced up at me, a curious look in her eye as she changed subjects abruptly. "Do you know how he was hired on to the company?"

I sucked in a breath and let it out thoughtfully. "You mean the bit about Dane sort of taking him on as an apprentice and teaching him the ropes of the engineering world?"

"Yes, that," she said. "He told me the story that night as we sat at the bar. I think he was trying to explain something to me, and the more I thought about it, the more I realized he was trying to pay it forward. That's why I never said anything. At first glance, I thought maybe he was trying to sell information on the company to the highest bidder—" her jaw clenched tightly—"something I might have done in a former life."

"But he wasn't," I said. "He was trying to take on his own apprentice and pay forward what Dane had done for him."

"Exactly. He's met this friend religiously every Wednesday night for the last six months. I imagine he was taking this person under his wing and guiding him along in the same way that Dane did for Trey."

"Why wouldn't he tell Dane?" I wondered. "Why would he do it on the sly?"

"I don't think it was on the sly, I think he was just prepping the friend for a job interview. I imagine that in time, Trey would've asked Dane to open an interview slot for his friend. Most new hires come from personal recommendations, so that is an entirely likely scenario."

"Why would he bring real-life technology into it?" I asked. "I mean, it must have been against Trey's contract to expose confidential documents to anyone."

"Yes, of course it was," she said. "Hence the reason I had to make a choice. But that night, I warned him. I told Trey I trusted my friends and kept them close, but I kept my enemies even closer."

"What did he say?"

"He told me he wasn't an enemy, and I believed him," she said. "The next day he apologized, and we carried on. When he continued his Wednesday night meetings, he made sure I watched him lock up every piece of technology."

"He could have been lying."

"He could have," she acknowledged. "Lord knows he has enough information in his head to be dangerous. If Artur got ahold of him..."

We both froze.

"You don't think maybe Trey's friend could have connections to Artur," I said, tapping a finger against my lip. "Could there be a second spy?"

Stacey's face went white. "I don't know why I didn't think of that. It's very possible Artur preyed on Trey's helpful nature. I think—maybe... it's best I contact an old friend. I think you should go."

I stood, downed the rest of my latte. "Keep me posted?"

She smiled. "Do you think Mr. Clark would be upset if I cancelled my afternoon meetings?"

"Absolutely not." I shook my head, then had a sudden idea. "But if you have a minute to spare, I think he could use your help."

Her face went even paler than before. "Is he in trouble?"

"Just business," I said hurriedly. "He's in some sort of negotiation stand-off with a German company. He says his language is rusty and the culture is different. Didn't you say you spent a few years working for a German company?"

"Oh, but I couldn't barge in. That's none of my business."

"No," I said. "But Dane keeps telling me the company is my business, too. Come on, follow me. After the Germans, maybe you and Dane can have a little chat about your old friend Artur and see if he's paid a visit to the states recently or had contact with anyone here."

"Perfect," she snarled, then recoiled. "Sorry, I shouldn't be bitter. But if he's involved, Miss Pink, things are worse than I ever imagined."

Chapter 16

*T*hings *are worse than I ever imagined.*

I replayed Stacey's last words over and over again as I rushed out front and climbed into a waiting SUV. I'd helped Stacey blow off her one p.m. exit interview by leading her into Dane's meeting with the Germans.

Under normal circumstances, I wouldn't have dreamed of overstepping my bounds in such a way, but in this case, I suspected that Stacey could really be of help to Dane. She was polished, intelligent, and proficient in German. I was none of those things, so I wasn't helpful, but hopefully my idea was a good one.

With any luck, it'd get Stacey and Dane back on the same page and smooth over the bumps I'd created earlier in the day. There was the added layer of them discussing Artur and his possible involvement in Trey's disappearance. The more I thought about it, the more I worried Artur or someone on his team had conned Trey into trusting him slowly but surely, receiving drips of information as Artur planned the bigger pay off.

A million dollars was just the beginning. The actual payoff would be something priceless: revenge for stealing Stasia from under Artur's sticky little fingers and the knowledge that he'd outsmarted Dane Clark, his biggest rival. After all, that's what Artur was famous for—that's what had brought Stacey to the Clark Company in the first place, and the duo had failed. If Artur was like most men I knew, he didn't like to fail, and he wouldn't have taken the loss easily.

"Hello," Babs said, prompting me into looking up for the first time since entering the SUV. She grinned. "Your moral support team is ready to go. Mrs. Dulcet said Dane couldn't get out of a meeting, but have no fear—we're here"

"That's sweet, but really—it's no big deal. You both didn't need to rearrange your days to come with me," I said. "I'm just pointing at a few pretty flowers and then putting the order on Dane's credit card. How hard can it be?"

Mrs. Dulcet and Babs looked at one another and then burst into laughter.

An hour later, I understood why.

Amanda Clark was waiting for us at the gardens when we arrived. She wore a stunning white skirt with a glorious white jacket and even a little white hat with netting across the front. She looked far more like a bride than I did, despite my lacy tank top, and in fact, the staff congregated around her instead of me. Amanda and staff had already begun discussing each and every flower in detail while I sort of meandered the gardens with Babs.

"They've been talking for an hour," I said, kicking a stone on the ground as I glanced at my phone and was stunned to see how much time had passed without a single person coming to speak to me. Aside from a quick hello, Amanda hadn't even acknowledged my presence. "I don't even know who's supposed to be helping me. How is there that much to say about flowers? They're all pretty. Smoosh some together into a bouquet. *Whabam.* Done."

"A gardener somewhere is taking huge offense to what you just said." Babs leaned over, her fingers resting daintily on a tall, deep purple calla lily. "Oh, but aren't these gorgeous?"

"Of course! That's what I mean. They're all pretty. This place is spectacular."

We strolled underneath a fragrant trellis of roses: yellows and oranges, reds and blues, even a green and a black variety of rose that I had never known existed. Mrs. Clark had insisted on coming to one of the most prestigious botanical gardens on this side of the country. I could've picked dandelions and felt just as giddy, but she wanted only the best at her—or rather, her son's—ceremony.

Tufts of decorative grasses whispered against one another as they filtered daintily over the edges of the path. Ruby red apples burst into color on one of the trees, arching over the walkway with grace while droplets of orange punctuated a nearby citrus tree. Bushels of blooms I couldn't name danced in little cottage-like arrays along the building's quaint brick structure, looking as if the very buildings had been imported from the English countryside.

"Lola," Mrs. Dulcet said, catching up to me. "Have you found anything you like yet?"

I shrugged. "I like them all."

"Which means no," Mrs. Dulcet said. "You'll know when the right one comes around. Just keep walking and browsing."

I flicked my eyes over to Amanda Clark. "It's not like I have a choice. She all but shooed me off an hour ago and told me to 'look around' while she took care of things. I've been meaning to confront her, but she's had one staff or another hanging onto her every word for the last hour, and I don't want to cause a scene."

"Just find what you like," Mrs. Dulcet counseled, "and then bring it to her. It's very hard to argue for what you want if you don't actually know what you want."

"Yowza," Babs said. "I've gotta write that one down. That's very deep, Mrs. Dulcet."

"Speaking of things you like, have you tried the brownies yet?" The butler's red hair almost blended in to a display of poppies behind her. "They've been in the freezer for some time, as have Mrs. Fredericks. I'm not trying to rush you, but you haven't eaten either of them."

I guiltily thought back to my Nutella binge in the middle of the night. I'd been too lazy to check the freezer—except to stick one hand in, remove ice cream, and put it back. "I've been a little preoccupied."

"But I'd really appreciate some sort of consensus on the brownies," Mrs. Dulcet persisted. "This competition is really important for the sake of my mental health, you should know—and if Mrs. Fredericks—"

"That's it." I pointed. "Those are the ones."

"Um, er—*those*?" Babs squinted. "You mean the flowers on the other side of the fence?"

"Yes, the sunflowers." I smiled, feeling happy at the very sight of the fat, bright blooms. "I just want a few sunflowers in my bouquet—I'm sure of it. Nice and simple."

"Er—" Babs glanced at Mrs. Dulcet. "Lola, those are the neighbors' flowers. They're not even part of the gardens."

"Great, then they'll be even cheaper," I said. "You think I can walk over there and ask if they'll let me buy some sunflowers?"

Mrs. Dulcet looked baffled. "You have all of these exotic flowers to choose from, and you want to pick from the neighboring garden?"

"These aren't me," I said, gaining confidence the longer I stared at those brilliant yellow petals peeping curiously at me. "I'm simple. Sunflowers are sunny, and they remind me of Dotty and the Sunshine Shore, and everything that's important to me. I'm just as happy seeing a sunflower as I am spending huge amounts on an exotic bouquet."

Babs studied me, then the flowers. "You're right," she said. "Those are totally you. Shall I go with you to visit the neighbors?"

"That would be delightful," I said in my most fake British accent. "We'll be right back, Mrs. Dulcet. If Dane's mother asks about us, well, we'll be right back."

She gave a weak looking nod.

Babs and I scampered off next door where we found a lovely young couple with two small children. The mother bounced a baby on her hip and the father chased the older boy through the long grasses of the front yard.

"This looks like a nice family," Babs said. "Maybe it'll bring you good luck to use their flowers for your wedding."

The mother was absolutely delighted when we asked about her gardens. When Babs went on to tell her it was Dane Clark getting married—yes, the King of Castlewood—she just about passed out from excitement.

"I just think he's gorgeous," she said, shifting the baby further back as if the little guy could understand. "I had a huge crush on him when I was in college. We'd love for you to use the flowers for your bouquet. Don't you dare offer to pay us, either. Just come on over and pick a few whenever you like. In fact, grab one now to take home. You can test it out with your dress. Fred! Get the girls a sunflower, will you? She's marrying Dane Clark, and they're using our sunflowers for the wedding. Isn't that great?"

"Sure," said Fred, and went over to snip a sunflower. He delivered it to us with a flourish. The little family of four waved good bye as Babs and I returned to the gardens.

Babs raised her eyebrows at me as we rounded the corner to where Mrs. Dulcet waited. "That settles that."

"Except for her," I said, nodding toward Amanda Clark. For the first time all morning, she wasn't surrounded by staff. They'd left her to examine some exquisite looking long-stemmed roses and pussy willow branches. I took one fortifying look at my sunflower. "I'd better go talk to her."

"You've got this, honey," Babs said, and then sent me off with a firm smack to the rump.

I glared at her over my shoulder, straightening out my expression the closer I got to Mrs. Clark. When I reached her side, I made a noise of appreciation for the flowers. "They're beautiful," I offered. "Pretty colors."

"Blech," Mrs. Clark said. "They clash like peanut butter and ketchup. I thought they had professionals here who knew their flowers. Instead, they've sent the three stooges. Do they not know who I am?"

"Then it's a good thing I've got the flowers sorted!"

"You do?" She glanced my way with a flick of her eyes. At the sight of the yellow bloom in my hand, she wrinkled her nose. "What is that?"

Her tone of voice made it seem as if I was offering her a smelly old dishtowel for a sniff. My knees positively trembled with nerves. I'd never spoken with Dane's mother on my own, let alone stood up to her.

"Mrs. Clark, it's a sunflower," I said, twisting the stem around. The bloom was as big as my face and as bright as a highlighter. "I'd like to have a simple bouquet of a few sunflowers. We have permission to pick them fresh from the garden next door on the morning of the wedding. As a bonus, it's free of charge!"

Amanda hesitated for a moment, inhaling a deep breath. Then she let it out like a burst of hot air and broke into a raucous laugh. I'd never seen the woman laugh so hard. "You're funny, Lola. I see why Dane says you have a sense of humor."

"I'm serious," I said, "I really like them."

"They're weeds."

"They are not weeds! And even if they were, they are beautiful," I said, feeling very defensive of weeds all of a sudden. I had the strange feeling I was somewhat of a weed in Mrs. Clark's perfectly cultivated garden. "They remind me of my grandmother. And they're bright! And fun and lively. They're perfectly fitting for a wedding on the Sunshine Shore. Most importantly, I love them."

My last statement was made a bit like a toddler, my chin tilted out firmly. Mrs. Clark didn't seem at all receptive to anything I'd said and merely stared blankly at me.

"Mrs. Clark, I need to talk to you about a few things," I said, my arms falling by my sides, the bright petals dangling around my knees. "This whole wedding business is getting out of control. Dane and I are simple—we want a simple wedding."

"Simply elegant," Mrs. Clark said, finding her breath. "That is the Clark way."

"Like it or not, Dane is a Clark too, and he has his own style. Soon enough, I'll be a Clark as well."

"Lord knows you have your own style," Mrs. Clark said, fanning herself. "You are not cut out to be a Clark, Lola. You are only becoming a member of the family because Dane has fallen for your...unique spirit."

Her words stung. "Frankly, I don't want to be a Clark if that requires 'simple elegance' and 'perfect etiquette' and a 'fun-free zone.' I want to have a warm and happy house, and if we have kids—they're watching movies, Mrs. Clark! They will sometimes eat popcorn and come into the house dirty. And, if we're not Clark enough for you, then maybe Dane would consider changing the company name to the Pink-Clark company. Has a nice little lingerie-store ring to it, don't you think?"

I hadn't meant to get so worked up, but my thoughts had been simmering for a while. Ever since I'd begun to crack the rough exterior of Dane Clark and expose the fissures of damage his mother had done underneath, I had harbored a bit of resentment for Amanda Clark. To this day, I couldn't be certain Mrs. Clark had ever kissed her son's forehead or hugged him to her in an embrace.

"You know what?" I said, on a roll. "I think we'll have a beach wedding. Just friends and family. A nice breezy dress, maybe a flower crown. I might even go barefoot."

I didn't really want a flower crown, and the sand on the beach was scalding hot—only tourists tried to go barefoot—but a part of me knew the hippie nature of my choices would really irk Mrs. Clark. Then again, the sunflower had already done the trick. She was well on her way to envisioning me as a flower child dancing naked under a full moon—I could see the horror in her eyes.

"Fine," she said with a snip. "If this wedding is a joke to you, then I will let my son know my concerns with the marriage as a whole."

"Mrs. Clark, I'm sorry. I didn't mean all of that, but yes—I wouldn't mind a beach wedding. I really do want sunflowers. I'm negotiable on the flower crown and the bare feet," I said carefully, "but my point is that the wedding is supposed to be about us."

"The wedding is about the Clark name, not about *you*," she said with a snip. "Media will be there. Investors. My husband's business contacts. I'm not introducing them to a daughter-in-law with a flower crown!"

Her voice grew more and more shrill as she spoke until I finally had to wince and step back. There was no way to misinterpret her meaning. "I understand you think I'm not good enough for Dane, and I've come to terms with that. I don't ask that you love me, I don't even ask that you like me, but I do ask you to respect your son's choice to love and marry me."

Mrs. Clark gave a negligible shake of her head, but she kept her mouth shut.

"Even if you dislike everything about me, you can't deny that I am so in love with your son," I said, my lip quivering. I tended to do that when I tried to imagine how much I loved Dane. It was a huge, intimidating vastness that I couldn't quite comprehend—that's how much I loved him. "I can't convince you of that any more than I already have. The rest of this—how everything goes—is up to you."

"You mean the wedding?"

"No! I mean our relationship. Me and you, Mrs. Clark."

"We don't need to have a relationship," she said. "I thought you were coming around when you planned the gala for the festivals, but now, you've taken ten steps backward."

"I'm sorry you feel that way," I said. "And I hope you'll come to our wedding."

"Hope I'll come? I chose the invitations."

"I know—that's the problem. You're choosing everything, and you haven't even consulted me. Like it or not, Mrs. Clark, we'll share a last name soon. Your son loves you very much, but his loyalty will be to me, as your husband's loyalty is to you. That's the way it should be."

Mrs. Clark merely cleared her throat. "His loyalty is to the Clark name and our family. You are fitting into us and not the other way around."

"You weren't a Clark!" I said. "You were just like me once upon a time. You married into the family. Did Randall's mother treat you like this?"

From her silence, I wondered if the answer had been yes.

"Well, I'm sorry then," I said. "I don't know if she broke you down and forced you to change, but if she did, that's a shame. I happen to like myself just the way I am, Mrs. Clark—and if that makes me a weed in your garden, I'm sorry."

"Me too."

I gave a guttural sigh. "Fine."

"What?"

"Fine," I said, clutching the thick stem of the sunflower to my chest. "If you want the ceremony and the dress and the flowers and the shoes, we'll do it. You can plan everything you want, and I will just show up."

"Now you're speaking sense."

I had another retort hot and ready, but I felt tears brimming at the back of my eyes and decided to turn and leave while I was somewhat ahead. Even as I stormed off, however, I felt the fury build, my fingers clenched. The ceremony didn't bother me—the fancy dress, the etiquette, the what have you. It didn't bother me she wanted me to play a brief role on the stage of Amanda Clark's life when in public.

What bothered me was the sadness.

My future mother-in-law despised me. Maybe I shouldn't have let someone else's opinion bother me, but it sucked knowing I wasn't wanted. Like it or not, soon this would be my only family. I didn't expect to get a mother out of the deal, but maybe a hint of grudging respect or friendship. Instead, I was the ugly duckling of the Clark family name, and according to Amanda Clark, I would never be good enough for her son.

"What's wrong?" Babs asked, reaching down to scoop up the flower I'd let fall as I rushed past her. "Where are you going?"

"Forget about it," I said. "It's not really my wedding; it's just a show. I want to go home."

"Oh, Lola—" Mrs. Dulcet reached for me, but I merely shook my head. "Let me talk to her."

"No, I was supposed to be able to convince her to like me, but I failed." I found Semi waiting for the car. "It doesn't matter—I have business to take care of, and the clock's ticking. Let's go."

"Wait—ma'am! Please!" A voice called from across the gardens, and a young man in dirtied jeans and a stained T-shirt jogged awkwardly across the lawn. "Are you Miss Pink?"

"Yep," I said. "I'm certainly not a Clark."

The young man had beads of sweat on his head from the hot sun. "I have a delivery for you. Phone order, just called in."

"From who?" My heart pounded, and I wondered if this was Mrs. Clark's passive-aggressive form of apology. It would fit her style.

"There's a card, ma'am," he said. "I'm not sure—I was just asked to deliver the flowers to the pretty woman getting into the black car."

I fumbled with the card, finding my name scrawled across the front of it. What I found inside was not an apology. If anything, it was the exact opposite.

Lola Pink—

We meet tonight.

Come alone or Trey and Dane will die—slowly.

Bring your purse. More information to follow.

—A secret admirer

"Oh, are those flowers from Dane?" Mrs. Dulcet clapped her hands. "Maybe that boy has learned some romance. I always knew your rom-com movie education would be good for him."

"Yeah, exactly," I said faintly. "That's it. Actually, I should—ah, get home to him."

Babs stared curiously at me but had the smarts to remain silent. "I'll go to the castle too, maybe have a bite to eat with Lola while Dane finishes his meetings."

"Wonderful," I said, catching a glimpse of the battered sunflower in Babs's hand.

She quickly deposited it outside the car when she caught me staring, and then Semi cranked the car into gear. As we left, the tires rolled over the bloom and smooshed its fine petals into dust.

Chapter 17

Semi cleared his throat on the drive home. "Has anyone heard from Annalise lately? I thought she might be here today."

"Oh, you big oaf—she's stalking you," Babs blurted. "She's madly in love with you. Sweep her off her feet already, will you? You both want it."

The car fell into absolute shocked silence .

"Sorry," Babs said. "I'm a bit on edge. What I meant is she'd like to talk to you, Semi."

He gave a nod, and that was the extent of the conversation for the rest of the drive home.

After unloading from the car, Mrs. Dulcet wisely let her brownie arguments slip away as she hurried into the kitchen. Semi stood outside the vehicle looking lost while Babs pulled an apologetic face after her outburst in the car.

"Semi, can you have my bike ready for me?" I asked, more to give the poor man something to do as opposed to my need for it. Then again, there was a possibility I'd need it sooner than expected. I hadn't decided what to do about the note in my hands, or the fact that my fingers trembled every time I glanced down at it. "I have an errand to run this afternoon, and I don't want to bother Dane."

"Miss Pink, I think he would prefer—"

"I can use the fresh air," I said pointedly. "I need some thinking time."

"Some thinking time wouldn't hurt you either, Semi," Babs said, and then slapped a hand over her mouth. "Sorry, I really need to shut up more often. But in all seriousness, if you have any romantic feelings left toward Annalise, well, don't be afraid to act on them."

"Babs," I warned. "Now is probably not the best time to be discussing this."

"No, I know I shouldn't interfere in someone else's relationship in the first place," she agreed. Then she turned directly to Semi and continued anyway. "But it's so difficult seeing the two of you apart when you both seem miserable. I mean, Annalise is miserable. I guess you've never really told me how you feel."

Semi just stared at Babs.

"How about that bike?" I asked, giving him relief from the conversation. "You have a lot going on, and Babs isn't pressuring you into doing anything."

Once Semi disappeared, Babs and I let ourselves into the castle and came to a stop in the entryway.

Babs looked expectantly at me. "What's next?"

"Not here," I whispered. "We have to go—Dane, hello!"

My instructions to Babs were interrupted by my smiling fiancé who was strolling toward the front door flanked by three men and Stacey. They all had smiles on their faces.

"I'm hoping your grinning faces mean the meeting was a success?" I asked carefully. "How did everything go?"

"Excellent," Dane said, pulling me toward him and planting a celebratory kiss on my forehead. "You were brilliant Lola—bringing Stacey in to help was exactly what the meeting needed."

"Hooray!" I cheered. "I am so glad. Congrats to both of you."

"How was flower shopping?" Dane asked, a look of concern flicking across his face. "Did everything go okay?"

"It was fine. I'll fill you in later," I said. "Anyway, I don't want to hold anything up—you all look busy."

"Actually..." Stacey cleared her throat. "Dane, if you have a few minutes, there is something I'd like to discuss with you."

"Of course," Dane said, glancing toward me. "Unless there is something else pressing?"

"Have a ball," I said, trying for lighthearted. "I'll come find you after, Dane. Call me when you're done."

I knew Stacey's meeting with Dane was the most pressing thing at the moment. She could loop Dane into our theories about Artur while I figured out what to do with the dang card from the flower shop.

"I'll be in my office," Dane said quietly. Before turning away, he discreetly let his finger trail down my arm. It left small sparks as it descended, and his lips pressed a soft kiss to my forehead, then a lingering one to my mouth.

Both Stacey and Babs had vanished by the time we parted in the hallway. It was like I'd gone into a little trance at his touch and completely forgotten we'd had company in the first place.

"Wow," I breathed. "That was so nice. You are so nice. I love you, Dane."

"Is everything okay?"

I squeezed my arms around him and pulled tight. "It will be."

"Lola—"

"Got the Oreos." Babs popped back into the hallway after pilfering cookies and milk from the kitchen. "Whoops, you two aren't done yet. Hurry it along, will you, Dane? It's girl time."

Dane gave a perfunctory nod in Babs's direction, his eyes scanning the cookies. He wanted to comment, I could feel it.

"Go ahead," I said on a sigh. "I know you need to get it off your chest."

"Those things are full of preservatives," Dane said. "The amount of fat and sugar in one cookie, let alone an entire box of them—"

"It's a line," Babs said. "Us cookie connoisseurs call it a line of Oreos. You know, it's our drug of choice."

"You're a bad influence on my wife," Dane said with a shake of his head. "If we were to have a child—"

"Are you pregnant?" Babs turned to look at me. "Is that why there's all this talk of a flowy wedding dress? I knew it. You're glowing."

"That's exhaustion," I told her. "I'm not pregnant."

"You might have been pregnant?" Dane asked me. "And you didn't say anything?"

I reached out and snatched the Oreos. "Not pregnant, never have been, not planning on it in the very near future. I need a cookie."

Leaning onto my tiptoes, I smacked a kiss onto Dane's cheek. He returned it, lingering longer than usual in an effort to show Babs's who was boss. They had a semi-passive-aggressive power struggle every now and again. In some ways, they were too similar to get along. I had a friend type, apparently, since I loved them both.

"Yeah, yeah, we get it—you're in love." Babs took my arm and pulled me away just as Stacey returned with two lattes—probably Mrs. Dulcet's handiwork.

I took one last glance over my shoulder at Dane, knowing he wouldn't want me handling the kidnapper on my own, no matter what the words on the page said. If I let him see the card, he'd find some way to transfer responsibility for it to himself, and I couldn't let that happen.

The lives of two men balanced precariously in my hands. I felt as if I'd been given a precious snow globe and told to walk across a tight rope. If it fell and shattered, the man I loved would die.

With a shudder, I led Babs to the bedroom that used to be mine. Everything was still as it had been: The space shower was some weird, partly functioning piece of technology in the bathroom. The regal bed had fluffed pillows and a fat comforter that were ready for my weary head. The walk-in closet remained decked out with clothing that would fit my body perfectly. Yet somehow, it all felt foreign.

Moving in officially with Dane had felt right from the first moment I'd slipped into bed with him. It was as if I'd never known anything else. As if there'd been no bumps or hardships on the way to getting there, as if the universe had somehow destined me to find my way beside Dane. My life before him seemed to belong to someone else, just like this room.

"Spill."

I could barely hear Babs's command over the ripping sound of her tearing into the cookies. She pulled a tray from the nightstand onto the bed, loaded the sweets and milk glasses on it, and dunked.

"Something's not right, Lola," she continued around a mouthful of crumbs. "I've known you forever and something is up with you today."

"You mean besides the fact that Dane's mother hates me?"

"She doesn't hate you," Babs said. "She's just really set in her ways and can't get over the fact her son is marrying a hippie. Or a free spirit. Or just... you know, someone fun. You're not a society type, and that's a good thing—you don't have to change. Either she'll come around or she won't, and that'll be her loss. I give her until grandkids, and then all her holdouts will collapse."

"Great," I said dryly. "I have to bribe her with children."

"Hey, the fruit of your loins is a very powerful thing," Babs said, working through cookie number two. "Sit down and stop stalling or I'm going to gain fifteen pounds, and I have to wear a bridesmaid's dress in a fancy wedding—in case you haven't heard."

"Semi's brother is missing, as you know."

"You told me. Any updates? Did he turn up? I did some digging on Trey, and I've been meaning to tell you, that kid has a past."

"I know," I said. "But we don't think that has anything to do with the reason he's gone."

"Really?" Babs sounded legitimately surprised. "I mean, the kid used to hang around with the wrong crowd. If he got back in touch with them, or crossed them in any way, I can see how things could get ugly."

"I thought so too, but the more we've dug into it, the more we suspect that's not what happened. We are almost certain Trey was kidnapped, and I think there's a chance it had something to do with Trey's work at the Clark Company." I reached for a cookie and proceeded to fill Babs in on what had transpired the night before, along with my lack of sleep and a few of our suspects. At her surprised face, I shook my head and swallowed the rest of the Oreo interior. "Unfortunately, that's not the end of it."

"You're telling me that some Russian company—a competitor of Dane's—might be behind Trey's disappearance?"

"It's very possible," I said. "Stacey's meeting with Dane right now is to go over that possibility as we speak. I figured she might want some privacy, seeing as it's her ex-fiancé and all."

"That's not fair—I want in on the action," Babs said. "I took the afternoon off work and everything to go to the gardens."

"We have something even bigger to deal with than a wedding," I said sadly. "And I'm going to let you in on the action. But if I do, you *must* promise you'll keep it a secret. No matter what."

"Fine." Babs heaved a huge sigh as if I'd asked her to sacrifice herself to the gods. "If I must."

I pulled the note out from my purse and handed it over. Her facial expressions fluctuated as she read through the message. I could tell when she started from the beginning a second time because she went through the same emotional rollercoaster all over again.

"What?" she finally concluded. "Bring your purse? What the hell does that mean?"

"I've been thinking about that the entire way home." I pulled my purse onto my lap. "At first, I was almost certain it had something to do with identification."

"You think he's going to whisk you off to another country?!"

I shook my head. "That'd be stupid. If he wanted to do that, he should've been smart enough to have a fake ID, and if his intention was to kidnap me, he'd know that the police would be tracking my IDs, credit cards, etc."

"That doesn't explain what he wants."

"I think he's been watching us, and I think he wants this." I pulled out the small translator device I'd accidentally swiped from Stacey's demonstration. "It's a prototype and not ready for market, but in the hands of the right person it could do damage. With the right tools, a competitor could make a whole new product faster than the Clark Company, and Dane would lose millions if not more."

"Someone like Artur," Babs said. "Evil genius and all."

"We don't know that, but it seems to be the likeliest solution. If it's not him, I don't know who else it would be," I said hesitantly. "On the plus side, if Artur is simply after the chip, theoretically, he won't hurt me or Trey once he gets it."

"And on the negative side?"

I winced. "He's already broken his promise to release Trey once, and he's killed a man already."

"Poor Fat Jim." Babs gave me a tentative look. "You have to show Dane. He'll know what to do."

"You promised," I reminded Babs. "I shouldn't even be sharing the note with you, but I'm trusting you to be my backup, Babs. You gave me your word you wouldn't tell anyone."

She groaned. "That was before I knew the extent of it!"

"A promise is a promise," I said, "and speaking of promises, I told Dane I wouldn't go running straight into the arms of a kidnapper without telling him first. Or something like that. So, I'm going to write him a letter. You have to stay behind and give it to him."

"I can't do that."

"Give me half an hour from the time I leave the front door, and then give him this. Hopefully, I'll be back with Trey safely in tow before that ever needs to happen."

"I can't do that," Babs said. "I can't let you go alone—what if it's a trap? What if the kidnapper's after you?"

"I will have Semi handcuff you to this bed if I need to," I said dryly. "I don't have a choice. Did you not read the consequences if I show the letter to anyone else? The kidnapper will go after Trey and Dane."

"I know." She gave a shuddering breath. "But there's another way, there has to be. We can figure something out."

"We haven't been able to yet," I said. "Plus, Stacey and Dane are looking into Artur as we speak. Their time is better used tracking him, trying to get the jump on Artur in case he gets away with Dane's technology. He'll need to be hunted down, even if we get Trey back safely."

"I'd rather him steal technology than you," Babs said. "Can't you just mail the device to him? Get a good old-fashioned courier service to take care of this crap?"

"He likes to have control," I said. "He's a hands-on sort of kidnapper. Babs, I really don't think there's a way around this. I'm sorry."

"I refuse. I will scream if you have me handcuffed to this bed."

I put my finger on the note, accentuating the word die.

"If he kills Dane, what's the point of anything? Money, love, life..." I shook my head feeling my eyes well with tears. "If the situation were reversed, Dane would do the exact same thing for me. That's what a marriage is, isn't it? Equal partners?"

"Uh, yeah, for doing the dishes," Babs said. "Not sacrificing yourself to a kidnapper and murderer."

The purse on my lap began to ring. I fished around for my phone, and with trembling fingers, I hit the speaker button. "Yes?"

"Did you like your flowers?" The robotic voice-changer spoke clearly. When I didn't answer, he continued. "Leave now. Meet me at the second bend in the road where you found the key. It shouldn't take you long by bike. You have twenty-four minutes to arrive before I start killing people."

I hung up the phone which was unnecessary because the kidnapper had already disconnected. With a resolute glance at Babs, I stilled my shaking hands and raised my jaw in a defiant way—faking my confi-dence.

"You can help me or not," I said. "I have work to do."

Chapter 18

The next four minutes passed in a blur.

I took three and a half of the minutes sweating over my letter to Dane, eventually forcing myself to scrawl down a half-explanation and a half-apology that would have to do for now. I knew Dane would be upset that I didn't consult with him first, but I also knew he'd have done the same thing in my position. I wouldn't toy with his life. That was non-negotiable in my book, and it superseded my promise to not run straight into the kidnapper's arms.

Meanwhile Babs paced across the room, crumbs spewing from her mouth as she chomped unknowingly on cookies. A waste of calories, she'd mumbled, since she wasn't tasting them. I didn't enjoy putting her in this position. I knew the quandary she was suffering between: Loyalty to me, or her best effort to prevent me from doing something stupid. If I were in her shoes, I'd be suffering in the exact same way, minus a few of the crumbs.

I shoved the note into the matching envelope I'd found in the rustic little desk tucked against one wall and hesitated. Glancing at the bed, I debated leaving it on the blanket at the foot of it.

"Oh, give it to me," Babs said, snatching it out of my hand with a sniff. "Of course I'm going to help you. Even if I think you're a stubborn twat."

"Thank you," I gushed. "I—that means a lot to me. I wouldn't do this if there were any other way."

"I know." Babs clutched me to her. "Be careful."

I caught a whiff of sugar and roses and fresh outdoor air. I hugged her tighter. "I will."

"I'm not giving you thirty minutes," Babs said. "I haven't figured out how long exactly I'm giving you, but you better get a move on before I change my mind."

I nodded in understanding. "Thank you. And tell Dane—"

"Yes, yes, everyone knows you love him, Lola. Your public displays of affection say it all. Now go before I come to my senses and handcuff you to the bed."

I cruised through the castle, pushing past or leaping over anything in my way. I elbowed a random staff member on accident and bounced off the wall as I stumbled.

"Sorry," I hollered over my shoulder as I barreled toward the kitchen.

I came to an abrupt stop when I heard Dane and Stacey speaking. They were having their meeting with the door of a small conference room propped open, their words carrying out. Judging by the severity of their tones, they were discussing Artur.

"How can we contact him?" Dane asked. "Do you—have you ever tried to get in touch with him since..."

"No." Stacey's response was sharp. "I figured your resources could check to see if he's traveled to the States recently."

"There are ways around flying commercial airlines," Dane said, equally saucy in his response. "Private jets, aliases—I'm sure you're aware."

"I have no clue which route he used—we never traveled together for obvious reasons," Stacey said coolly. "But I imagine we must find out fast. Trey's been gone what—nearly forty-eight hours? Artur is patient...until he isn't. He'll be antsy and will make a move soon."

If only they knew, I thought grimly. Then I jumped as a hand touched my shoulder.

"Everything alright there, Lola?" Mrs. Dulcet chirped. "Are you and Babs enjoying your girl time? Would you like some wine sent to your room?"

I noticed the conversation in the other room had faltered. Panic set in—I had to move before my entire plan was ruined. There was no other backup plan.

"Actually," I murmured, keeping my voice down as I nodded for Mrs. Dulcet to follow me. "I have a quick errand to run and am going to clear my head outside. Babs is taking a quick nap—rough day for both of us."

"Shall I get Mr. Clark—"

"No, I don't want to interrupt," I said, waving my hand. "He and Stacey are probably figuring out what to do with the Germans. You know, business."

I gave a hearty chuckle and Mrs. Dulcet didn't quite chime in, but she nodded along.

"Very well then," she said. "Semi has just pulled your—ah, bike around front."

"Excellent."

I didn't pause for a goodbye, well aware I was pushing it by taking so long to leave. I knew I'd have to will my legs to pedal extra hard to reach the second bend in the road near the back of the Clark Company property in time. It couldn't have been a coincidence that it was the same spot chosen as where Annalise had spooked Darius. This play confirmed that whoever had hired Darius also had Trey. The connection still baffled me.

The only thing that remotely made sense was if this whole thing was a trap...

My heart pounded. A wave of stupidity rolled over my shoulders. If Trey was waiting for me, that would mean almost everything we'd done so far was pointless. It would mean we'd played right into his hands. Maybe this had been a con all along. Maybe I was the one meant to be kidnapped this whole time, and the rest of the mess had been a carefully laid ploy leading me into the mouth of the beast.

All he would have to do was tighten his jaw, and he'd have the Clark Company on its knees, and I'd be lucky to stay alive...

Or, it could be Artur on the hunt for technology. Maybe this was as simple as it seemed—a quick trade: Trey for the prototype. Easy peasy. Dane's company might be out a lot of money, but that was a trivial cost to pay in order to save a life.

Or maybe, it was someone else entirely. Someone like: "*Billy*?"

My voice rattled as I skidded around the second bend. I stopped mere inches away from where we'd found Darius's grated down car key. I blinked, struggling to understand as I set my bike down.

"What are you doing here? Did you get..." My mouth went dry as Billy stepped from the passenger's side of an average looking blue mini-van—probably lifted from an unsuspecting family on the Shore—and pointed a gun at me. "Drop the bike and get in the van. Did you bring the purse?"

"I don't understand," I said. "What are you doing here? Do you have Trey? Is this—are you behind everything?"

"I assume the prototype you lifted from Stacey is in the purse, isn't it?" he asked, skipping straight to business. "Don't worry, I was watching more than you know."

"Did you follow us that first night back from Trey's?" I asked. "Have you been behind everything?"

He looked cross. "Yes! Why's it so hard to believe I could come up with a master plan that would actually work? You know, it doesn't matter. Get in the car and show me the device on the way. I don't want to waste time on your boyfriend's property."

"He's my fiancé." I tried to sound offended and strong as I cracked open my purse and took several steps forward until he met me in the middle of the road. As I glanced over his shoulder, I caught sight of a figure in the front seat. "Trey?"

Trey's eyes flicked back to me, but he didn't meet my gaze.

"Trey doesn't talk much anymore," Billy said, snatching the bag out of my hands. "Let's get rid of this, just in case you've got any other surprises in there."

Billy tossed my purse in the front seat of the van before withdrawing a set of handcuffs from his waistband. "Turn around."

"But—"

"Now."

I turned, closing my eyes as I felt the click of cool metal against my wrists. *Billy*? My brain worked overtime trying to piece things together. Had Artur roped him into this in an attempt to exploit an old friendship of Trey's? The payoff had to be big; I'd bet Artur would pay a huge sum of money to get back at Dane for stealing Stacey and foiling his attempt to corrupt the Clark Company. Artur would have been planning this for ages, no doubt.

"Get in," he instructed. "You try anything, and Trey gets a bullet. Don't you, buddy?"

I slid into the van's middle row, keeping my eyes focused on Trey. Semi's brother was a much smaller version. Trey wore glasses, though one of the hinges was broken and they sat lopsided on his face. He was handcuffed in front of his body with enough room to maneuver the steering wheel.

Billy pointed the gun at Trey. "Drive. You know where we're going."

"Are you going to tell me what this is about?" I demanded as the vehicle eased forward. "At the very least, I deserve that. I brought you the purse and tech like you wanted. Let Trey go."

"I will, but my plan is not over yet."

"Why kidnap me? You know Dane won't let this rest. He'll come after me at any moment now. We were supposed to meet—he will know I'm gone."

"Don't worry. This won't take long." Billy gave me a thin smile. "Just a little cleanup, I'm sure you'll understand. Everything will work out okay for you, Miss Pink, I promise."

"Who are you working with?" I shifted, glancing out the windows for any sign of Dane or Babs. Technically Dane shouldn't be aware anything was wrong yet, but maybe Babs had gotten impatient and given him the note early. "Who put you up to this?"

"That's what's wrong with you all," Billy snarled, his eyebrows pinning together. "That's what's wrong with this whole world. Write off the poor, the lowlifes. Surely, we can't accomplish anything. Once someone's taken a stumble, it's impossible to get back up—is that it?"

"No, Billy—that's not what I mean. What was your incentive to kidnap Trey? You have the tech—so what? It would take a huge company and millions of dollars to do anything with it."

"Trey and I were good old pals back in the day." Billy's eyes flicked toward the driver's seat. "Lifted cars, small heists, dabbled a bit in the drug trade. And then this one outgrew us. Decided he was too good for the crew. We had a good thing going, didn't we, Trey?"

Trey gritted his teeth together and glared at the road. Apparently, he'd used all his words and hadn't refilled the well.

"This one got recruited by his brother and Clark. They hauled his ass up to the castle, cleaned him up, taught him some fancy math—before I knew it, he'd gotten himself the hottest condo on the Shore looking down on the rest of us."

"It's not like that," I said. "He worked hard. Everyone at the Clark Company works incredibly hard. If he was recruited, it's because Dane saw the potential in him. Trey's brilliant."

"Is he any better than me? *Really*?" Billy shook his head. "I could've done it too. I could've had the condo on the hill, but I wasn't chosen because I wasn't lucky enough to have a big brother with connections. It's not fair I'm being punished because I don't have family in the right places."

"You're not being punished for anything," I said. "Trey's success has nothing to do with you. That was all about him."

"Well, I don't like to watch other people find success while I linger around," he said. "You saw my place. It's a rat's nest. I have to have a roommate to make ends meet. I'm getting old if you haven't noticed. I'm staring down the barrel at thirty, and I don't want a roommate anymore. But the Shore's expensive."

"I thought you got a real job."

"Right." He sniffed. "The gas station didn't pay enough, so I had to find funds elsewhere."

"The rumors of a *new* drug dealer in town—that's all false, isn't it? There's nobody new moving in—it's just you, upping your stakes. That's why you were involved with Fat Jim."

"Bingo," he said. "I decided to open a new line of business. Fat Jim knew about it, which was fine. We had an arrangement."

"Then something went wrong," I said, puzzling through the pieces. "We went to visit him and got to talking about Trey. Fat Jim put two and two together because he knew the two of you went way back. He figured it out: Your new line of business wasn't only drugs, it was kidnapping. He was on his way to break the news to us, but you got to him first."

"The man couldn't keep his trap shut," Billy said, horrifyingly unremorseful. "That's what I paid him to do—help sweep things under the rug when they got out of control, but he decided he didn't want to have anything to do with kidnapping. Decided it was below him. As if the man had any moral ground to stand on."

"And trying to do the right thing got him killed," I said as a wash of sympathy rolled over my shoulders. "I don't have a particular soft spot for Fat Jim, but that was cold of you to do."

"It's my fault." Trey spoke for the first time, his voice hoarse. "If I hadn't gone and trusted this idiot in the first place, none of this would be happening. I'm sorry."

"It's not your fault," I said, and then clarified. "I don't think. What do you mean you trusted Billy?"

"He means I came to him," Billy interrupted. "I'd heard the story—I was friends with Trey, remember? Semi interfered to keep his moron brother from overdosing, Dane Clark took a liking to the kid, and then he got rich. Well, I wanted to get rich. I asked Trey if he'd help me get on my feet."

"And because Trey is a good guy," I said, feeling the anger furl in my stomach, "he decided to try and pay things forward just like Dane had done for him. You exploited his good intentions."

"I exploited his stupidity," Billy said. "I had him really going for some time, teaching me programming, giving me all these lessons in engineering. I told Trey I wanted a job interview, but that wasn't exactly true. I just needed a way inside the gates."

"Then Trey got suspicious?" I pressed.

"You got it. See, I wanted to rekindle an old business partnership, but Trey refused," Billy said. "I got him to show me a few real business plans for the purposes of 'education', but then I pushed too far, and he was onto me. He left me no choice but to do something about it."

Trey jerked the car into a particularly hard left-turn, and I watched the familiar countryside as we climbed higher and higher above the shoreline and away from the castle.

"I had a feeling he was going to give up mentoring me," Billy said, "and I couldn't let all of my hard work go to waste, so I had to make a move. As for the actual technology, well, I don't have to understand it in order to sell it to the highest bidder."

"You won't get away with any of this," Trey said. "They'll find you."

"Dane Clark isn't a murderer," Billy said easily.

"He will be if you lay a finger on me," I said evenly. "And the same goes for Semi if you touch Trey."

A brief flash of panic flitted over Billy's face, but it passed quickly. "Guess I'll have to take my chances at this point."

"Not if you let us go now. We can pretend we didn't see who took us," I said. "Right, Trey? We'll give you a twenty-four-hour head start before we suddenly remember."

"Not Trey. It's too late for my good little Samaritan." Billy reached over and stroked a finger playfully, horribly, down Trey's face. "He's gone over to the good side. I figure, why go over to the good side if it's so much work? One quick kidnapping, a cool couple mil, and I'll take off from the Shore and start somewhere else. Somewhere I won't be the bottom of the barrel for once."

I was peripherally aware of the car picking up speed, going faster and faster, but I chalked it up to anticipated nerves. I focused on Billy as my heart raced and my palms began to sweat.

"Don't worry," Billy said casually, glancing out the window. "When I kill you, I'll let you be the hero, Miss Pink. Trey will be the villain."

"You can't—"

"The demo device will be missing. I'll leave a wad of cash on Trey's body—just enough so everyone will believe he sold it for a quick buck. His fingerprints will be on the gun that kills you, and then he'll shoot himself."

"Nobody will believe that," I said. "Why would he go through all the effort, score the cash, and then off himself?"

Billy shrugged. "Let them wonder. Maybe they'll chalk it up to his good conscience, or maybe they'll suspect it was foul play. I don't really care either way because I'll be long gone with a new identity and way more cash than you've ever dreamed of, Miss Pink."

"I'm marrying Dane Clark," I said. "I understand what a lot of money means."

"True, but it's not yours—not yet. You can't hold it in your hands, spend it as you wish, pay to become another person." His eyes gleamed at the thought. "What are you doing?"

Billy's gaze swiveled to Trey. It wasn't my imagination; the car had indeed been speeding up. Trey had done it in such a way that Billy hadn't noticed until it was too late. The car was passing ninety miles an hour when I looked.

"You're going to kill us anyway," Trey said, his eyes flicking toward the rearview mirror. "I might as well do it first. With your permission, Miss Pink."

I had a split second to make my choice—no answer was a good one. If we parked, that gun would be on my forehead and then Trey's—we already knew that. Billy had told us, and he wasn't going to have a change of heart. He'd already murdered once, and he'd do it again.

While I rapidly processed all of this, I looked into Trey's eyes, and I saw something there. Determination, the will to live—something. And I understood. I gave him the subtlest nod just as Billy made his move.

"You idiot!" Billy screeched, startling both of us. "You're going to kill us all!"

Billy jerked the emergency brake from the center console of the vehicle, driving the car into a crazy spiral. My head jerked as my body slammed against the seatbelt.

We skidded off the road, the car flipped. It rolled over, jostling us, throwing our bodies like limp rag dolls as airbags deployed in every direction. We flipped again, screeching to a stop after barreling through hedges, bushes, and narrowly missing a tree.

We landed upside down along the side of the road, the roof groaning and creaking as the vehicle stabilized. I collapsed, letting my body dangle, broken and bruised, bleeding from somewhere, suspended above the top of the car—now the bottom. Trey hung limply in the driver's seat, his cuffed hands dangling before him.

A rustle came from the passenger's seat, followed by another *thunk*. My view was blocked, but Billy must have kicked the door open because in the next second, he stood outside. His nose looked a broken bloody mess and his left wrist hung at a distorted angle. In an almost comical twist of events, he had the purse slung over his opposite shoulder and a gun sitting in his right hand.

"Trey!" I shouted. "Trey, wake up!"

Semi's brother stirred, blinked, but remained unresponsive.

"You thought you could kill us all," Billy said, raising the gun to point it at me. "But you only sped along the inevitable. Last words, Pink?"

"Trey," I shouted again. "Wake up!"

This time, he woke. His eyes flickered open, though he appeared dazed and disoriented. Out of the corner of his eye he caught sight of Billy pointing the gun at me, and it shifted something in him. He tried to focus and found his voice.

"Lola," he said gruffly. "I'm so sorry. I can't move. I would—I would take the bullet for you."

"What's the auto-detonate code?" I'd gotten the idea on the car ride over, but I hadn't been sure how big the blast from the auto-detonate function would be, and I couldn't risk trying to signal Trey with my escape plan. "The auto-detonate feature on your prototype, Trey."

"If you're gonna shoot," Trey said, ignoring me as he yelled at Billy. "Shoot me first, you bastard. Lola is innocent." Then he lowered his voice. "The code is *Escape-0911*."

"Escape-0911!" I screamed. "*Escape-0911!*"

A monotone, robotic voice began to chant: "Voice Activated Detonation: Demo A—Terminate in 5, 4, 3—"

The detonation countdown sequence was interrupted by a bullet rocketing through the car. It plunged into Trey's shoulder. His tortured cry of pain was drowned out by the ringing in my ears. Billy stumbled as he reached down for the purse, looking confused as to where the robotic voice was coming from. We'd probably all suffered slight concussions, and now on top of it, we were deafened by the reverb from the shot that had hit Trey.

"—2, 1!" The device finished the countdown before Billy could locate it in the bag.

Billy realized what was happening just a second before the last command finished. With urgency, he ripped the purse from his shoulder, but it got caught around his elbow. Just as he began to fling it, the device exploded, sending my purse into the air in a flaming ball of fabric.

Billy yanked his hands back, his fingers likely singed as the gun fell to the ground. Unfortunately, the blast was not large enough to put him entirely out of commission. Within seconds, he was reaching for the gun and raising it toward me.

The roar of an engine cut him off. He scowled, turning to flee at the sound of car brakes screeching to a stop somewhere behind the van. I was at once relieved and disheartened—he hadn't managed to kill me, but he might get away. Trey, however, was not so lucky. He was in bad shape; I could hear it in his ragged breaths.

Dane appeared seconds later and began wrenching doors open. I didn't see Semi at the car, so I imagined he'd taken off in pursuit of Billy. From somewhere in the distance, Babs screamed her lungs out as she presumably chased after both Semi and Billy in a crazed (and very futile) effort to help.

"Lola," Dane said, catching me as I fell out of the car. "I got your note. You are so..."

"Idiotic? Moronic? I know, I'm sorry," I said, clutching him. "Let's discuss that later. Trey needs to get to a hospital, and we need to get after Billy before he kills anyone else. He's hurt and on a rampage."

"I was going to say brave." Dane kissed my forehead. "And selfless."

By the time Dane got me out of the car, Semi had returned. Out of breath, he explained Billy had gotten away.

"I couldn't find him anywhere—I'll get him later. Where's Trey?" Semi asked, his eyes flicking toward the car. "Is he..."

"He's alive," I gasped. "But he needs medical care. And Semi—he saved my life."

Semi didn't wait before wrenching open the driver's side door and extracting his brother's limp body. He held Trey in his arms with as much effort as it would take to hold a pillow. "I'll get him to the hospital—you take Babs's car."

"Wait for me!" Babs held her shoes in her hands as she ran back across the grassy fields. We were just outside of Trey's neighborhood. We'd likely have been headed to Trey's condo where Billy had planned to orchestrate our murders.

"I'm taking you to the hospital," Dane warned as he put me into Babs's car. Apparently, Dane and Semi had tried to convince her to stay back after she'd passed along the note, but she had chased after them anyway. "Keys?"

Babs handed over her keys and climbed into the backseat. "Seriously, girlfriend. You look horrible, and you probably have a concussion."

"I'm just tired," I said. "I'll go after we chase down Billy, I swear. We can't let him get away."

"Where would he have gone?" Dane asked. "Any idea?"

The three of us sat in stumped silence for a second.

"I guess we should just start driving," I said. "He's on foot, so he can't have gotten too far. He's definitely inside the perimeter of the Sunshine Shore."

Dane gave a subtle nod of agreement and put the car in gear, waiting until Semi pulled out ahead of us with the black SUV and careened toward the hospital with Trey. Then Dane pulled onto the road, driving as smoothly and efficiently as he ran the rest of his business. Religiously, we drove up and down every street in the surrounding area looking for any sign of disturbance.

We all jumped when Dane's phone rang. He briefly checked the number and frowned. "Hmm."

"Who is it?" I asked.

"Unknown number," he said. "But nobody has this line except those who have my business cards. And I only give these cards out to..."

"Answer it," I demanded. "Just in case."

Dane put the phone to his ear. The voice on the other end blared loudly and familiarly. "Yo, is this Dane Clark with the titanium business card? This is some real James Bond stuff, you know."

"Darius," Dane said, his eyes flicking toward me as he hit the speaker button on his phone. "Look, it's a bad time right now. Can I call you back?"

"Sure, brother. Maybe you can just relay a message to your gorgeous girl."

Dane cleared his throat in a no-nonsense way. "Sure."

"I need some help, and I think she might like to see what I have here," he said nonchalantly. "I accidentally shot my landlady."

"You mean Billy?" I screeched in the background. "He went *home*?"

"Yeah, he didn't think I was home, and he came in here with guns blazing. Well, as you know, I was taking a...well, I was doing my business on the toilet. Good thing I keep the gun in the toilet. I got one shot off because the dude was trying to kill me! Good thing he missed, huh?"

I sat in stunned silence.

"Anyway, I hit him in the foot, and then I tied him up in the bathtub. He's sort of complaining and bleeding, and I'm a little worried about calling the police."

"Um, thanks for the call," I said dumbly. "We'll be right there to handle everything. You won't get in trouble, I swear."

"Yeah, but the gun isn't legal."

"You stopped a murderer," I said. "We'll work something out, Darius."

"Well," Dane said, disconnecting the call. "I guess we found him."

"Damn roommates," Babs said with a shake of her head. "You never know who you're gonna get, do you? Maybe you meet your best friend. Maybe you live with a murderer. Talk about a crapshoot."

Epilogue

"**A** or B?" the judge asked. The room was silent as a tomb. "Everyone must make a choice."

I glanced over at Babs who was sitting next to me. "Who are you voting for?"

She covered her paper with an arm and scowled. "No peeking at mine. Eat your own damn brownies."

"The brownies are eaten," I said. "I just don't have my vote. They're both equally good."

"Well, I've made my choice. You make yours." With a flourish, Babs jotted down her answer and then stood. "I'll be back."

Babs trotted to the front of Shades of Pink wearing a pair of hot pink pants and a light pink shirt in honor of the store's final day of construction. With a grin, she dropped her vote in the bin up front and scurried over to compare notes with Annalise, who had also voted already.

I thumbed my pencil against my mouth, trying to peek over at Dane's paper. He, too, shoved an arm across his answer, so I stalled, glancing around at the newly finished storefront.

The construction crew had finished work on Shades of Pink earlier this afternoon, so to celebrate, Mrs. Fredericks and Mrs. Dulcet had scheduled their brownie bake-off on location and gathered as many local residents as they could to flood my new space with fanfare and excitement.

"You can peek at my paper if you'd like," Darius said, sidling over toward where I sat with Dane. Darius waved his paper in my face. "But I'm not claiming to be smart about brownies or anything. Plus, I couldn't decide, so I voted for both. Free food is free food, you know."

"You can't do that," I said. "You need to pick one."

Darius shrugged. "Darius isn't very good about following the rules."

"Obviously," I said. "But maybe... you could think about it? You did promise the police."

"For the right price, I'll think about it," Darius said, raising an eyebrow as he jutted a hip not fully covered by his sagging jeans against the table before me. "Your fiancé hiring? I bet he could pay my right price."

"If I'm ever looking to hire someone with your skillset," Dane said. "You'll be the first to know."

"That's great, man." Darius gave him a salute. "Thanks again for all your help with the police the other night. I'm glad my little accident was sorted out."

By Darius's little accident, he meant shooting the man who'd kidnapped Trey and killed Fat Jim in his bathroom. While at it, Billy—the mastermind behind it all—had also tried his best to end my life, along with Trey's, so he could walk away from his little scheme with a million bucks in cash and a tech gadget he could sell for a lot of money on the black market.

Fortunately, Billy hadn't made it far from the scene of our car accident. The police found Billy whimpering in his own bathtub—handcuffed to the faucet and whining about a piece of his little toe that probably wouldn't grow back—thanks to Darius's quick reaction time. And the fact he had a gun stashed in his toilet.

The police had been more than a little confused at the situation, but after they took statements from me, Dane, Semi, Trey, Babs, and Darius, it had become clear that Billy was the man they wanted. Which made it quite easy for Dane to gently convince the cops to look the other way for Darius's little mistakes which, in the scheme of murder and kidnapping charges, were minimal.

Grudgingly, the cops had made Darius promise he'd find a real job and lay off the tourist scamming, and in exchange for his help wrangling Billy in for capture, they would let the charges slide. So long as he handed over his gun and drug paraphernalia. The choice was an easy one to make.

"Well, I guess I better go get another brownie or two," Darius said with a shrug. "I've already forgotten how they taste. Peace out, you two lovebirds."

"This place looks great," Dane said, leaning back in his chair and smiling over at me once Darius had slipped out of earshot. "Are you happy with how it turned out?"

I held a hand over my heart. "Happy? I'm speechless. Everything is perfect. I think—" I cleared my throat. "I think Dotty would approve."

Dane reached over and lovingly rubbed my shoulder. I leaned into him, still very concerned about my brownie vote. Sunset had hit a few minutes prior, bathing the room in a wash of oranges and pinks and purples. Huge, full-length windows spanned the store in every possible location, letting in light from all angles at all times of the day.

Walls had been knocked down to create an open space with only a small section cordoned off for personal use. The rest of it contained a coffee bar, gorgeous racks that would be covered with sunglasses, and plenty of squashy furniture as a tribute to the cozy, welcoming space that had naturally drawn visitors to Dotty for decades.

Biting down on my pen, I quickly made my choice and hurried up to cast my vote at the ballot box. We'd appointed Gerard as the judge this time around since he was unrelated to both bakers and unbiased. The rest of the vote would be anonymous.

"How are you feeling?" Stacey daintily dropped her vote into the box behind me. "I heard whispers about something happening the other night—I've been meaning to stop by sooner, but Mr. Clark had me on a flight to Germany, and I just got back."

"Oh, I'm fine," I said, pointing to my head. "Mild concussion, but what's new?"

She gave a dainty laugh. "So, you caught him, then? The culprit?"

I nodded. "It wasn't Artur. I'm really sorry I doubted you, Stacey. I hadn't meant to put you through all that. It sucks to have to revisit a painful past—I know."

"I understand." She blew a breath out and tucked a hair behind her ear. "I'm just glad everything's out in the open now."

She reached behind me and grabbed two glasses of champagne from the table. Someone had popped open a few bottles and poured a whole tableful of bubbly for the room. She handed me one.

We clinked glasses and shared a smile. We were interrupted by a soft-spoken voice as the next person in line excused themselves and dropped a note in the box. It was Trey.

"How are you feeling?" I asked him as Stacey politely faded into the background. "I'm glad you were able to make it tonight."

Trey gave a tense smile and gestured to his sling. "I've been worse."

I nodded, struggling with an appropriate topic of conversation. Despite our bonding moment over the auto-detonate feature, I didn't know the man, nor did I have anything in common with him except for Semi and Dane.

"Have you decided about your job?" I asked. "I know Dane would really like you to stay on with the Clark Company."

"I don't know," he said. "I resigned for a reason in the hospital. I don't deserve to work for Mr. Clark. He's already given me plenty of chances."

"Nobody blames you for what happened," I said. "You can't blame yourself for the actions of Billy. He was jealous and ruthless and smart enough to be dangerous. That's not your fault."

"If I hadn't offered to help him," Trey said, "or if I hadn't shared tidbits of the things we were working on, he never could have taken advantage of Mr. Clark like that."

"Look, we all make mistakes. You were trying to do a good thing. Nobody has thought twice about it, okay? Trust me. Dane would really like you to stay—I'm sure of it."

"I'll consider it," he said with a half-smile. "And thanks, Miss Pink. For all you did. I still don't think I deserved to have you risking your life for mine, but I appreciate it."

"Then do me a favor," I said with a wink. "Don't quit your job. Have a little faith in the people who have faith in you."

"People, people, the vote is in," Mrs. Dulcet trilled. "Take your seats, please."

I took my seat as did everyone else while Mrs. Fredericks droned on about the rules of the competition. Gerard took his place as esteemed judge at the front of the shop and dutifully began calling out votes while Richard of The Lost Leprechaun and his girlfriend Stephanie were in charge of documenting the tallies on a whiteboard.

Dane pulled his chair closer to me and put his arm around my shoulder. He leaned in, his breath tickling my neck as he whispered. "How long do you think they'll keep that up?"

I snickered, glancing to the back corner of the shop where Annalise sat in Semi's lap, wrapped around him like a beanpole climbing a trellis. The two had been inseparable since Annalise rushed to the hospital at the news of Trey's injury. They'd had plenty of time to talk while Semi's brother went through surgery and recovery—too much time, as a matter of fact. Apparently, they'd talked so long all their words ran dry and they were left with nothing to do but make out and hold hands.

"Three months," I said. "Then maybe they'll be tolerable."

Dane grinned an easy smile. "Speaking of making out, do you think we can sneak out of here early?"

I gave him a look of mock horror. "And miss the final vote?"

"I rigged it," Dane said. "It's going to be a tie. Now, can we go? I have something to show you. I'll have you back before the party's over, I promise."

"But it's my own party."

"Live on the edge," Dane said. "Come on, it's out back."

"Out back?" I stood out of mere curiosity. "What's out back?"

Fortunately, we'd both been seated near the front door, so our sneaking out was fairly feasible. Everyone else was focused on the brownies and the outcome of the vote. The rivalry apparently was a much bigger deal on the Sunshine Shore than I'd ever realized.

"Are these from you?" I almost stumbled over a bouquet of flowers that'd been left on the front steps. "Don't delivery people knock?"

"Must not have been heard over the roar of the crowd," Dane said, his eyebrows furrowed. "And no, I didn't send you flowers."

My hands shook as I opened the card on the array of sunflowers. The bouquet itself was beautiful, but the last time I'd received an arrangement, it'd almost led to my death.

Dear Lola,

Congratulations on your new store. I have no doubt you will succeed.

Regards,

Amanda Clark

I gave a wry smile at the sunflowers, bringing them in for a sniff before cradling them to my chest. "They're from your mother."

Dane's eyebrows couldn't have gone any higher. "My mother?"

"I think we've, ah..." I hesitated. "Reached a little truce."

"What happened at the flower store the other day? You never did get around to telling me."

I gave a shake of my head. "It doesn't matter now. We'll figure things out. By the way, what do you think of a beach wedding?"

"My mother would die."

"That's what I thought, too," I said with a sigh. "It might be nice though, don't you think? Just small and informal, and—"

"She'll get over it," Dane said, sweeping me into his arms. "I think it sounds perfect. Now, can I show you my surprise?"

He was almost childish in his excitement, his hair ruffled and shaggy, his eyes a bright, bright blue beneath the stars. He took me toward one of his SUVs, dragging me by the hand, and clicked the trunk open with his keys.

"Close your eyes," he instructed severely, "and don't open them until I tell you."

I did as he asked, listening carefully to a series of clunks, clanks, and curses. I had no possible idea what he might be doing except playing in some weird band that banged on pots and pans to make music.

"Okay," he said. "I have to explain."

"Should I open my eyes?"

"No, wait!"

"Too late," I said with a laugh and let my eyes open. My jaw dropped at the sight of Dane. "What the hell are you doing? You hate bikes!"

Dane Clark, billionaire and tech genius, sat on a bicycle seat—fully protected by a bike helmet, elbow pads and knee pads, and a goofy grin on his face. "I, ah—" He cleared his throat, somehow maintaining his manliness and dignity despite the silliness of his attire. "I wanted to show you that I would do anything for you."

I burst out laughing. "And next time an awful kidnapper makes me bike after him, you want to be ready to help?"

"Hold on—next time?" Dane shook his head. "There's no next time. But maybe after I practice some more, we could take a ride along the beach. Just for fun."

"Let's see what you've got, hot stuff," I said, clapping my hands with a delirious sort of happy giggle, "Ride 'em, cowboy!"

Then Dane Clark kicked off the ground and began to pedal. Someone, probably Semi, had fastened stupid little tassels to the handlebars of the bike and the little beads that *clink-clink-clinked* as the tires went around.

He tumbled into the sand ten feet later.

I ran over, tackled him, and smothered him with kisses. "You're the sweetest thing, you know that?"

"I can't ride a bike, but you're going to marry me? You're the saint." He pulled me in for a breathless kiss. "I know this was silly, Lola, but I mean it. I would do anything for you. I'd get married on a beach, trade my life for yours—hell, I even broke my diet and ate two brownies for you tonight."

"If that isn't love," I said, "I don't know what is."

We lay sprawled like a pair of teenagers in the sugary sand, the cool, soft grinds of it gentle against our skin. Dane ran his fingers lazily up and down my arms as the light beat of music in the background signaled the vote was over and the festivities had kicked into party mode.

"It's a beautiful night, isn't it?" I murmured, glancing up at the stunning array of blinking, winking crystals of light. "The stars are gorgeous."

"Who needs stars," Dane asked, rolling over to face me, "when I've fallen in love with the sun?"

My eyes stung with the emotion in his voice. "Oh, Dane. Stop. You're going to make me cry and my mascara will drip and I'll need to wear my new Angelo's sunglasses at night. That's no way to debut my most fabulous shades."

"I mean it." Dane was undeterred by my pleas, stroking my lip with his finger. "You're the brightest part of my life, Lola. Thank you for loving me enough to run straight into a kidnapper's arms to spare my life."

"You would have done the same for me."

"Yes, but Lola," he said on a murmur. "You've saved my life more than once."

"You're the brightest spot in my life," I whispered. "Just marry me. That's all I've ever wanted."

THE END

Author's Note

Thank you for reading! I hope you enjoyed spending a little more time in Castlewood with Lola and Dane. To be notified of the next release featuring Lola Pink, please sign up for my newsletter at www.ginalamanna.com[1]. In the meantime, stay tuned for more in the Magic & Mixology, The Hex Files, and Lacey Luzzi worlds coming soon!

Thank you for reading!

Gina

Now for a thank you...

To all my readers, especially those of you who have stuck with me from the beginning.

By now, I'm sure you all know how important reviews are for Indie authors, so if you have a moment and enjoyed the story, please consider leaving an honest review on Amazon or Goodreads. I know you are all very busy people and writing a review takes time out of your day—but just know that I appreciate every single one I receive. Reviews help make promotions possible, help with visibility on large retailers and most importantly, help other potential readers decide if they would like to try the book.

I wouldn't be here without all of you, so once again—*thank you*.

---

1. http://www.ginalamanna.com

List of Gina's Books![2]

Gina LaManna is the USA TODAY bestselling author of the Magic & Mixology series, the Lacey Luzzi Mafia Mysteries, The Little Things romantic suspense series, and the Misty Newman books.

List of Gina LaManna's other books:

The Hex Files:

Wicked Never Sleeps

Wicked Long Nights

Wicked State of Mind

Wicked Moon Rising

Wicked All The Way

Lola Pink Mystery Series:

Shades of Pink

Shades of Stars

Shades of Sunshine

Magic & Mixology Mysteries:

Hex on the Beach

Witchy Sour

Jinx & Tonic

Long Isle Iced Tea

Amuletto Kiss

MAGIC, Inc. Mysteries:

The Undercover Witch

Spellbooks & Spies (short story)

Reading Order for Lacey Luzzi:

Lacey Luzzi: Scooped

---

2. http://www.amazon.com/Gina-LaManna/e/B00RPQD-NPG/?tag=ginlamaut-20

Lacey Luzzi: Sprinkled
Lacey Luzzi: Sparkled
Lacey Luzzi: Salted
Lacey Luzzi: Sauced
Lacey Luzzi: S'mored
Lacey Luzzi: Spooked
Lacey Luzzi: Seasoned
Lacey Luzzi: Spiced
Lacey Luzzi: Suckered
Lacey Luzzi: Sprouted
The Little Things Mystery Series:
One Little Wish
Two Little Lies
Misty Newman:
Teased to Death
Short Story in Killer Beach Reads
Chick Lit:
Girl Tripping
Gina also writes books for kids under the Pen Name Libby LaManna:
Mini Pie the Spy!